On Board Out Of Singapore!

VERN RIGBY: He'd made one dive too many, but his terror of the depths was matched by the dangers aboard the **Sally Lou.**

HARVEY DODD: The forever playboy, his fortune spent, he remained insatiable for money and weird kicks.

BEATRICE DODD: Sleek, blonde, and bitchy-eyed, she liked cocktail hour and bed-time best—and Harvey least.

JOHN SIM: On the beach for years, the tough old skipper knew this was his last chance to get fat.

TAPLEY: A little man with a big mouth, he had a burning need for the kind of wealth that would make him tall.

LING-PO: Chinese cook and former Red terrorist punk, he was a good hater but a bad friend.

CHINA GIRL: She began in a Singapore brothel and ended up aboard the **Sally Lou,** up for grabs.

THE RED FATHOM

Robert Edmond Alter

WILDSIDE PRESS

The Red Fathom

Published by Wildside Press LLC
www.wildsidepress.com

THE RED
FATHOM

PROLOGUE

The first shark wasn't much, and the two behind it were even less. Barrel-bodied, black-tips wending a casual course across a shelf of millipore which was perforated like old pink lace. It was only a mama shark taking her tads for a swim. They went past Vern one-two-three, ogling him with three starboard eyes, glassy, myopic and saucerlike.

Vern panned the glass-encased, bat-winged camera after them until their papercutter snouts poked through the screen of the sea's color spectrum and they blended with the blue obscurity of the middle distance and vanished.

He didn't think much of them, but he was just as glad that his partner, Jimmy Nolan — armed with a CO_2 gun and finning a fathom under him — had decided to leave them alone. It was the Red Sea; a poor place to go asking for trouble. It was considered the most dangerous water in the world because of its over-abundance of man-eating fish. That was why the oceanography people were interested in the region, and why they had hired Vern and Jimmy Nolan to help them catalogue the breeds.

Sometimes Jimmy was a little too enthusiastic for Vern's blood. He wasn't content with standing back and observing a hornet's nest with patient interest. He wanted to kick it over and see what made it buzz. But this time he let the black-tips go.

Jimmy jackknifed and went hitch-kicking for a coral castle, his exposed flesh milk-green in the submerged twilight, a sporadic column of silvery bubbles spewing out from his exhaust hose like fat crystal beads. Vern tilted the camera's wing stabilizers and angled after him.

7

A large dentex cut from beneath a coral elbow and looked at Jimmy with something akin to horror in its startled eyes. Jimmy couldn't resist it. Vern heard the gun go *tzzzaaang* as the harpoon slithered out of its channel, saw it stand bright and keen in the turquoise water, and then it was standing jauntily in the portside of the fish and the dentex went off like a bucking bronco, whipping the line right along, streaking purple zigzags of blood across the blue walls, then Jimmy rearing back with the gun, backfinning until he was standing vertically against the points and elbows and shoulders and shelves of the castle, and Vern cutting in with the camera, triggering the action, then catching a shot of Jimmy slamming against a coral elbow, and now man-blood mingling in the water with fishblood. It was a good fight.

Jimmy came step-step-stepping with his fins as though climbing translucent stairs. Vern could see his face mask, the grinning eyes. He pointed at Jimmy's bleeding right arm, but Jimmy shook his head. To hell with it. Nothing. Vern pointed upwards and they started finning, the dead dentex tagged along like a subdued dog on a leash.

Now the broken silver disk of the sun on the surface right above them, and then the sudden consciousness (no man knowing from what primitive sense, too undefined to be understood) of something wrong, of danger waiting. Vern pulled his eyes away from the silver ceiling, looked down at Jimmy rising beneath him, then out and around the blue world—and saw it.

It was a twenty foot tiger shark, a massive chunk of barrel-like tanned muscle: skin a pale yellowish-brown with dark brown transverse bands; plate eyes bugged with that peculiar look of suspicious awe as he glided across a tall bed of purple sea rods, following the prison-striped pilot fish that rode securely in the compressible displacement above his great snout. Then it was two tigers, then three.

Vern hooted in his mouthpiece and pointed down. Jimmy's mask glinted up at him, then winked out as he turned his head to look. The tigers spread their bomb-fin pectorals and stopped. They were in a phalanx and they looked like three dirigibles. They were staring at the dead dentex.

Jimmy — Vern shouting, *My God, no!* — jackknifed and went kicking toward them, hooting shrilly.

It frequently worked on reef-dwelling sharks; but these were from far-out. They didn't give a damn for man, fish or noise. The leader hunched up, then snapped out like a whip

8

and took the dentex off the line with one swipe. They came on, swimming through the sagging blood swirls, the leader spitting out fragments of fish and the others sweeping them up like garbage men following a litter-bug.

Jimmy corkscrewed, getting out of the leader's path, and blundered against the starboard tiger. The shark made a rolling pass at him, jerking its head savagely aside, and peeled off gracefully, working its jaws like a buzz saw.

Even at that distance Vern heard Jimmy's cry in the mouthpiece.

Now the port tiger veered and nosed into the fan of blood and caught Jimmy by the middle, and the leader whipped back because the dentex had only been an appetizer, and he went for the skindiver and the other shark with his mouth open like a shopping bag. The port tiger was in an epileptic dance: body twisting, tail kicking, head shaking from side to side like a terrier taking a gopher. And then they were both doing it and the starboard tiger slashed in too, as Vern let the camera go and started down himself, his hand going for his knife. Then he stopped, saying, Jesus, what am I doing here?

After that it was impossible to see anything in its proper perspective, because a nightmare has no spatial relation to dimensions. There was a great thrashing of bubbles, and broad streamers of blood, and fins flapping, and sleek glints of muscled tanned skins and all of it was churning over and over like a Catherine wheel. And once, a mouthpiece bobbled upwards on the flaring airhoses, spewing a silvery foam; and once, a human hand reached out of the welter of bubbles, blood and fins, stretching, clawing, for Vern.

And that was all he wanted of it. That was all his libido would stomach and he knew it wouldn't stomach it for long, and that meant doing it in his mouthpiece. But it wasn't the nausea so much as it was the bred-in-the-bone animal fear that finally triggered him out of there like a shell from a trench mortar.

With a sickening rush he went kicking upwards. His head splintered the pane of the surface and he bobbed high in the water, spitting out the mouthpiece, shouting — not words, only a hysteria of sound — feeling, seeing the clean, bright strength of the sky going on around, and dropped down again, treading frantically now (knowing what was happening right under his fins and praying *Jesus Christ don't let it happen to me*), holding up his right hand to the oncoming rowboat.

The two Nubian boatboys and Wilson, one of the minor

9

wheels of the oceanography group, grabbed him by the wrists, armpits, hair, anything to haul him over the gunwale and get him out of the water. Then he was all limp and soggy and collapsed on the floorboards and could feel the dark-skinned hands stripping the mask from his head, fins from his feet, scuba gear from his back, weight-belt from his waist, and he kept flinching from their touch as though the hands were teeth.

"My God, Rigby!" Wilson's voice said, and then again but this time saying "man" instead of "Rigby" and the third time only "My God" and keeping it up until it sounded like a litany to despair: mygodmygodmygod. . . .

Vern needed a drink so badly he felt he would have to commit suicide on the spot if he didn't get one. But they didn't keep a bottle in the boat and so he had to settle for one of Wilson's cigarettes. And it was all he could do to get it lighted and it seemed to bumble all over his mouth every time he brought it up to his lips in his shaking hand.

Circumspectly, as though his head and eyes were trying to keep a secret from the mutely screaming man cowering inside his nerveless body, he turned his head and looked at the flat blue water. Off the starboard quarter a widening stain of deep purple was spreading on the surface.

"Poor Nolan! My God, poor little Jimmy!" Wilson's voice unrolled on and on like a straight-away horizon-bound highway. "Are you all right, Rigby? My God, man, did they get you too? Are you—"

Vern shook his head. "I'm all right," he said and his voice sounded like something that had been stepped on.

But he wasn't and he knew it. Thirty minutes ago he had left the boat and he had been Vern Rigby, professional diver. Now he was back in the boat, but he wasn't the same man. He had left a piece of himself down there in a red fathom, and he didn't know how he would ever get it back again.

Mythology has been written in tomes most curious, and bibliophiles have rejoiced in bringing to light translations of that hazardous voyage to Colchis, made by those legendary sailors in a ship called the Argus. *But I know of real Argonauts — alive and in our century — who are willing to run to the edge of Beyond in a borrowed rowboat with a two-dollar watch for a chronometer if necessary, and dive naked to the bottom of the sea with a piece of glass and a strip of rubber for diving gear, to seek for the ocean's Golden Fleece.*

It is men of this caliber with whom I would form a partnership: for they are inevitable men, as inevitable as death.

Fergus . . .

PART 1

It was a morning like any morning: bright, warm, a brisk breeze coming off the bay, bringing the faint tang of salt and something of the narrow harbor streets. If you were young and in love, or if you were healthy and wealthy, it was a good morning. If you weren't, it was just a morning. And that's all it was to Vern.

He lay on his bed and blinked his eyes against the sunlight which came through the open window in a squared, opaque block. He knew he could close his eyes again, resettle his brain on Nod's rounded shoulder, and roll down into the dark land of sleep for another two hours, and it was tempting, too tempting. So he didn't. To the down-and-outer, to the man who could no longer face himself or his failures, sleep was an opiate, a brand of partial suicide.

He rolled onto his back and looked at the ceiling with its network of cracks that looked like faces. Then he remembered he had been dreaming again of Jimmy Nolan and the shark

11

(he had evolved it to that in his mind: one shark, the symbolic embodiment of his fear) and the Red Fathom.

"So," the doctor he had finally gone to see in Bombay had said to him, "every man has a mental Achilles' heel in his make-up. In one form or another. The particular manifestation with each particular individual is unimportant. So it comes down to this. First, the trauma. Then, either learning to accept it and live with it, or—putting off the necessity for having to be brave as long as possible, knowing all the while that the decision to face it will have to be made eventually in order to continue calling oneself a man. And knowing, too, exactly what it is going to be like when it is faced."

Like hell on earth, Vern thought.

He sat up, aware of the doleful complaints of the cot's rusty springs, and turned his sleep-grained eyes on the familiar, sickening room. It was a Chinese rooming house with a misconceived European facade, belonging to one of the back sections of Singapore — a sort of international skid row. A paint-chipped dresser stood across the room from him. It held a washbowl of limpid water and an empty square gin bottle. His shorts and one sock encircled the base of the bottle. He could taste the sour perfume of last night's gin in his mouth.

Sleep still buzzed hazily in his head, merging with the outside sounds. He left the cot heavily, letting the part of him that was awake drag the rest of him to the washbowl. The water, then towel, on his face helped a little.

He pawed through his odds and ends for a cigarette, but it was a waste of time. So he dressed and left the building quietly via the side entrance. There was no sense in calling the Chinese proprietor's attention to his departure. He would start cracking his meaty ivory knuckles and worry about Vern's rooming bill. "Allatime dlink, dlink, dlink," he would murmur accusingly. "No money. Allatime no money."

The place he was heading towards was a minor bad habit with him. But it was cheap. You could buy anything there from a drink to a girl. The former sometimes made you puke green bile, and the latter frequently came with VD.

Vern sat down at one of the little tables and ordered a French breakfast, mostly coffee and cream. He was the only person seated in the cluster of zinc-topped tables. A large group of the inevitable slumming tourists were at one end of the bar. They were very loud, a little tipsy, and flashed money around like proud battle-banners. The girls made shrill little laughs like two fingers high in the scales, and they had turned boldly appraising, wanton eyes on Vern when he had walked in. One of them, very bleached, very hippy and breasty, had said, "God in heaven, what a hunk of — did you see his eyes, May? They make you want to . . ." But he had walked beyond the range of the words by then and all he heard was the shrill laughter running the scales.

So I make the girls want to, he thought ironically. But he had also noticed that he made their men want to punch him in the nose. They had looked him over with cold, jealous contempt. A bum, their eyes had said. A big stud bum. He waited for his coffee and ignored them and their women too.

Down at this end of the bar were two Chinese whores. They were sitting sidesaddle on the tall, spindly-legged stools and were wearing the traditional high-necked, skirt-split, silk-sheath dresses of their trade. A stubby Limey seaman from one of Her Majesty's ships was standing between them, between their crossed legs, and he was making free with his hands and buying the drinks and having a hell of a good time.

The girl on Vern's right had the thick, flat features of her Mongolian ancestors, and she wasn't much to look at. But the other one probably had a little Nordic in her, and she was something more. The split in her skirt was as high as the law would allow and it showed almost as much leg as a bikini. Sitting one-buttocked on the stool, which threw her right hip out toward Vern, there was something about her that made him forget to order cigarettes when the boy brought his coffee.

She had a long Occidental leg, rare in an Oriental, and he was having trouble keeping his eyes off it — his mind too; thinking now of how soft and silklike a girl's inner thigh was, how like a . . . Cut it out, he said. You don't have the money for it.

But the girl didn't mind. She was watching Vern (even though the Limey was getting annoyed), and every time she caught him looking she would show a little more and smile and wet her scarlet lips with just the tip of her tongue, first upper then lower, and finally she was getting downright wiggly on that damn spindly-legged stool until it reached the point where he knew she would be slinking over to offer, "How about it?" So he grinned and shook his head at her because he couldn't afford it. But he hated to do it.

The Limey came over instead. He hitched up his bell-bottoms on the way by exerting pressure with his inner wrists, a

13

John Wayne gesture. His eyes were as nasty as a disturbed moray's.

"'Ere," he snapped, checking his progress at the edge of Vern's table. "That bit of fluff your sister or somethin'?"

If Vern stood up he would have eight inches on the sailor. But he didn't. He smiled and shook his head. "Sorry," he said. "Just resting my eyes."

"So rest 'em on somethin' helse, myte, before I give 'em a bit of the black!" The stubby sailor took another hitch in his pants.

Vern had grown tired of the ridiculousness of the scene. "All right, mate," he said shortly. "Better get back to her now before she goes cold."

The Limey didn't like that. Being a small man who of necessity existed in a seamy environment, he was constantly alert to fight anyone, anytime, anywhere. Primitive anger was his edge on life. It gave him the momentary illusion that he actually was the rough, tough, capable son-of-a-bitch he always wanted to be.

But there was an interruption and Vern turned his head away. Someone had just come in the door.

There was something about the man, perhaps the way the seedy clothes hung on the tall angular frame, that reminded you of a fierce old giant who had outlived mythology, who, because of his savage nature, had been too damn stubborn to lay down and die. He stood spread-legged, just inside the doorway, with the vivid blaze of morning backing him, square fists akimbo, and panned his eyes over the room.

The girl who had made comments about Vern turned and looked at the man and made her eyes wide with mock awe. "Holy mother," she said in a deliberate stage whisper. "I thought Bully Hayes died in the last century!"

One of the men tourists thought that worth a laugh and started to, but the man in the doorway moved his head and looked at him and the tourist decided it wasn't so funny after all. His gaze went away like a rag snatched from a clothesline.

The old giant looked into the room again, his eyes narrowed by countless years of sea- and sun-squint. Then he dropped his fists and walked over to Vern's table.

"Vern," he said. "Remember me?"

When he smiled it looked as though it pained every feature, yet Vern felt that nothing could ever hurt that face. Fists and marlin spikes, belaying pins, broken bottles and the sea itself

14

had hammered the flesh and bone into bumpy cast-iron. He was the inevitable white man who dwells where the pavement ends; ageless, with a hint of youth; looking anxiously, from young eyes, for something out of life—like a passing spoke of sunlight on a distant shore searching for the power and beauty and passion of the Beyond.

He remembered Sim. He had worked off one of Sim's boats during the salvage period after the war. That was before Sim made a few mistakes; before his reputation went to pot over a barratry charge.

"Hello, Sim," he said. "Sit down."

Sim didn't. He gave the Limey a flat look. "You finished here, son?" he asked. "I've got business with this man."

The Limey thought about it and decided what the hell. He'd made his point. He'd shown the two whores just what a rough-and-tumble little bastard he was. So he said, "He's all yours, dad," and turned away, once again repeating the wrists and pants action.

Sim glanced toward the whores, the glasses and the bottles, and came back to Vern. "The square-face got you on the skids?" His tone was blank.

Vern looked at him sharply. "Would you like to taste my coffee?" he offered. "If you find any gin in it, drink it."

Sim turned smoothly, as though his heels were oiled ball bearings, lifted a chair out from the table and sat in it.

"You know me. I always get to the point. I got to know if you're worth a damn or if you've turned rummy."

Vern looked away. There wasn't any sense in losing his temper with Sim. "Do you have a cigarette?"

"No. Cigars. You know me. Look here, I've got a job for you. No wages. It's either shares or it's bust."

"You mean a diving job?"

"What else?"

The tiger shark, long, swollen and sleek, its great maw showing the double row of disorderly teeth, drifted ghostlike from Vern's subconscious. He fixed his eyes on the Chinese girl's bare leg to dispel the red mushrooms of blood swirling in memory.

"I haven't been under in a year, Sim." But he wasn't really speaking to the old seaman.

Outside in the street the noise of Singapore gathered and trembled on the hot air. Rickshaws rattled their desperate ways; horns blared round, mellow notes; the garble of the black, yellow, brown and pale mingled and won supremacy of sound with a monotonous sing-song insistence. There was romance down there on the quay. Below the windows of the company buildings were the stepping-stones to adventure. Who had said that? he wondered idly. Some kid just out from home probably. Some starry-eyed little bastard with a stomach full of untested guts and a hip pocket full of fresh money.

Sim's hand moved aimlessly across the tabletop, into Vern's line of vision. Then he was aware of the old man's voice.

"—sure, I'm a topside man. I know where I belong. But you can find as much danger on a clean deck as you will under the waves. I've heard the tales they're spinning about you. Gutless, they say. Afraid to step into a bathtub without somebody standing hard by to hold your hand. Horse manure! You can't pull it over me, my son. One hungry shark and a lost partner ain't going to drydock you for life."

Vern started rummaging his pockets for a cigarette. "Tell me about it," he suggested.

Sim smiled slightly and placed his hands in his pockets, leaning back. "You were in on the *Prince Ferris* salvage job, two-three years ago, weren't you? Remember a little Jap diver called Haki? Little, squinty, bow-legged gook, savvies pretty good English?"

Vern actually discovered a crumpled cigarette and nodded as he smoothed it into cylindrical shape. "Vaguely. We didn't have much to do with each other. Lot of divers on that job."

"Yeah. Well, this gook was working for the Pearman outfit a few months back, doing salvage on a sunk steamer. He ran into something when he was under. Something that some friends of mine think is worth a heap of coin."

Vern lit the cigarette, studying Sim through the smoke swirl. He checked the obvious ear-marks of the seaman's financial status: scuffed tennis shoes, faded oil-stained dungarees, the clean but carefully repaired white shirt, and thought, Sim is desperate.

"You ever hear of the Seven Madonnas?"

Vern nodded. He'd heard but he didn't know them. They were an island group beyond the Black Belt, an archipelago with New Guinea for its head and New Caledonia for its tail. It was east of the Santa Cruz group, where the curve is, where the Pacific seems to deny the existence of the earth. It was out of bounds for trade and civilization alike. Even the war had

16

passed the remote volcanic structure by and left it in savage obscurity.

Sim paused, rubbing one of his sea-grained hands across his mouth, staring at the nothingness of the west wall reflectively. He snatched the hand away suddenly and tucked it back on his hip.

"The gook," he said, "had a little trouble finding the steamer. While he was blundering around down there he stumbled on another wreck — an old girl: I mean *real* old from his description of her. Well, you know how them Japs are — crafty, always nosing around for a possible buck. So Haki thinks he just might of stumbled onto something worthwhile, so he keeps his yap closed, which ain't hard for a gook."

Vern said nothing. He saw where the drift was taking them. And he wasn't interested. Pipe dreams. He'd heard a hundred of them. But it bothered him to think that Sim was actually so desperate he was willing to clutch at straws. He had thought of Sim as someone a bit special, and this new let's-run-to-the-end-of-the-rainbow picture wasn't right.

Some of what he was thinking must have reflected on his face. Sim suddenly cocked his head to one side and stared at him with narrowed eyes, his smile like the thin mouth of a sadist.

"All right, Vern. I've got you pegged. You think the old man has lost his grip, eh?" He raised his huge shoulders, squaring them, bringing his head and neck between the humps in a catlike stretch. He relaxed all at once and said:

"I came out here when Christ was a corporal, boy. And in my time I've heard so goddam many lost-treasure tales you could start a lending library on them and make money at two cents a day. But I only tried two of 'em, and both was in my first year. Since then I've been like any old seadog: I've scoffed. But, my son, this one has some authenticity behind it."

Vern shrugged. "Try me."

"All right, here's what she looks like. The gook figures the old girl might be one of them Dago ships: so he clams up like only a gook can do, hangs around until the salvage job is done and then goes on his way. Well, he wanders around for a while wondering what the hell to do with it and finally takes his tale to this Fergus fella. You know, Donald Fergus? No? Well,

17

he's one of them whatayoucallem fellas—you know, a man that roots around for old bones and junk?"

"Archeologist," Vern said. "Paleontologist? I don't know which."

Sim dismissed the importance of the terminology with an abrupt nod.

"Yeah, got a string of letters and periods behind his name that would plug a latrine. Well, anyhow, he's a pretty good head. He's bugged on buried loot, lost temples, old wrecks, all that crap. Spends all his time scratching around in the dirt, digging his nose into old records and logbooks. People are always coming to him with little bits of information they want to sell, and that son of a bitch seems to know right off whether the stuff is worth a goddam or whether it's all bilge."

He paused, cleared his throat, making a sound like a car grinding gears, and looked around for a moment as if he were going to spit somewhere. He did, but it didn't matter. That's what the floor was for.

"Anyhow, Haki finally takes his old wreck to Fergus and those two buckos put their heads together. What they come up with sounds pretty good. The *Habanera*, a reconverted collier, came out of China in 1810, touched at Mindanao, the Admiralties, then ran on down the Belt and started east. The ship went aground in the Seven Madonnas and sank, no hands lost."

Vern smiled slightly. "What cargo was she carrying? Rice? Teak? Rattan?"

Sim grinned, showing a black starboard gap among his broad square teeth. "Something like that. But she also had a box of jewels — rare old Manchu sparklers, my son. Fergus got all the facts. They're all in print. You can read 'em anytime you feel the urge. As far as the archives show, the swag has never been recovered."

"As far as the archives show."

"What the hell, son; you take a chance you'll make it through the day every morning you leave your bed, don't you?"

Vern dropped his cigarette on the floor and snubbed it out with his foot. It sounded better, much better, but he couldn't see where he fit in.

"What's it to me? You have Haki. He'll find the wreck again. He can recover the box for you."

Sim looked like he had just been handed the lid off an old

garbage can. "Something happened to the Jap when he was down there. No, he don't know what, or if he does he ain't saying. You know how them gooks are: superstitious little bastards. Says he don't want to dive again."

"Shark?" Vern said quietly.

"Oh, for crysake. Look here, there's other things in the sea besides sharks. Leave it alone, can't you? No, it wasn't no fish. I asked him. It — aw hell, he don't know what it was. A feeling, I guess."

Vern nodded. He thought he knew what it was. Atmosphere-reaction, he called it. A common ailment among divers prowling alone in wrecks. Suddenly every passageway, every open door, every black compartment was a waiting place for nameless terror. The wreck became the diver's breeding ground of fear.

"There're other divers, Sim," he said. "Any of them have a better reputation than mine."

Sim hunched over the table, elbows down, wrists crossed. He looked at Vern. "I figured you were hurting. I've heard it mentioned that the big outfits aren't offering you much lately."

There was an understatement. Vern smiled wryly. "Thanks, Sim. But let's not hedge with it. You've never let friendship stand between you and a pound note. This *Habanera* deal means quite a lot to you, I'd say. Why are you willing to risk it with a spooked diver?"

Sim held a long, flat stare, then grinned, letting it spread through his battered face like a wolf showing his fangs.

"Smart, ain't you? All right, my son, I'll level with you. The Seven Madonnas are within French jurisdiction, and you savvy their law governing treasure trove. Anyone holding back information concerning treasure is subject to fine and imprisonment. Oh sure, they'll help you root it up, and maybe they'll buy it off you at reduced face value — maybe not. But the people I'm in with sort of figure like me. We'd stand a much better show in the U.S."

"The people? You mean Haki and this Fergus?"

"I mean them, and I mean the Dodds — man and wife. Also the crew. I guess I didn't give you the full lay. Fergus has got a few pounds, but not enough to outfit an expedition like this one. So he's got these two friends, young couple, swank stuff. You know the breed: 'I'm a playboy from Gotrocks, New York, and I don't think I know you, do I? Or do I want to?' And a sleek, bitchy-assed wife who looks like she'd lay anyone

19

and goes around with her nose higher than a skysail like it was the last thought in her mind."

He grunted and rubbed his mouth with his thumb.

"Well, between you, me and the sternpost, I don't think they're as well-fixed as they like to spend. But anyhow, they bought old Phillip's schooner, the *Sally Lou,* remember her? You worked off her once, I think. And they sort of putter about in the old tub and amuse themselves between bed and bottle by skindiving and underwater photography and all that.

"Well, Fergus went to 'em and gave 'em the pitch. His knowledge and coin matched by their ship and help. And the Jap of course, because he's the only one that knows where the *Habanera* went down. Then they came my way and offered me the skipper's berth."

Something new, startling, to Vern, came into Sim's eyes. It had nothing to do with the tough, old man-of-the-sea, or with youth looking eagerly for the flicker of sunlight on a distant shore. Simply quiet desperation.

"I wouldn't fool you. I'd have taken the berth without the Manchu kicker. But they're giving me a share. And, son — I *need* that coin. Need it bad. I'm on the beach."

Vern looked away, looked at the blazing doorway between two dingy windows, then along the darkly-stained, grease-crusted bar to the two leg-exhibiting whores, then down at the rugless, butt-littered floor.

"And all of these people," he said, "they're all willing to skip the treasure-trove law?"

"Yeah. All of them. I guess they got their reasons."

The schooner *Sally Lou* was moored in the red eye of the sunset at the extreme end of a crowded quay, sandwiched between bulging godowns that stood rank and file for acres around. Vern wove a path along the littered quay and went to the edge to throw a cigarette butt into the water. And it wasn't easy to find even that much room between the sardined boats. He stayed for a moment to watch the river traffic.

Cargo-carrying lighters bearing spices, oriental woods, coconuts, rubber and palm oil, shuttled between quays and anchored freighters. An endless parade of commerce. It was amusing to him to see the European touch — battered pith helmets on the heads of Oriental lightermen. But the noise and bustle of the river was dissatisfying. He turned away with a sense of aimlessness in his libido. Everyone was busy. If they weren't busy at honest toil, they were busy begging. And he felt about as active as a cigar store Indian.

He had worked off the *Sally Lou* in 'fifty-five. She was an old-fashioned girl with raised poop and fo'c'sle. A storeroom and the galley stood forward of the cargo hatch in the waist. There was no after house, only a boxed skylight and a companionway leading down to the saloon in the stern. She had a 110 Diesel, as he recalled, for auxiliary. It wasn't much good for a ship of that size and had the annoying habit of conking out whenever the crew was depending on it.

But mostly he remembered the smell of the old ship: the brine, grease, old work clothes, mouldy canvas, and something else — something that was a hangover from her more evil days when she had been a black-birder in the recruiting trade for the Queensland plantations. That kind of smell was the most enduring. Nothing could ever rid a ship of the taint.

But she had also had her gay days: like the time before World War I when Raze Dalls, the pearl poacher, had been her skipper. Raze and his crew of don't-give-a-damn-for-man-God-or-VD bully boys had visited a little island belonging to the Tanimbar group in the Banda Sea. The bully boys had gone ashore with their Snider rifles and dynamite sticks in their belts and the smouldering cigars for the fuses in their hard mouths, and they had brought the natives a boatload of square-faced gin that would make Bacchus stitch up the bottom of his pants before he tried a second swallow.

The square-face took care of the native males and the bully boys took care of the females. They fetched twenty of them aboard the *Sally Lou*. Good God how they fetched them . . . drunk, screaming, fighting, by the hair, by the ankles, by anything that was handy and plenty was because the girls were all naked, and that's the way they put to sea.

It's been said that the ensuing orgy would have had the ancient Romans sitting up and taking down notes — in shorthand: that for the next two weeks the sun hid its face in shame while the *Sally Lou* kicked up her own personal little typhoon, bellowing, brawling, boffing all the way down the Timor run. And by the time they staggered into Lombok, where they pushed the girls overboard and into the shallows, one girl had committed suicide with a straight-edged razor and

21

another had gone blind on the square-face and a third had gone mad and was raving about snakes and eels, but they were all too drunk to understand the symbolism, and two of the bully boys were dead from knife fights and one, presumably, was overboard because they never did see him again, and that nine months later — give or take a week or two — there were no end of half-caste babies born on Lombok.

And that was only one entry on the seamy pages in the *Sally Lou's* logbook.

As Vern approached the plank a Chinese boy came from the galley and hoisted a pail of thick amber slop over the starboard rail. It splashed sharply and then spread in greasy clots like leprosy on the already clouded water. The boy straightened his back with the empty bucket still in its pouring position and looked at Vern.

In the dusky light Vern had to look at him twice before he decided he didn't know him. He was short, stocky, with a sleekness to his tight skin that bespoke good health. Twentyish, Vern thought. A cold-faced punk trying to act like a Chink hood. All he needed was an unlit cigarette in his mouth and a raincoat collar turned up around his neck.

Vern nodded. "Hi. Skipper aboard?"

The boy watched him without expression, then righted the slop bucket and turned away. "Aft," he said, barely.

Superior little bastard. He probably belonged to the Dodds. Sim would never stand for that breed of insolence from his hands. But it wasn't Vern's business. He went aft, pausing to glance at the clutter of diving gear that had been dumped carelessly in the scuppers.

There were three diving helmets and they looked like relics from a harbor antique shop: archaic old daddies, Cyclops-eyed, round copper-headed monsters. He checked them professionally. Starboard and port windows and one topside, rigged for phone—sending and receiving. Three suits of tanned twill, two ply, with rubber between. Lengths of air lines, life lines. He turned and looked inboard, seeing the compressor and airpump just abaft the cargo hatch.

Very neat, he thought. All ready for business. All ready for the sharks and the squids and the bends and the amusing moment when the goddam air line fouls up.

"Hello, Rigby. Reminiscing?"

He looked aft and saw a tall, tapered silhouette standing by the break in the poop. His mind paused, waiting for memory

22

to catch up with the Negro's face and name. Then he remembered.

"Hello, Sully. Are you a part of this?"

The cream-and-coffee Negro moved away from the steps and approached with light catlike steps. He had a cigarette in his lips and a pale smear of smoke over his mouth, and because of the smoke his face was drawn down a little to one side, to match the business-like rake of his cap. He had the proud, ruthless, lonely aspect of the man who owns nothing except the clothes on his back. Nothing was his; not the plot of earth or length of deck his feet walked. No door opened to his key; no mailbox bore his name. He didn't offer his hand because even their acquaintanceship was on a loaned basis. It didn't belong to him.

"I'm Sim's mate," he said. "He gave me the berth yesterday."

He might have added that it was his first berth, other than the beach, since he had been released from a penal colony: something to do with running arms to the rebels, Vern had heard, but something which he had closed behind him like the cover on a dissatisfying book.

"I hear you're going to dive for us."

Vern made a twist with his mouth. "Maybe. Where's Sim? Below?"

"Aye, waiting for you. They're all there." Then he smiled and Vern had the impression he almost winked. "Watch out for Mrs. Dodd, diver. She has a restless eye."

Mrs. Dodd must be some kid, Vern thought. Or maybe all seamen just naturally have dirty minds. But he knew that wasn't so. Seamen, out of all walks of men, were the most innocent: perhaps because they were more detached from society, like cowboys. "What do you care? What good would it do you?" Vern said, and started away.

"You mean because I'm an off-color?"

It was in the voice, all of it: the curse of Ham, the blindness of those long-dead, Bible-thumping, money-grabbing Yankee slavers, the thoughtless casualness of all those long-ago white men who had carelessly slurred the enunciation of the word Nigger into a curse far more meaningful than bastard or son-of-a-bitch.

Vern stopped, turned around, and came back. He felt hollow, like a man going into a fight.

23

"Did I say it?" he asked angrily. "Did I even look like I was thinking it?"

Sully hesitated, but couldn't quite unbend. You have to hold some things sacred, even if it's the tattered banner of owning, having, loving nothing. There is always the proud ruthlessness:

"All right, diver. Forget it."

Vern had a healthy edge on six feet, but he had to look up to hold Sully's gaze. "Sure." But he couldn't—because Sully couldn't. He turned again and went aft.

Sully stood flat-footed on the deck, watching the diver climb the steps and head for the companionway. Alone, he turned and looked at Singapore, at the company buildings with their flags, orange-tiled roofs, and the great, square white bulk of their bodies. The white man's world. The British square at the back of pagan beyond. The last outpost of dying imperialism. His mouth grimaced and he looked away. He was getting touchy, and it was an emotion he couldn't afford. If you were going to be a *Negro*, then you acted like a representative of a proud race. But if you were going to be the other, a nigger, then you acted like a teen-aged colored punk from Harlem who took offense at every innuendo, supposed or not.

He started forward and saw the Chinese cook watching him from the galley door. He didn't like Ling-Po, didn't like the snotty expression on the punk's cold face. It was a risky look to wear anywhere, because there was always some tough nut just waiting to wipe it off. He suspected he would have trouble with the China boy before long, but it could wait. He wasn't looking for a row.

Ling-Po's obsidian eyes flicked from the mate to the poop deck, his lips curling in a soft, practised sneer. "Another white bastard, eh?" he suggested softly.

It was the wrong thing to say, at the wrong time. Sully was too close. Something—maybe the imagery of Vern Rigby who, because of his own problem, was neither black nor white; maybe because you couldn't act like a Negro and react like the other—sparked in Sully's brain and he grabbed for the cook, bunching up a fistful of white shirt and apron in his square dark hand and yanked the youth in, towering over him by a clear foot.

24

"Keep your filthy little gook mouth closed!" he hissed.

He wanted to say more but too many words were tumbling through his mind and he knew it was hopeless to try and sort them into coherent sentences, and so he threw the cook back into the galley, propelling him with the full push of his arm, and stamped off without a second look.

Ling-Po's back hit the edge of the sink, hard. His elbow plowed through a clutter of pots and pans and he slipped to the deck butt-first, ducking under the rain of cooking utensils, for the moment not capable of thought, his equilibrium caught in a tinny bubble of clashing sound. Then the last pot clattered into reposed silence and he realized he was on the deck, and that his back, elbow and rear were shooting sharp flashing little stabs of pain to his brain.

A bone-handled butcher knife lay near his right foot and that was all the suggestion he needed. His eyes blazed wide, centering on it, and he came up in a scramble, snatching the knife from the deck, his left hand clutching at the edge of the sink, and he knew that it was going to be now and that if it was now, then what would follow would be the end of him, and yet that didn't matter at all.

But he stalled like a Ford with a faulty fuel pump, even as his feet were ready to start him, and the knife ready for the underhanded swing, because the door to the storeroom opened with its familiar need-to-be-oiled screech, and when he turned his head he saw the girl standing there staring at him.

She said nothing, but then she seldom spoke, not even during the frantic twenty minutes each night on his bunk in the storeroom when he muttered and gasped curses and endearments of passion and all the angry, hungry, demanding sounds of need. She stared at him blankly, her face painted and diamond-sharp with mascara and lipstick and hooped earrings, and that was the only part of her that really looked clean. Her yellow silk sheath was the same one she had been wearing the night she had propositioned him in the doorway of the lantern-maker's shop (a hell of a place for it: no privacy, no bed, not even a blanket, just there in the dark doorway, British-style) three weeks ago.

But what could you do? Dirty or not, he needed her. It was life, wasn't it? It was normal. Man needs woman. And ever since he had made his frantic departure from Kuala Lumpur he had been dead broke. The *Sally Lou* had served as a hide-out but not as a source of money. That white capitalistic bitch Mrs. Dodd had told him he could live and eat on board the schooner, but that they couldn't pay him any wages, not just then, but perhaps later. Yeah, later, in a pig's prat. Well, he'd take care of that end himself. He'd get his. But until then . . .

"What do you want?" he snapped at the girl. "There's nothing wrong. I slipped and fell. Go back into the room."

She did, soundlessly, closing the door slowly on her diamond-bright face which seemed impervious to time. The latch said click.

He turned around and threw the knife at the sink. He wanted to smash something, anything. He took a few aimless steps across the deck and stopped. His eyes were smarting and he cursed himself for acting like a woman. They would pay — oh yes, they would all pay. Not only the scum on this stinking schooner, but every last bitch-mother's son in the Dutch East Indies. And the yellow, brown and black who bootlicked them would pay also. And there was so much to pay for, so very much.

Now he was remembering the two little British boys he had played with when he was a child, when he had lived on their father's rubber plantation in Perak. Tuan Harold and tuan Peter, products of the superior race. When they had grown tired of their play they had turned to teasing him. "Ching-chong-Charlie," they would sing, and they would laugh, point at him, and jab him with sticks to get him to cry.

But some years later it had been his turn to laugh. That was when the Red terrorists were raiding the plantations. Ling-Po had been along on the raid against the plantation where he had spent his miserable childhood. Yes, that had been very nice, very satisfying — especially the hand grenade through tuan Harold's bungalow window, and the yellow flash and gray blast of smoke and the scream that had sounded like the shriek a dog makes when it is being mashed beneath the wheels of a truck.

Ching-chong-Charlie to you, tuan Harold.

The saloon, or cuddy, was crammed between the skipper's quarters aft and the two tiny staterooms forward. It was locker-walled, timber-beamed, and bare-decked. A long table, complete with benches, extended from the butt of the mainmast. Sim and four men were sitting around the table talking smoke at each other. Each man had a beer can standing in front of him like a tin hitching post.

26

Seeing Vern, Sim smiled and laid his cigar on the edge of the table. He stood up. "Come on down here, Vern. Been waiting for you. This here's Mr. Fergus." He overturned a fist toward one of the men. "Mr. Fergus, Vern Rigby."

He was a bald one with snapping eyes gleaming through plate-glass windows rimmed with horn. A little man, narrowed and brittled by fifty-odd years of poor health. He was a scholar and lived in another world.

"How do you do, Vern?" He smiled warmly when he extended his hand.

"Fine, thanks."

"And Mr. Harvey Dodd, Vern," Sim added, as his fist curved to portside.

Sim had been right. Harvey Dodd was the forever playboy. His mama-boy face was almost too cute to be true, especially in a man of thirty. But there was something wrong with the eyes, something behind them that was old and a little haunted.

"Glad to have you aboard, Rigby," Dodd offered.

Vern smiled and shook his head warningly. "I haven't made Sim any promises. I told him I'd talk with you people."

"You remember Haki, Vern," Sim cut in.

The Japanese diver stood up, placed his hands carefully at the seams of his trousers and bowed his burr-head slowly. He smiled, showing his glittering collection of dental gold.

"So nice, Mr. Ligby. So nice that we should meet again," he said graciously, striking each sibilance with a sharp little hiss.

Vern looked at the last man. He had the look of a young to-hell-with-you-and-everything beachcomber. He hadn't shaved in days and he held an unlit cigar in one corner of his mouth. He was thin to the point of being emaciated, and no taller than Haki. "All of me," he hummed softly, his city-wise eyes flickering over Vern's size and clothes, "why not take all of me?"

"This is Tapley," Sim said off-handedly. "We're talking him into shipping with us before the mast. Him and a Dutchman he's got for a pal. I told Mr. Fergus that we could run the ship ourselves, but he wants to do things right."

"Let's hear more about the shares," Tapley suggested. He hadn't stood to greet Vern, and now he looked away from him without a sign of interest.

Sim paused for a count of five. He picked up his cigar and inspected it. "If you don't like the lay, laddy, you can hoist out of here. I can find some other swab to work for wages."

Tapley grinned impishly. "Sure you can. But I don't see you
27

doing it. I wonder why not?" He turned his head and looked at the other men speculatively. "You took the part that once was my heart —" he hummed easily.

"Don't try the high-hand with me, my son," Sim advised. "Yeah, there's a reason why I'm not looking for seamen with papers in order. But I'm not ready to tell that reason yet. I know you, know your breed. That's why you're here, and why Sully, the Chink, and the Dutchman are here. You're on the beach, blacklisted."

"Like yourself?" Tapley suggested, grinning.

"What about the shares?" Vern asked quickly. That Tapley ought to wise up. He was built too toothpickish to herd a tough old hand like Sim into a row.

Sim put his cigar in his mouth and talked around it.

"Fifty-thirty-twenty. The Dodds and Mr. Fergus take the lion's share. You'n I and Haki take the middle, and the boys forward split the hind."

Vern looked at Sim. "They take fifty?"

"Yeah, sure. That's all right. There's enough to go around. Nobody is going away short."

Vern turned to Mr. Fergus. "What do you think this trove is worth, Mr. Fergus?"

The scholar smiled easily, shrugged. "Hard to say. Quarter of a million perhaps. I wouldn't worry about it, Mr. Rigby. I think it's quite possible that we'll all end up rich."

"I won't, Mr. Fergus," Vern assured him. "I won't worry about it at all." He turned to Harvey Dodd because he didn't want to hear any more just then, and said, "Sim tells me you're a skindiver."

Dodd smiled, crinkling his eyes, dispelling the nameless tragedy they housed. "I play around at it. Spearfishing, camera work."

"What sort of a gun do you use?"

"A CO_2 Jet-Com. Lots of wallop to it. I have a peripheral vision mask. Do you use one? I like the exhaust valve setup. You have diving gear of your own, I assume?"

"Sure. In the hock shop."

"Same place we all came from, sport," Tapley said. Then he laughed and stood up. "Okey, dad," he said to Sim. "I'll get Ernie and we'll be down here tonight, kit and caboodle. Tell you what, though: a pound note would clear up a few pressing little matters that are bothering Ernie and me right now." He grinned. "You can deduct it from my share."

Sim's look was flat as he reached for his hip pocket.

"When we're in port, my son, you can call me *Sim*." He touched the name deliberately. "But when we're at sea you'll make it Captain, and you'll tag a Sir to it as well. Am I clear?"

Tapley turned his grin to Vern and winked. "My, we *are* proper. Aye, aye, Skipper."

Something began clicking a slow rhythm along the passageway. Vern looked up, realizing that the sound was being made by a pair of high-heels. The clicking missed a beat, as from a stumble, then continued. Mrs. Harvey Dodd.

From the first he thought her cold. She stepped out of the passageway and paused by the highboy, looking at them emptily. She was dressed, severely, but not plain. Cultivated class, he thought. Her hair was blonde, metallic. And though her mouth was sensuous, the eyes were dead, without promise, and he wondered just what it was that Sim and Sully had seen in her to make them think she had hotpants. Then he woke up. Infidelity was often an amoral bi-product of apathy.

When she started into the cabin, he noticed something else about her. She was being too careful with her movements, with the plastic set of her features. Drunk, he realized, and wondered at his surprise.

Tapley laid his head back and stared at her along the line of his nose. "You took the part that once was my heart," he hummed. Then he seemed to forget that he was leaving. He sat down again.

Harvey Dodd stood up, leaning against the edge of the table, his eyes critical as he spoke to his wife. "Bea, this is Vern Rigby. My wife, Rigby."

She paused pointedly, smiled slightly in Vern's general direction and inclined her head, a glossy wave slipping across her right eye. For a moment Vern thought she was going to fall.

Her eyes slid to the table top, to the beer cans, and blinked slowly as though in acceptance of an unspoken fact. "Oh — it's the cocktail hour. I'll join you." She reached for a glass and a bottle of bourbon in the highboy.

Vern glanced at Harvey. The playboy was still leaning against the table as though abandoned in suspension and not certain of how to get his feet down on the ground. He watched his wife with a tight expression that just bordered on anger.

"Bea," he said *"Bea —"*

She turned quickly, too quickly. For a split-second she did start to fall, but she recovered instantly. One slim, nyloned leg shot out and the highheel spiked her balance.

"Yes, dear? Were you about to say something amusing?"

She poured two inches of amber bourbon into the glass and started toward the table. She didn't look at Vern when she spoke.

"Harv always says the most amusing things, Mr. Rigby. Really he does. It's the reason I fell in love with him so — so very long ago."

This is nowhere, Vern thought. Nowhere at all. This is capital T trouble. Sim must be crazy.

Bea Dodd stopped by a captain's chair at the head of the table, facing all of them. She looked at the young beachcomber. "I haven't met this gentleman."

"Tapley. He's one of the crew."

Tapley raised his beer can to his grin. "Welcome aboard, shipmate," he said.

"Shipmate." She tested the word. "Now there is an endearing —"

"Bea." There was no question of Dodd's anger now. "Why don't you sit down before you fall?"

With an innocent smile Fergus turned smoothly to Vern and said, "The Seven Madonnas were named by the old Spanish seafarers who first discovered them. They thought the group was the most beautiful, serene, and of the purest aspect they had seen. Virginal. Did you know that?"

Vern knew what Fergus was trying to do and he admired him for his tact. Aside from being a pacifier, the scholar was trying his best to put Vern at ease in this unfamiliar and troubled atmosphere. But his mind wasn't completely on what the bald man was saying. Bea Dodd was crossing her legs, keeping them close together, so close he could hear the rub of the nylon.

She ignored him pointedly as she tugged at her skirt, squaring it snugly about her knees. The way a high class whore, pretending she isn't a whore, would do, Vern thought. He blinked his eyes away.

"No, I didn't know that, Mr. Fergus." But he knew some other things, and he suddenly thought, My God, it's warm in here.

30

"That's nice," Bea Dodd said. "Very nice. Harv will like that. He knows all about virgins."

"Bea —" her husband started again.

"Let's get back to cases," Sim cut in harshly. "I think everyone is squared away now except Vern." He turned to him. "What's your course, Vern?"

It wasn't good. It wasn't good at all. It would be a trouble voyage. A whackier crowd of misfits would be hard to find. But perhaps that was why he should do it. Perhaps this was where he fit in. The gutless wonder.

But there was a bigger reason why he was holding back. Like Sim had said: You can find danger enough on a clean deck. And the danger was the tipsy blonde. If he went with them he would make love to her. He knew that, knew she would see to it. And then — the wind blew and the stuff flew, and then it hit the fan.

But there was something else that went a little deeper, that he was half-heartedly ashamed of because it seemed outdated. He had a bred-in-the-bone conviction that you shouldn't make love to another man's wife, especially if you liked the guy. Somehow it just wasn't the thing to do. What was it Jimmy Nolan used to say about those wild booze orgies he had attended in Frisco after the war? Everyone doing his level best not to lay some other poor bastard's wife — and sometimes succeeding.

He looked up. They were all watching him. Bea Dodd smiled and asked, carelessly, "Calculating your end of the treasure Mr. Biggy?"

I'd like to show you just how big, sister, he thought.

"It's Rigby," he told her, and stood up. "R-i-g, as in righteous."

He looked at Sim. "I'll think about it. I'll let you know."

Sim looked worried. He held up a blunt finger, making the gesture a sign of warning. "We ain't got all the time in the world, son. We're clearing out in the morning."

Vern nodded and turned for the companionway. He wanted to get away from there, away from the girl with the brass hair and the slim, careful legs. "I'll let you know. Goodby," he said to the others.

Fergus stood up and followed him. "One moment, Vern. I was thinking you might let me see you later tonight — after you'd thought about it by yourself for a while. I think I might

31

be able to point out the advantages this voyage could hold for you."

Advantages. Vern kept his eyes off Bea Dodd and smiled.

"Sure. You can talk if you want. But I'll make up my own mind." He gave Fergus the address of his room.

Tapley clumped up the steps, going by them, shooting a parting remark. "Better come along, sport. Loan sharks can be as bitchy as saltwater ones." Then he passed through the scuttle, leaving his tuneless hum behind. "All, all, all of me."

A moment later Vern came up into the darkening evening. Singapore was now a wonderland of many-colored neon abstractions, dazzling in its night jewelry. He started to move toward land and saw that Tapley had stalled by the gangplank. Then he saw why.

The Chinese boy had been replaced in the galley doorway by a Chinese girl. She was standing there, the galley dark behind her, staring at the night city. She paid no attention to Tapley, nor to Vern when he reached Tapley's side.

Standing next to Tapley was like standing beside a tall drinking fountain. He had to look down, and he spoke in an undertone.

"Who's that?"

"Cook's woman. Nice little bit, eh?"

"Woman or wife?"

Tapley grinned. "I said it the first time. She used to work in one of those play-for-pay houses in back of Sago Street. Wonder why she gave up all that fun for the gook cook?"

They went down the plank to the quay, and Tapley seemed to suddenly realize that Vern was towering over him. He looked up and said, "This is a little too much like Mutt and Jeff. Let's break it up."

Vern couldn't tell whether he was bitter about it or not.

"Reminds me," Tapley said. "Hear the one about the midget who married the tall lady from the circus? Sure: his friends put him up to it! See you around, sport!"

Fergus liked Rigby. He was indifferent about Tapley. The little seaman was the usual South Sea riff-raff with a few added idiosyncrasies. But the diver he liked. Pity he had lost his nerve. Or had he? Perhaps he merely thought he had. Now, Mr. Haki — there was a man who had lost it completely and, he suspected, permanently.

He went down the steps and noticed that Sim had left. The Dodds and Haki sat at the table like the three points of a triangle, creating a static atmosphere out of their silence. Donald Fergus smiled. Mr. Haki was either day-dreaming or he was a very stupid man not to realize he was a third wheel.

Fergus felt sorry for the Dodds, wished he could understand the psychological gap that existed between them. Was it the boy's weakness, his inability to stand on his own feet in a man's world? Somehow, Fergus doubted it. Harvey Dodd had never had to stand on his feet until now when his inheritance money was almost gone. And Fergus knew from the talk around the Colony that the Dodds had never gotten along, even when there had been plenty of money. What was it then? The girl's drinking habit? No, there had to be a cause for the effect.

He shrugged. It was beyond him, and it wasn't really his business. He approached the table with a smile.

"Mr. Haki, I thought perhaps if you were not busy, we might go over my charts again. Get a sort of preconceived idea of what we are up against. I mean by way of currents, depth . . ."

He was amused by his own words. Mr. Haki, he knew from earlier experience, was always most gracious, most helpful — with everything except pointing out the exact wreck-site on the charts. It was only, as Mr. Haki explained it, that he had never been a seaman and did not understand charts. Mr. Haki was a very cautious man.

Haki looked up, the light from the deckhead lamp catching silver sparks off his glasses, and bowed his burred head. "So pleased," he hissed.

Harvey Dodd watched the two men walk off companionably. The fox and the snake, he thought wryly. Then he forgot about them. He looked at his wife.

He ran his eye down the line of her legs, stopping when he reached the open-toe network of her pumps. Something twinged through his body, stiffening him: a minor thrill of sensation like a weak current of electricity, positive but not painful. Sensuous, he thought. My God, but she is. Even now after five years. But why does she have to hate my goddam guts?

"Bea," he said, softly now, almost imperatively.

She started as if the name had jabbed her. Then she relaxed as though she were going to fall apart, and reached for the bottle.

"All right. In a moment," she murmured.

But already he knew it wasn't going to be worth it. To some other, perhaps, but not to him.

Vern walked slowly through a new section of Crown Colony apartment buildings. Each building looked like its brother and each apartment offered its inhabitants a window and a private balcony in the front. The balconies were vivid white against the coral-colored walls and rose neatly in tiers of three, jutting out from the face like futuristic diving boards for a gigantic swimming pool. An arcade with orderly, glass-fronted shops ran beneath the apartments on the sidewalk level.

He stopped and looked in a dress shop window. In one corner a pale, legless mannequin wore a sheer-nylon negligee of powder blue that contrasted shockingly with the corpse-white of her painted body. He thought of Bea Dodd, activating her into the blue negligee and upstairs in one of the apartments, and himself with her. A phonograph would purr mood music at them. Only one light would be on, softly. She'd be standing in the center of the room, her visible breasts rising and falling as she watched him . . .

He leaned his face against the cold glass pane and closed his eyes. Cut it out, Rigby. Walk, sap. Walk it out. He turned and started down the arcade again.

He didn't see any sense in kidding himself. He wanted her, and the trouble was he knew it was there waiting for him and he was walking away from it. She meant no more to him than one of the little Eurasian whores he used to assuage his natural desire. But her skin was fair, her nose wasn't flat, her eyes didn't slant, her breasts . . .

Jesus, he said. Jesus.

He pushed his way down crowded Sago Street in Chinatown, where jaywalking was the rule, letting the rickshaws, trishaws, and pedicabs clatter out of his path, and turned into an international bar.

An obscure, insignificant blur of faces mingled with the heavy smoke clouds. Their mouths vociferated in a bedlam of dialects, and laughter covered every octave from a gutteral chuckle to a high screech. Many individual parties at the far end of the room blended into one huge party of drinkers, smokers, talkers, bitter argumentative cursers. In the faces of all the girls was the same hardened expectation of the possibilities that the environment and circumstances called for.

Vern looked around to see if that Special Girl was there and got the impression that she was — with a tipsy, pawing-under-the-skirt sailor in an active corner — but that he was ten years too late. She was listening to the sailor who was talk-talk-talking, and she wore that certain fixed smile that meant she was trying to keep from screaming, and her eyes were distant and blank and like eyes that didn't belong to a human being. She didn't seem to be at all aware of the hand under her skirt.

A part of Vern was made up of the romantic souvenirs of his imaginative boyhood, and for an absurd moment he thought of walking over there and saying to the girl, *Come with me*. But he didn't, because even if he did they would both know that it was just for tonight, that tomorrow morning they would have to leave the rumpled bed and face living again. And living meant earning money. And besides, she was already dead; so far dead that he doubted if she really wanted to return again.

He shoved up to the bar and said "Rye."

He looked at himself in the streaked mirror that caught every glint of light in the room and threw it back to dazzle the eyes of the lookers searching for themselves. His reflection showed him a tall, tired man with a shadow over his eyes. He turned wearily away.

He looked at the other faces, at the vari-colored faces that were different yet somehow suggested kinship, like a band of stupid brothers outshouting each other in an effort to obscure their mean little souls. All of their eyes had the same stare, quick or slow, brown, black or green, a concentrated emptiness.

Here's to you, kinsmen, he toasted them silently.

A girl, who looked as if a Javanese mother had misbehaved with a European father one night in the scrub, edged along the bar. She stared at Vern's motionless reflection for a moment, then turned to smile aggressively at him. Her eyes, he noted, had come from the parent with the white touch. She was short with long black hair hanging far down her back, stocky, with tight yellow skin that glowed. She wore a Western dress that covered only the extremes and a pair of spike heels that were similar to the pair Bea Dodd had worn.

"You buy dlink?" she asked.

35

He smiled and placed a hand on her hip, liking the tactile feel of the dress, observing that she wore nothing beneath it.

"Sure, sister of mine."

She laughed coquettishly, cuddling against his chest, rolling large eyes up at him. "You come along me later, maybe so?" she offered. "You like me fine?"

"Fine," he said huskily. "Just fine. But in the dark. It must be in the dark."

But the dark helped nothing. Nor did closing his eyes and trying to pretend that the girl under him was Bea Dodd. The girl who had sprung from the indiscreet Javanese mother seemed to think that conversation was the best part of the carnal act, and she chattered along in her peculiar singsong pidgin with no regard for commas or periods, and her voice had the cadence of water filling a bathtub. And on top of that the female scent was far from being a white female scent, but belonged wholeheartedly to the mysterious East; betal and spice and everything not so nice.

And when it was over and finished and she brightly asked, "More? You like more?" he shook his head and straightened up and felt sick. Then she thought perhaps she could help talk him into another round and he had to push her damp hand away. "No more," he said curtly.

The windows like French doors were open on the night and on the night-running city, and the moonlight came in like a quiet silver-haired cat looking for a spot to curl up and nap. He looked at the girl on the bed, ivory-toned now in the moonlight, the outline of her large soft breast standing up like a pale tent against the darkness of the room.

Snowy breasts fitting into champagne glasses . . . thighs like a wild white mare. Where had he read that?

He shrugged and stood up, looking for his clothes. Time to pay and go. Paying for nothing, going nowhere.

"You come back again sometime, ah so?" Her drowsy, companionable voice lulled in the shadowy darkness.

"Yes," he lied. "Sometime."

While in the same part of town, though in another house (a

house well established for the purpose and known as the Abode of Everlasting Joy), Harvey Dodd enjoyed himself profusely and expressively under the warm, stale glare of an electric light with three Oriental girls (also well established for the purpose), wearing only three pairs of jade earrings.

And this was Harvey's way and it was as necessary to him as water was to a fish.

In the beginning, the Genesis of Harvey Dodd, he had been a spoiled, precocious, too-sweet-looking brat, living the pampered existence of a rich man's son. That had been Phase One in his life and he always looked back on it with a fond sense of euphoria. Then some naughty little schoolmates had whispered to him that there was a difference between boys and girls and, with rough diagrams hastily and excitedly drawn, had showed him what the difference was and what they thought was supposed to be done about it.

That started Phase Two.

The longing, searching, wanting, needing; the wild day-dreams and fantastic night-dreams; the secretly-collected treasure trove of magazines depicting provocative-looking young girls in various stages of undress, and the ever-expanding stack of four-by-five glossy photographs showing erotic behavior of bedroom athletics; the constant wondering when, *when*, for God's sake? When would he meet a girl in the voluptuous flesh who would be willing to do with him what the girls in the illicit photographs did.

And then on one of the 365 nights of his fifteenth year, he miraculously found Phase Three in the backseat of his father's car, parked at the country club along with all the other Buicks and Cadillacs. She was sixteen and home for vacation from one of the best finishing schools, and she liked his boyish good looks and witty manner, and even though she was as green as spring grass at it, the frantic fumbling, panting, whispering, wet-kissing gyrations made Harvey believe that this was the total accumulation of all his childhood dreams.

Unfortunately, he had never dreamed that the girl's father would find out about it. But he did and he told Harvey's father, and suddenly everyone seemed to know. Then the shrieking recriminations and the wails of anguish, the red-faced fathers and the fainting mothers, and the smelling salts arriving on silver trays via secretly amused butlers; and finally, conclusively, Harvey being sent to Europe under the watchful eye of a male tutor and a male guardian.

But Phase Three was not to be thwarted by such minor obstacles. Money, Harvey soon discovered, bought anything — even the eyes of the tutor and the guardian. And in Europe there were French girls and Italian girls and Spanish girls and Serbian girls and tall, thin, stately English girls from across the channel. And so the tutor and the guardian were happy with their share of the Dodd money, and the various girls were happy with it too, and Harvey was so happy that he never did return to America but passed out of puberty and into manhood there on the orgy-loving Continent.

Then, on the Riviera, he met Bea Sloane.

She was an expatriate and her early life had more or less followed the same materialistic pattern of Harvey's. She could just as well have been the sixteen-year-old girl in the back of Harvey's father's Buick: only in her case she had been seventeen and the car had been a Cadillac, and the boy's name had been Billy or Tommy or Jimmy, she couldn't remember. Only now the family funds had dissipated and Bea was on her own, in a manner of speaking. But she was beautiful and cultured and worldly and the type of girl that rich people liked to have along. So she went along and didn't worry too much about tomorrow but let it take care of itself.

All of their friends thought that Harvey and Bea were a perfect match. Such a fine, young, healthy, handsome couple they made. Such refinement, such breeding. They might very well represent the furthermost evolution of the young upper class. Bless their darling hearts, just two pampered, pretty little children: the world's sweethearts.

And then Bea and Harvey made the mistake of being hoodwinked into the same belief. "Let's settle down — to each other," they said, starry-eyed. "Let's marry and make the world a playland. Let's loll around on the ivory beaches in the warm south-wind days and make open love and drink Napoleon Brandy. Let's live in a pink and white villa over the bay and drink calvados in the mistral nights and make more love. Let's . . ."

And so they had, and so Phase Four.

It had been a long, interesting street with many pausing alleyways, leading from the Riviera to Singapore, and it had taken five years. But it had only taken Bea five weeks to realize that Harvey had a problem: a pathological sexuality so intense that almost anything sensually suggestive triggered it and he

38

had to be assuaged and right now. And if it wasn't right now, then there was no living with him.

Certain things, she discovered with dismay, caused a reaction in him like snapping on a light switch: highheels, nylons, garters, black panties (or green or blue or white,), bras, sheer negligees, too-short skirts, too-tight sweaters, a gesture, a movement, a look. You name it, he'd try it. And after a while she learned that whenever she wanted a rest from it, she would practically have to dress in burlap and make like the Hag of the Hesperus.

Then too, his physical expression to the reactions took devious tributaries to the norm. At first, for her, it had been different, exciting: a reaching, creeping, searching for carnal expression, for something unmentioned which perhaps strained to go beyond physical limits. And there had been experiments — she tentative in the beginning, growing bolder, lustier, then realizing that they weren't experiments to Harvey. He *knew* what he was doing. He'd damn well been there before!

But the experiment in the bathtub had been the final straw. After all, a girl, a normal young wife, should be allowed to take a nice hot, soapy bath in peace. But no. Harvey came into the bathroom for some reason or other, wearing nothing but his wedding ring and a bright glassy look in his eyes, and had stood over the tub staring down at her. Then, without a word of warning, she was no longer alone in the tub. And there simply wasn't that much room (it was an undersized tub in an undersized Sevilla hotel), and the jarring, unexpected rush of it forced her face under the foamy water and she got it in her eyes and nostrils and mouth, and she came up gasping and hitting at him and trying to push him off, and she thought, What in the hell *is* this?

Then they had a supreme fight, and the essence of it was this:

"You don't want a wife! You want a dirty little degraded whore!"

"You stupid little bitch! Every normal man does. That's what he expects of his wife in the bedroom!"

"Not four and five times a day, every normal man doesn't! And not in a bathtub, either! Nor in the middle of the living room floor, nor over the edge of the breakfast table! *Bed*room? We haven't used a bedroom since the day we were married!"

39

And then he had slammed out of the hotel room and she had known quite well where he was going and what he was going to do there; and he did, and many times after that in many different lands.

Now it was their last night in Singapore and Bea was alone in her cabin aboard the old schooner, while Harvey was in the Abode of Everlasting Joy and he was far from being alone.

And it was strange and different: wild as savagery at its fever-pitch, erotic as a pimply-faced highschool-boy's daydreams. Hot, moist bodies coiling, writhing, snaking over crumpled sheets, breasts against chest, mouth glued to mouth, loin to loin; then everything breaking, dissolving, regrouping again, sensuously crawling feeling . . . stand back and look and the activated scene loses its state of being, its identity with flesh, humans, love . . . hothouse plants entwining, strangling each other through a need of expressing living life. The last and Final Phase.

It was after midnight when Vern returned to his room. He didn't know if he felt better or if he was going to be sick. He was dead broke, he knew that. His last pound note had gone to the Eurasian girl. Somehow the knowledge didn't disturb him. Maybe, the monitor of his mind suggested craftily, it's because you know you have an ace in the hole — Sim's offer. He shook his head in annoyance and opened the door.

Immediately, even though the room was like the womb of an inkwell, he knew he wasn't alone. He closed the door, stepping quickly to one side, and put his back to the wall.

"Rig?" A voice cracked the black stillness.

"Yes. Rigby. Who is it?"

"Hit the light, sport."

He reached for the switch, wondering what the little seaman wanted of him. Probably a touch. That was a laugh. The single overhead light snapped the shabby room into dull dimension, suggesting more of its sordidness than pure daylight could ever show.

Tapley sat in the cane-bottom chair near the window, the only chair. He rubbed his eyes and grinned at Vern. "Got a smoke, sport? I'm ready to roll coffee grounds — if I had coffee grounds."

"No. What do you want? I'm tap-city, so I'll save your asking."

Tapley set his head on one side, studied him. "Been back here tonight, sport? I mean since you left the schooner?"

Vern leaned against the door and folded his arms. He was in no mood for nonsense. "No. I scrounged along the quay for a while until I found some old fishheads that a couple of leprous Malays had discarded, for my dinner. Then I went into a public urinal where I think I caught something. And then went down to Sago and bummed a few shillings from the rickshaw boys so I could buy myself a glass of wine. I've been nursing the one glass ever since. Does that fill out today's chapter for you?"

Tapley grinned, hunched forward on the cane-bottom. He wagged a finger toward the cot. "You got a buddy boy over there. Another visitor."

Vern looked at the cot. A man was lying quietly on top of the blankets. Donald Fergus. Vern frowned. Why in hell was he sleeping there? Then he remembered that he was supposed to see Fergus that night.

He placed a hand on Fergus' shoulder and shook. "Fergus — wake up, Mr. Fergus." He looked again at the scholar's face, at the eyes. They were open, dead open.

He stepped back, wiping his left hand on his pants. Absently he felt that the hand was contaminated. So, he thought, you've touched dead men before. But this was different, this was . . . No, he couldn't believe that Fergus was actually dead. He sat down on the cot and felt for a pulse.

"I've already gone through that bit, sport," Tapley's voice called him back.

He straightened and looked around. Tapley was smiling a queer little smile, his eyes wary. His lips moved slightly as he hummed. "Your goodby, left me with eyes that cry."

"You want to tell me about it?" Vern suggested with implication.

"Hey! Don't hand me that score. I found him just like that."

"You came up here and found him like this?"

"Uh-huh, dead in bed. I blew the schooner same time you did, remember? Then I went down to my digs and told Ernie, my partner, the scoop. After that I wandered around the Settlement for a while by my lone." He paused and cocked a hand pistol-like at Vern.

"Tell you what, sport. I'm a cautious little bugger.
41

Somehow this deal didn't smell right. It spooked me. So when I ran into Rob Hanks — Navy diver, you know him — he told me where you was living and I scooted up here. I knock on door. Door drifts open. I stick head inside and spot bingo on the bed. Scared me for a minute. I thought it was you."

"Thanks for the concern. What time did you spot him?"

"About an hour ago. You didn't do it, did you, sport?"

"No, I didn't do it. And I've got an idea — it's a sneaky sort of idea, I admit, but there it is — that you *know* I didn't."

"Hey-hey, you're trying to push it on me again. So help me, Rig, I found him just like that. Roll him over; you'll see that someone aced a shiv in his back."

Vern left the body alone. He said, "What did you hang around for?"

"I told you, I wanted to see you."

"Why?"

Tapley rubbed at the lower half of his face. Then he pointed at the cot. "For reasons like this, I guess. I dunno, something about the whole deal bugged me wrong. Those people. What a screw-loose outfit. And there's always something risky about partners and lost treasure. Know what I mean? It ain't like any other kind of business."

Vern nodded. He could understand that.

Tapley stood up and took a quick nervous turn around the room. He looked at Vern and stopped, as though he'd reached a decision.

"I guess you know why I'm such a gate mouth," he said.

Vern looked away. He felt his pockets for a cigarette, then remembered he was out. He didn't like confessions. It embarrassed him to have people haul out their souls and toss them at his feet for inspection. He knew why Tapley had a big mouth.

"Sure," Tapley said, "it's a cover up. Same with any little guy. We've got to act tough so people will forget how goddam little we really are. We got to come out swinging with our mouths. We got to point out everyone else's defects and keep 'em all so confused they won't suddenly wake up and say, 'Hey! You're a shrimp, ain't yuh?' Yeah. But you know all this. I could tell first time I met you."

"All right," Vern said. "So we've all got our defects."

Tapley nodded. "That's right, Rig, we all do. Some of us are short, some fat, some crippled, some ugly, and some of us are perfect outside but shot to hell inside."

Vern looked at him sharply. But the little man's expression was blank.

"You were going to tell me why you came up here."

Tapley looked impatient. "Jesus, I just did. Don't you see it? I want in on this treasure deal. I've goddam got to be in. I'm on the rocks. But I don't go for that bunch of nitwits. I looked 'em all over real careful and decided that you were the boy for me. Wake up, Rig! I'm saying I trust you. I want to be your buddy boy. If something goes wrong I'll stand behind you, and you'll stand —" he grinned, "— in front of me."

Vern smiled. "What about your friend? What's wrong with him?"

"Who? Ernie? Nothing. But when God said brains Ernie thought He said trains, and he missed his. Anyhow, I came up here because I was afraid you were going to walk out on the play. I came to see if I could get you to change your mind."

Vern glanced over his shoulder at the wax-like form lying behind him. "You were lucky. That's why Fergus came." He paused, reflecting, trying to recall something that bothered him. Then remembered.

"If I recall correctly, you were the only person near us when Fergus asked if he could come see me tonight."

Tapley smiled crookedly and shook his head reprovingly.

"Easy, easy. There you go again. Let's not make a habit of it, huh? He could have mentioned it to any of them after you'n me left. Any of 'em."

Vern was looking at Fergus again. He had liked this man, and someone had put a knife in him. He had to admit that he liked Tapley, too, and Sim and Sully. And was someone waiting to put a knife in them as well? Funny, now that he thought of it, he liked Haki and Dodd also. And Mrs. Dodd? He frowned and shifted his eyes. He was caught up in this thing, inexorably, and it was something he couldn't turn his back on and walk away from.

I'm a victim of friendship, he thought self-mockingly.

He stood up and looked at Tapley. "I'm not going to take the tumble for this." He motioned his head toward the cot. "When they find him, I want it to be in some other place. Even if I'm out to sea."

Tapley wet his lips as though tasting them.

"You want to dump him somewheres? You're in, then?"

Vern shrugged. "Looks like it hasn't been left up to me. I'm going to carry Fergus down to the docks and put him out of sight. You want to help me?"

Tapley wiped his hands slowly along the sides of his dungarees. He smiled abruptly and moved toward the cot.

"I'd carry him out of here by myself, if I could. Give me a hand with him, sport."

Sim looked at their faces, touching each one with his stern eyes. They were sitting about the table in an aura of tense silence, bathed in the warm cuddy light. Together now, all except the gook girl (Ling-Po kept her in wraps) and Donald Fergus. And Vern had said that the scholar was lying inside a rotting fish shack under a pile of burlap on one of the nameless little quays.

Sim was not a layman philosopher in the sense that Rigby or Harvey Dodd might be, but forty-eight years at sea among ships, seamen and savages had given him a wise composure on the vicissitudes of life, and he found Fergus' last resting place grimly ironic. He knew that books and scholars had their definite, necessary niche in the world, but they weren't his meat. He could get along with or without them. But it bothered him, vaguely, that a man of Fergus' intellect, breeding and education should end up forgotten on some filthy wharf under a pile of stinking burlap. It was a fitting end for a seaman, not for a scholar. He suspected that at times fate was too tricky.

Now, studying the ring of silent faces, he saw the uneasiness and the unspoken fear that crouched in their hearts and minds. And it disturbed him because he knew he was fighting an intangible, and that was worse than quelling a ten-man mutiny single-handed. If he couldn't bring them out of this web of doubt and suspicion it was quite possible that they would throw up the deal and call it quits.

Spineless, he thought. What do they know of fear, of trouble? He wanted to clutch the edge of the table in his great battered hands, shout at them in his quarterdeck voice, drum sense into their heads. He didn't. He spoke quietly with admirable control.

"I know what you're thinking. You've got it in your noodles that someone here in this cuddy slipped Fergus' hawser for him. Well, I don't think so. I think he was done in by some gook hood or beachcomber for whatever could be found on him."

"Why in my room, Sim?" Vern asked.

"Why not? Someone trailed him there. Maybe some gook

44

that lives in that flea house. Who knows? You said yourself his wallet and watch were missing." He paused, looked at them with authority.

"My sons, when you've lived as long as I have you'll find that life is nothing but a big poker game. The guy sitting next to you gambles all and loses. His cards go against him and he runs out of chips. So he drops from the game. But you don't stop playing because his luck ran out. You say to yourself 'That's tough,' and 'I'm glad it wasn't me,' and you go right on playing because the stakes are high and because you still got a chance to win.

"All right, let's look at the brass tacks. Let's put Fergus in his proper place in this game. He was necessary in the beginning to help build up the pot. But now the pot is right, and it's sitting there smack in front of you, and Fergus has dropped out. See the play? Fergus don't matter no longer."

He paused, watching them, seeing that they didn't like it, and yet knowing that they recognized the callous truth.

"We've got a ship. We've got a crew to handle her. We've got Haki to show us the place and Vern to dive for us. Now what are you going to do? Throw in your hand because your shipmate left the game — and you with aces?"

Bea Dodd rattled the ice cubes in her glass, dispelling the sudden hush that followed Sim's question. She smiled sweetly and looked at her drink when she spoke.

"You are very eloquent, Captain Sim. Very eloquent indeed. It would behoove my husband to listen to you more often. I suspect that if he did he would incorporate you in one of his stories; one of the stories that he is always going to write — someday."

Harvey Dodd looked up with a start. He had been listening absently to the clink of the ice cubes, thinking they sounded like strips of Chinese glass shaking in the wind. The simile had bothered him because he realized he was very tired of the Orient.

"Bea," he said warningly. He glanced surreptitiously at the others before settling his eyes on Sim. The old man was watching him stolidly.

I wish I could have your strength, sea dog, he wanted to say. I wish I could have your power of purpose. You're like an older, more battered edition of Wolf Larsen from *The Sea Wolf*. Perhaps Bea, in her bitchy way, is right. It would behoove me to listen to you.

45

"I see your point, Captain," he said aloud. "It's brutal, as I suppose is your way, but it's honest. I do have a stake in this game, and I'm going to play it to the end."

Bea Dodd set her glass down and clapped her hands. "Bravo!" she cried. "The young man from Back Bay comes through with family crest flying! He sets aside childish things and takes up his cards — as the good captain would phrase it — and says, 'Damn the torpedos! I double the bet.'"

Vern grimaced. She wasn't *that* drunk. He wanted to reach out and slap her. Automatically he said, "Why don't you relax, Mrs. Dodd? This isn't any too easy for your husband. I imagine Mr. Fergus was a friend of his."

For a fraction of a second her black pupils filled with a dull red light. And when she looked at him, he thought he saw something in them that was beyond the present, something that reached into the past when she had been innocent, more fragile.

"Thank you, Mr. Rigby, spelled with a righteous. As long as we're going to be shipmates, you must promise me that you'll speak right up every time I say something to my husband that you don't approve of. Perhaps you'd care to move into our compartment with us in order to be certain that you don't miss any untoward remarks I might imprudently make."

It was much too long a speech for her to attempt at the moment. He could see her breaking up after the tenth word. And suddenly she did, as the last of it came out with a rush. Her face crumpled together like a cracked porcelain vase. She put a hand to her eyes, sobbed an almost inaudible gasp, and stood up. She walked out of the cuddy quickly, wobbling slightly, her heels clicking the deck brokenly.

Then Harvey stood up, his little-boy's face a tight indignant mask.

"There was no necessity for that, Rigby," he snapped. "I'll thank you to keep your goddam nose out of my personal affairs." He hesitated and looked at the others. "If you'll excuse me, gentlemen." He walked to the passageway, then looked back. "Decide the matter among yourselves. You know where I stand."

Vern felt so foolish he thought he was going to be sick. He wanted to stand up and kick himself. He wanted to walk away from the whole whacky crowd and forget he'd ever met them. What had possessed him to say such a stupid thing?

Tapley was grinning at him from across the table.

46

"All of me; why not try all of me?"

Sim's clear voice cut through the song. "I won't say she didn't have that coming, but you were out of line, Vern. Well, you know it, and there's no sense making a mountain out of it. Let's face the issue again. Are we going or ain't we?"

Suddenly Vern realized they were all watching him: the two Orientals, the two ship's officers, the two common seamen. What is this, he wondered. What am I supposed to be? Then he understood. All of them wanted to go, but without him they were wasting their time. He was their diver.

You crazy bastards, he thought. Don't you see how badly this thing is beginning? Can't you see where it will end? Don't you care? Are you all that desperate? Am I?

He stood up and nodded his head, answering for them. "We go."

Harvey Dodd opened the door to their stateroom and looked into the cramped cabin. It was outrageously small: a double bunk (which he didn't approve of) against the right bulkhead; a wardrobe locker and a small deal table, complete with mirror, along the left; between them, opposite the door, a white enamel basin.

Bea Dodd was sitting at the table, facing the mirror. She was in a negligee and she was without makeup. He didn't like her that way. Her face was too much like a young girl's, a young girl recovering from a long sickness.

She had been combing her hair, but now she was doing nothing. Just sitting, staring at her reflection in the mirror. Her eyes moved when he opened the door, seeing him. Then she looked at herself again. Her face was void of expression.

"Are you all right, Bea?" he asked.

"Yes. Yes, I'm all right."

He hesitated, feeling for a cigarette. He glanced at her face-reflection. "I put Rigby in his place. I told him exactly what I thought of him."

Her eyes shifted again, seeking him in the mirror. "Did you hit him, Harv?" she asked coldly. "Did you exert your manhood?"

He blinked, frowning, and looked away.

"Well, no. I didn't think that . . ."

"No, you wouldn't."

He was angry suddenly, unreasonably angry. He wanted to strike something; her, the bulkhead, Rigby. His head snapped up and he glared at her reflection. "Is that what you want? I'll go out there now and call him on deck, if you think I should. My God, Bea, I'm not afraid of the man, you know!"

"No," she said tonelessly, "that isn't what I want. I'm sorry, Harv. I know you're not afraid of him. Let's not talk about it."

He said nothing. He felt his pockets again. Then he went to his bunk for the cigarettes he kept on the small shelf when he wanted a smoke at night. His wife's bra and nylon panties were lying on the lower bunk. He paused, looking at them. He touched the nylon with his fingertips, stroking its smoothness, making it crackle. He straightened up, the cigarettes forgotten.

He turned, took two steps and placed his hands on his wife's shoulders. "Bea —" he whispered. He felt her flinch under his palms, and looked at her reflection in the mirror, not wanting to see what he knew he would see in her eyes, yet unable not to look.

She moved and his hands fell away. Her dark eyes were glistening as though filled with bits of broken glass, and her eyelids flickered as if it pained her.

"You just don't understand, do you, Harv? You simply can't feel about anything — except my body, can you?"

He stepped back, his stomach a tight little ball. He said nothing, saw nothing. He turned and walked out of the cabin.

Across the passageway, in the second cabin, Vern lay on his upper pipe berth and stared at the water reflection dancing on the deckhead above his face. The port was open and he listened to the far-off murmur of men's voices, the splash and gurgle of the harbor water where it slapped fondly at the schooner's counter, and the distant drone of the night-living city.

"Vern?"

It was Sully speaking from the lower berth.

"Yeah?"

"You ever been to the Black Belt?"

"In the war. Guadalcanal."

"I mean have you worked around there since the war?"

Vern said no.

The night music crept back into the cabin. He turned his head and looked at the open port. When he closed his eyes he saw Fergus' waxen face.

Sully sighed heavily. "I've been there often. From N.G. down to Caledonia. Strange, isn't it?"

It was a rhetorical question and Vern disliked them. But he said, "What is?"

"The Black Belt. A chain of islands peopled with Negroes; with Micronesians and Polynesians on one side of them and Indonesians on the other. How did the black people end up in the center?"

Vern didn't really give a damn. "Probably came from Australia. The full-blood natives are dark."

"Aborigines," Sully said with a touch of disdain. "They aren't the same. Haven't you ever noticed that? Anthropologists recognize the Australoids as a separate division of the human race."

Vern didn't care to pursue the problem, but the phrase: *a separate division of the human race* stuck in his mind. He thought of Sully and himself, Sim and Haki, the Dodds, the Chinese cook and his woman, and the two seamen, and the schooner nosing her way out to El Dorado far across the sea. A separate division . . .

"Yeah," Sully's voice lifted again, touching him in his drowse and stirring him slightly, "a chain of islands peopled with Negroes. Strange."

The old schooner *Sally Lou* ran out of Singapore under the first streak of dawn. Harvey Dodd, leaning at the taffrail with the wind rustling his hair, watched the sleeping city fall behind in their rose-tinted wake. The white company buildings with their orange-tiled roofs sat squat and somber along the quiet quay, pockmarked with their many windows and doors. Like so many cliff dwellings in a steep canyon, he thought. Then he straightened up, nodded at Sim and started forward.

The *Sally Lou* nosed down the middle of the strait, past Batam and Bintan islands and broke into the South China Sea with the sun standing over the bowsprit like a guiding beacon light. Harvey felt that something was expanding inside him, something new and glorious. Flight, he thought, is a matter of money; freedom is the will of God. But he was an agnostic and he smiled crookedly at his own thought.

Sim also smiled as he watched the young man go forward. He was doing some expanding himself. He glanced back at the purple hump of land with a scornful eye. Singapore Beach had not been good to him. Nor had he been alone. That beach had been downright crowded.

He looked at the flat, phlegmatic face of the Dutchman, Ernie, as he stood stolidly at the wheel. A stupid block of a man, he decided. The type that would follow a little loud-mouth like Tapley about. He wondered if Tapley garnisheed the Dutchman's wages. He'd seen that happen often enough.

He paused at the edge of the skylight and looked down into the shadowy cuddy. Vern Rigby and Bea Dodd were sitting alone at the table. Sim straightened up and smiled. He put a cigar in his mouth and strolled away to shout at Tapley about the slant of the inner jib.

Bea Dodd had dressed herself for a sun bath on the cargo hatch. She was clad in body oil, sun-glasses and a tight, sparse bikini. She had stopped for her breakfast in the cuddy and had remained there waiting for the sun, passing the time away with coffee and cigarettes. Then Vern had entered the cabin.

They sat across the table from one another and stared at their coffee cups. She crossed her bare legs, carefully, and he glanced up. His eyes lingered on her gleaming body involuntarily, moving thoughtfully over her smooth contours and pausing when they reached the Alps, where they swelled threateningly above the narrow strip of colored bra.

She looked up suddenly and caught him, and his embarrassment amused her. She knew the man. He might not like her, but he wanted her.

"Are you getting your eyes full?" she asked coldly.

"Yeah — both of 'em."

"You object to my attire?"

He frowned and looked at his cup. "Look, Mrs. Dodd. There are only two females on this ship, you know. You wander around here in that getup — with that figure — and it might cause some trouble."

She smiled icily. "Thank you for the compliment. Does it bother you?"

He grinned at her. "I know how you mean that, and you're right."

She opened her eyes very wide and childlike.

50

"Are you going to attack me, Mr. Rigby? Mr. Righteous Rigby?"

"No, I'm going to try to control myself, Mrs. Dodd. If I find that I'm weakening I'll have Sully lock me in my cabin at night. It will be hard — no double-meaning intended — but I'll try and remain righteous." He leaned back on the bench and lighted a cigarette and looked at her through the swirl of smoke.

"You remind me of a teen-age girl I once knew, Mrs. Dodd. She was very cute, very built and sexy-looking. She liked to act like a little whore, you know, tease the boys along. Unfortunately, the fat sweaty truck driver who snatched her behind his rig one night didn't know that she was only crying wolf."

"Thanks for the warning," she said stiffly. "I also knew an innocent teen-aged girl once. She knew nothing of men or life except what she had read in novels. When she was planning her first date, her mother, who was very strict, fussed and fretted until the poor girl finally cried, 'If you don't leave me alone I'll go out and become a wore!' Her mother couldn't understand her. 'You'll become a what?' 'A wore! a wore!' the poor girl cried. You see, she'd been so sheltered she'd never heard the word, only read it in books, and she tried to pronounce it with the W."

Vern grinned, sincerely feeling the grin this time. "That's a charming story. Are you going to tell me that you were that innocent little teen-ager?"

She stood up, looking pointedly bored. "Yes, I was. Who was the little switch-tail the sweaty truck driver raped? Your sister?"

She walked across the cuddy and disappeared down the passageway. Vern wrapped his hand around his coffee cup. The fact that he had no sister didn't block the intent of the insult.

Time passed. He smoked and sipped coffee and thought. His mind formed pictures, dissolved them, overlapped them, confused them. The girl, her half-naked body; Fergus, alive and dead; an ancient sunken wreck embedded in coral; savages with cartridges in their noses; the girl . . .

The Jap diver, Haki, came down the corridor and entered the cuddy. He acted surprised to see Vern sitting there. It had something to do with manners; they always acted that way.

"Oh," he said and hissed politely. "So sorry to bother you."

51

"No, not at all. Come in, Haki. Have some coffee with me."

"So kind, so very kind. Thank you so much. Please, I will not interrupt your thoughts?"

Oh for God's sake. "No. Please sit down."

"So nice."

They sat silently, contentedly, listening to the creak and give of the old schooner as it slipped along. Then Vern asked, "Were you in the war, Haki?"

The Jap diver smiled and his eyes, behind their thick sheltering windows, slid sideways as though he were looking warily at something that stood just back of his elbow. "Yes. I was infantry sergeant in the Imperial Army. So sorry."

Vern swallowed a smile. "Where? Guadalcanal?"

Haki hesitated. His eyes moved quickly, and he smiled again.

"Yes. So sorry. You were there too, please?"

Vern nodded, wondering if this strange little man and he had ever traded shots. It wouldn't be much of a contest today, he thought. I could crush him with one hand. Or could he? Maybe Haki would judo him all over the cuddy. Could be. He'd seen it happen before. Anyhow, it doesn't matter now, he thought. Times have changed. Today we're supposed to marry them.

"Tell me about the *Habanera*," he said.

Haki's eyes were suddenly harassed. He touched his thin lips with the tip of his tongue and raised a hand to adjust his glasses.

"It is very deep," he said softly. "It is down where the shadow is, where the weeds grow unhampered by the coral. It is, please, like nothing else I have ever seen. No, and do not wish to see again. It is a ghost place, you understand, please? There is a noise, a booming hollow noise, and there is a shadow above you, so large, so terrible! It — I will never go there again. So sorry for you, Mr. Rigby. So sorry that I cannot help you."

Vern said nothing. He sat holding his coffee cup, staring through the curling cigarette smoke, seeing the shark curving upward gracefully, coming out of the shadows, always coming.

The day's passage, though uneventful, had been profitable to

52

Harvey Dodd. He felt that his soul had become a free agent running with abandon before the rushing forefoot of the schooner, intent in the search of the farthermost mystery of mid-ocean solitude. He loved to rove the decks of the ancient schooner, loved the rise-and-sink motion under the soles of his shoes. The wind in his face and in his shirt, making a balloon of it, was clean and free. The salt on his lips and about the corners of his eyes was the spice of life. He was happy — as long as he didn't think of Bea, or of the others, the many, many others. He stomped along the deck, rolling with the cant of the ship, and he even nodded cheerily at the Chinese cook standing indolently in the galley doorway.

At dusk Sully came on deck with a battered guitar, sat himself with his back to the scuttle and strummed at the strings with a blunt, calloused thumb. Harvey was fascinated with him. The mate wore nothing but a pair of fouled trousers, greatly tattered in the cuffs, a sheath knife on his hip and a gold earring in his left ear. He threw back his head as his thumb whanged the strings and sang as though defying the wind song.

> "Only one more day, my Johnny,
>   One more day!
> Oh, rock and roll me over,
>   Only one more day!
>
> Don't you hear the old man calling,
> Can't you hear the pilot bawling.
> Only one more day, Johnny!"

He laughed, then — "Hi, Johnny!" he shouted, and his broad bare foot struck a *thump-thumathuma-thump* against the deck and his thumb raced and skidded across the strings.

Ling-Po watched the mate from the seclusion of the galley door, and sneered without a change of facial expression. Nigger, he said. Nigger, nigger! Then he turned and went into the galley, went to the sink and slid the louvered window aside and looked out. He saw Sully sitting and strumming, Sim standing complacently at the break of the poop, and Harvey Dodd leaning his back to the starboard bulwark, smiling at the mate.

A white brute, a black fool, and a capitalistic bastard, he thought. Fine shipmates for a man of the people. He grunted

53

and slammed the louver shut. He remained at the sink staring at nothing, immobile, semi-tragic, swaying unconsciously with the ship, feeling the power of the sea under his feet, listening to the sharp clatter of his pots and pans as they clinked tinnily one against the other, swinging like round black heads in the oneness of a primitive rhythm.

He hated the sea. It was frightening. Hated the confused, arrogant, hopelessly inept white people with their grubby little schooner and their lost treasure. He didn't belong here. He belonged on the land of his fathers', the vast, brawling, breeding East, fighting for those who were preyed upon by capitalism, superstition, ignorance, defeatism and disease.

But they didn't give me a fair chance, he thought bitterly. They turned against me as though it was my fault that the assassination ended on a tragic note.

The Central Committee had sent a request to his party cell for a man trained with a machine gun and he, because of his field experience with the plantation raiders, had been the obvious choice.

The Central Committee desired the physical liquidation of a certain VIP. Everything was arranged. All he had to do was follow orders.

It was known that on a certain morning at a certain time the VIP would be driven up to the doorstep of a certain house in his touring car. Ling-Po would be sitting in the backseat of a sedan which had been parked directly across the street the night before. He would have an automatic rifle and two clips of ammo. He would also have two men with him: a driver and a man with a hand grenade. The grenade was the *coup de grace*.

At precisely eight that morning the three of them had met on the designated street and had walked together to the parked sedan. A Buddha-bellied fruit merchant had given them a quizzical perusal from behind his display stand, but they pretended to ignore him, as the man who was to do the driving brought out his keys and tried the first one in the locked door. Nothing happened. The grenade man said:

"The other one, you fool. That's the ignition."

Ling-Po wet his lips and said nothing. His two helpers were from another cell. He didn't know them. They were young students and they gave him the impression that they didn't think much of him because he had never been educated. But he knew that it was little things like this business with the key that queered the best laid plans.

The second key unlocked the door. The driver slid in behind the wheel while he and the grenade man took the backseat. Right away he saw that a mistake had been made. He had expected the Central Committee to have enough sense to pick a car with a right-hand drive, seeing that he had to sit left-rear to cover the street with the submachine gun. But no: the sedan was an American-made Dodge with a left-hand drive. Now he'd have to be very careful about sweeping his fire or he'd blast open the back of the driver's head.

"You'll have to duck down before I fire," he told the driver. "I don't want to catch you in the sweep."

The driver looked at him, then at the grenade man, and said, "You'd think he was planning on tearing *our* car apart."

"Listen," he said, and he could feel a cold iron ball of anxiety beginning to form deep in his stomach. "He's going to have police and bodyguards in that car with him. I have to sweep all of them. A machine gun isn't a rifle. I can't just hold it in one position and take my time pecking them off one by one. I'll have to start at the windshield and sweep to the rear."

"All right, all right," the driver said irritably. "Sweep up the entire street if you must. Just leave this car in one piece." He turned a scornful eye to the grenade man. "Did you hear that? Sweep-sweep-sweep. Is that what they taught him in the hills of Malacca?"

The grenade man's eyes crinkled with amusement and he looked at Ling-Po. "Where are the weapons, sweeper?" he asked.

Ling-Po swallowed the anger in his throat. He was too nervous to backtalk them. He knew his voice would lose control. "Under the seat here," he said brusquely. He reached down and fumbled with the false seatboard, brought out the automatic rifle, the clips, and the grenade. And he groaned inwardly. Anyone with any experience knew that the Mills bomb, the serrated pineapple, was the most reliable. So what had the Central Committee given them? A bean-can shaped bomb. An old fashioned potato masher: all flash and noise and no fragments.

But he said nothing. He handed the bomb to the grenade man, who held it in his hand for a moment and stared at it without speaking, as though not quite certain what it was for or what he was expected to do with it.

But the automatic rifle was all right. He cradled it in his lap and worked the lock. Its slick oiled metallic motion gave him a spark of courage. Lowering his head below the level of the

55

windows he put his lips to the muzzle of the gun and blew with the lock open. He wished he could lift the barrel to the light and squint down it to see if the stupid Central Committee had left a wad of grease and dirt in it. But it seemed all right. He checked the cartridges in the clips and then slid the first clip into the gun. He placed the second one on the seat beside him and the gun on the floorboard.

He looked at his wristwatch and knew that the apprehensive time was going to crawl.by like a wounded snake. I wish they would hurry, he thought. I wish they would drive down the street now and park the car and let us get this business over with. This waiting will make me sick.

The two students were conversing quietly. They were discussing the tiresome old doctrine of the End justifies the Means, and were citing glowing examples of how this Machiavellian policy had helped the Party time and again. He felt that they weren't really listening to each other or to themselves. Their words sounded mechanical. He could tell from the nervous agitation of their eyes and hands that they were as afraid as he was. It's this waiting, he thought again. This waiting will make us cowards.

Then the grenade man suddenly slapped his shoulder and pointed a trembling hand. And he looked and saw the open touring car with all the uniformed men coming down the street, and the cold iron ball in his guts froze, solidified, as he lifted the submachine gun from the floor and set it in his lap, his hands fumbling for the forward and trigger grips. Then he remembered and snicked off the safety, thinking, What if I'd forgotten it?

"Down," he whispered, hunching the gun toward the driver.

Then the maddening thing that too often throws a monkey wrench into the smoothly spinning wheels of careful planning happened. The touring car was supposed to stop directly across the street from the sedan. There was no reason why it should not stop there: a broad space of curb had been cleared for that purpose. But, without any apparent reason, the driver stopped the touring car ten feet back from the proper spot.

He couldn't believe it. Everything had been arranged for him to sweep the car which was supposed to be parked directly across the street. And now his target was parked obliquely in front of him and he couldn't sweep because of the front doorpost.

"Pull up!" he cried at the driver. "Pull up!"

But they couldn't. A pickup truck was parked snugly in front of them. And the driver was already ducking, shouting, *"Do it!* Do it now! What are you waiting for? Sweep! *Sweep them!"*

The doors of the touring car were opening and its occupants, laughing, talking, taking their time, were starting to descend. In a moment it was going to be too late. Now the grenade man was pounding him on the shoulder with the potato masher, crying, "Get out! Get out where you can get a shot! *Hurry!"*

And he didn't want to get out there and stand alone and naked and vulnerable in the street, and yet knew that he had to and it had to be now. And why, Why, WHY couldn't the miserable Central Committee at least have picked a car with the rear doors opening toward the hood instead of swinging open toward the trunk? He fumbled it open, pushed it away from him, stepped down and around the standing-open door and raised the machine gun and squeezed, the gun going *bop-bop—bopbopbop!* feeling the quick liquid jerk of it in his shoulder and hands, smelling cordite, seeing the muzzle leaping, jump-jump—jumpjumpjump. And seeing, too, the windshield of the touring car dissolving with a splintering crash and the whocking bullets dancing up the radiator, hood, door panels, and men falling, spilling out, and pedestrians running, scattering everywhere in a hysteria of screaming hurry.

Then seeing the thing that he should have known from the very first would be there (the thing the Central Committee had undoubtedly known *would* be there but had written off as an insignificant example of the End justifying the Means), the armored car with a mounted machine gun. It came roaring down the street at him, the machine gun swinging right to left —*pupupupupupupup!* And he couldn't fight that.

Ducking, stumbling, lunging headfirst against that damned open door, the car being whocked and shattered to pieces around him, he toppled into the rearseat, screaming, "Get out of here! *Reverse!* Reverse the car—" before he realized that the driver wasn't going anywhere, ever. His head was tipped back on the curl of the seat and what was left of his crimson pulpy face was tilted toward the headliner.

The grenade man was screaming, not words at all, only a long ribbon of shrill noise. He was fighting with the door on his side and he was getting out of the car with the potato masher still in his right hand.

"Throw it! Throw it at the armored car!"

And he supposed the boy would have if he'd been given the chance, because he started to swing back his arm as soon as he reached the sidewalk, even though he hadn't remembered to pull the pin. But the machine gun whocked into him as if invisible clubs were beating the dust from his clothes, and he went down fast and spinning and banked himself against the fruit stand and that came down on him, the fruit spilling and bouncing and rolling everywhere.

Ling-Po grabbed the second clip and went out the same door in a crouching leap, squeezed himself against the side of the punctured car and started working his way toward the hood. The armored car had stopped in the street and was now trying to angle its machine gun on him. He ran in the direction the armored car had come from, hugging the row of parked cars and trucks, fumbling the second clip into the submachine gun.

Pedestrians, merchants, rickshaws, everything, everybody getting in his way, all of them screaming, hands reaching and plucking at him: a wall of humanity blocking his panic path to freedom. Without a conscious will of his own he swung up the gun and started chopping a hole, clearing them aside, melting them away with short *brap-ba-dap* bursts.

Now, alone and reliving the nightmare, he felt a shivery film of sweat on his narrow body. It had been a very close thing, and it had left him a defenseless loner. He hadn't had the nerve to report back to his cell. He knew what the Central Committee's orders concerning him would be. Later he had heard that fifteen people had died that day in the street from gunshot wounds. The VIP had not received a scratch.

"Don't you hear the old man calling,
Only one more day, Johnny!"

Sully's drifting, vibrant voice touched his consciousness. He raised his head and stared at the knife-rack above the chopping block. The long worn blades gleamed wanly in the gloom. Ling-Po's hands gripped the edge of the sink, making his knuckles bone-white.

Vern was alone in his cabin, stretched out on the lower bunk, smoking in the dark, thinking of Bea Dodd. She was, he had begun to suspect, merely a form of security for Harvey. In her body (oh Jesus, that body) Harvey could find a momentary refuge. So could any man, he thought, and it would be far better than alcohol. He smiled wryly and murmured, "I suppose after all that's what whores are for."

The door opened and he saw the giant form of Sully silhouetted in the passageway light. "Hey, diver. Sim wants you forward. He's cracked open a bottle of stuff and he wants to tip one for luck."

Vern came to a half-up position on his elbow. "Why forward?" he wondered. "What's wrong with the cuddy?"

Sully came into the cabin. He took one of Vern's cigarettes and placed it in his mouth, sat on the edge of the bunk and took a light from Vern's cigarette.

"The playboy," he said, "is at the wheel. Sim wanted to stay shy of the cuddy because of Mrs. Dodd. He says he's not looking for any trouble."

"Yeah." Vern didn't want to talk about Bea Dodd. He switched to, "Sully, how many of you people stayed aboard the schooner that last night in Singapore? I mean after Fergus went ashore?"

"I dunno. Me'n Sim and Mrs. Dodd and the three gooks, I guess. I wasn't paying any attention. Why?"

"I was just wondering."

Sully dragged deeply at his cigarette, then said quietly, "Why don't you leave it alone? The guy is dead. He's spilt milk. Let's worry about the living."

Maybe he's got something there, Vern thought. Maybe we really don't want to know the truth. We're afraid the reality will burst the dream. We want to close our eyes to Fergus' death and go after that treasure. Treasure is money and money is non-truth, because it buys respite from reality. I wonder what form Sully's shark takes?

The deckhand lantern made a warm island of shifting light in the snug fo'c'sle. The stolid Dutchman, Ernie, with never two words for anyone, was sitting on the edge of a pipe berth like a poor relation. Tapley stood nearby, smirking at nothing or anything, with a glass of amber liquid in his small hand. Haki sat on top a sea chest, hunching in on himself, brittle and mysterious like a porcelain image of an Oriental god. Sim held the center of the cabin, balancing his hard body nicely against

59

the rise and fall of the deck, his left hand on his hip, a whisky bottle in his right.

The blackbirder, Vern thought. The sea wolf.

"Hey," Sim boomed — he was in good spirits— "Where's that gook? The Chink. Fetch him down here, Sully. We're gonna tip one for a fair breeze. This is the moment when all hands got to stand by their goddam duty." He raised the bottle suggestively.

Tapley's grin punched deep corner pockets in his cheeks.

"I go you, Cap. And tell the mate to fetch down Miss Lotus Bud, too, while he's at it. I'm suffering from that rare Haywaiian disease—*lakanookie*."

"And you can go right on suffering from it, my son," Sim said good-naturedly. "Because I ain't having no pom-pom problems on my ship."

By the time Sully returned, Vern and the others had had two shots apiece and Sim was making the rounds again with the bottle, and already saying, "I guess we better secure a couple more a these. I'm as dry as old canvas in a waterproof locker." And Vern felt that way himself. He decided it would be a good night to get roly-poly drunk. Maybe then he could forget about the girl with the brass-helmet hair and the 39 chest. But he doubted it.

"The gook will be down in a minute," Sully said, holding out his glass to Sim. "I don't think he wanted to join us, so I told him it was your order." Then he grinned a square white-mouthed grin. "I think he was in the sack with Lotus Bud."

"What did I tell you?" Tapley cried. "Hell, he's the only bastard on this hooker who *don't* have a pom-pom problem!"

Ling-Po slipped into the fo'c'sle like an assassin, his eyes bright and wary and taking in everyone at once. He smiled, but Vern could see that the facial movement was as false as the brilliant smile of a prostitute.

Sim swayed over him, his square fists cocked aggressively on his hips. He surveyed the Oriental for a long moment coldly, as though he owned him. Then he grinned and became himself again.

"Well, doctor, you'll have to learn to jump when I pass the order for all hands to splice the mainbrace. But you'll savvy in time, my son. They all do. Have a drink."

Ling-Po's smile hesitated, then deepened. He made a slow nod with his head, his slitted eyes flicking from face to face. He excused himself, explaining that he had a bottle of wine in his galley and that he would go after it. But as he turned to
60

depart Tapley shifted in front of him, blocking his exit. The little man was grinning cockily, but Vern thought with amusement that he had more stagger than swagger.

"Look here, Charlie. How would you like to pick up a few extra bucks for yourself, huh? Now a nice bit of slantwise stuff is always worth —"

Sully swung his frying-pan hand into Tapley's back, creating a resounding slap that sent the tipsy seaman sprawling to the deck.

"What you drinking, mate?" he asked, laughing. "Deaf juice? Didn't you hear Sim's command?" He turned to Ling-Po. "No hard feelings, doctor. I'm sorry I manhandled you yesterday."

Ling-Po's mouth twitched a smile. He nodded again. "I'll get my bottle," he murmured.

There had been no malice behind Sully's backslap, only whisky humor. But Tapley didn't seem, or didn't want, to recognize this fact. He picked himself up from the deck, his ferret-face dark and tense, and retrieved his glass. He said nothing, looked at no one as he poured himself a fresh drink. He bolted it with a sudden angry gesture.

A brawl, Vern thought unemotionally. We're going to have a brawl.

The first bottle went by the boards, and then the second, and then the third, and finally there were four dead soldiers rolling and bumping around the deck. They raised their glasses and slurred toasts, belched and drank, worked their way through tongue-thickened jokes and long, involved dirty stories. They grew swacked together, creating a false aura of happiness about them that shimmered pinkly like a great glassy soap bubble.

Absently, Vern saw what it was that drew them together. They were tired and frightened and they were embracing in a weary gesture of defiance at the rest of the world, like naughty little children boastfully thumbing their noses at the shadows.

Suddenly the bulkheads and deck seemed to be throbbing, closing in on him. The lantern light became sultry, bathing everything in an evil sulphurous glow: a sick leprous yellow light with the quality of decay and horror in it. I'm drunk, he told himself. So very drunk.

"Too bad we don't have Miss Bikini Bea down here! The kid with the knockers." Tapley shouted suddenly, then giggled drunkenly. "There's a gal that will take a drink if she's got to knock you down to get the bottle. Say! A couple of shots in her and I bet we could get 'er to do a stip — a strip!"

Fuzzily, Vern thought about getting up and going over and giving Tapley a hit in the mouth. But he stayed where he was, trying to divine the reason why he should hit Tapley. I only want the girl, don't I, he asked. I'm not in love with her, am I? I am? No.

Haki slid limply from his seat and curled up silently on the deck. Vern looked at him and grinned loosely. Japs never could drink. They could fight like little bastards, but they never could drink. Here's to you little bastard soldier. Here's to the Solomons and all the bastards we left there. Here's to the bleached bones and the . . .

But he lost the thread of it down some bleary avenue of spastic thought. It didn't matter anyhow, because they were dead and so to hell with them. Let's worry about the living, Sully had said. And that meant him, Vernon Rice Bigby. Oh yes—big. And that meant a certain sexy-looking girl who was in one of the cabins on this very schooner! With 49s . . . now wait, now wait just a goddam minute. Was that right? *Could* it be right? 49s? Wasn't that stretching them a bit? All right, with 45s like two Colts ready to . . . So who was making all the goddam noise and why?

It was Tapley. He had decided he could take Sully.

"The bigger and blacker they come the harder they bounce on the goddam deck! Put up your dukes, chocolate man!"

But Sully only grinned and swayed. "Take it easy, little man. You'll just get hurt," he said affably.

Tapley grimaced and swung his small fist into the mate's dark face. Sully's head jerked back, but he still grinned. "Get it out of your shystem?" he asked.

Tapley tried it again, but this time Sully raised a hand and brushed the punch aside. He reached out and clipped Tapley's mouth backhand and Tapley went down like a bag of nails.

Vern told himself he should get up and do something to stop the brawl. But the connection between his mind and his limbs was fuzzy and the message wasn't getting through. Have I ever been this drunk before, he wondered.

Something was happening, something violent. He focused his eyes and brain on the scene. Tapley had become a wildcat, had thrown himself on Sully, kneeing, kicking, clawing, punching, head-butting. And now the drunken Dutchman was lumbering into it, shouting:

"Leave my mate lone! *Gott-verdummer!* Leave him lone!"

Oh, for God sake, he thought. Then, amazed, he realized he

was on his feet. He lurched toward the three-man tangle. His mouth was open and he was trying to tell them something, something that suddenly seemed very important to him.

Someone had hold of his arm, spun him around. He faced Sim. The old man was laughing, shouting. Vern heard his voice as from far away and wind-tossed. He could see the open mouth and the square blunt teeth and it seemed that he could also see Sim's words. They were like the balloon-speech in the funny papers.

"Let 'em go! Like old times. Crew goin' for the bucko mate! Few broken noses, teeth, heads . . . no harm done . . ."

He was away from the voice. The hand was gone from his arm. But the damned walls of the fo'c'sle were pushing in on him again and the evil sulphurous light was blazing in his eyes. Then he was facing the door to the hold.

He opened it, stepped into darkness, closed it, feeling now the whisky in his body like a savage in a cage, the burning, wild, blurred, laughing, howling, wanting-to-run need for escape and expression. Then — the faraway pencil-thin streak of white light under the aft door tipping slowly on its beam ends — he started walking, matching somewhat his drunken equilibrium to the drunken roll of the sea, feeling now around him and about and smothering him the all-encompassing hold, feeling it — because of its darkness and motion and the whisky, too — as the lightless, stinking, moist womb of the queen primogenitor, himself yet unborn and wanting to be but afraid to be, and knowing that it was impossible to remain where he was, and knowing too that what came next was worse.

He opened the second door and lurched with the list of the schooner into the corridor. Then he was facing the third door. The last one. He stared at it, at the cracking varnish-flaking wood, at the small square of louvers, each one like an eyelid one on top of another, all cast down as in shame. The knob was in his hand. He turned it, shoved it away. Last door gone.

Bea was on the lower berth propped against a bulwark of pillows, reading a paperback. She was in her panties and bra (knowing Harvey would be on the wheel for hours until Sim or Sully or someone remembered to relieve him), the bra a white satin affair standing up and out, not padded by man-made fabric and not needing to be. The panties were blue nylon, nearly transparent, glossy, taut across abdomen and hips. She said nothing, did nothing. She looked at him and her expression was blank watching, or waiting.

He came for her, canting against the deck, and made it. He

63

gripped the frame of the upper berth in his right hand, hanging there staring down on her. She looked up at him and he wondered passingly that she could do it for so long without blinking, while his eyelids were like birdwings in flight. He let the frame go and swung, dropping into the berth with her, half-covering her nearly bare body with his own, his left hand cupping for the right cone of bra, his right hand sliding up along her leg and onto her hip. He could smell the perfume of her body.

She was staring up at his eyes, only eight inches above her face. And he saw how it was going to be and there could be no mistake about it: even through the whisky he could see the ridiculous truth. It wouldn't even be by force, a method which had never held any attraction for him. It would be like a lonely degenerate making love to a pillow in an empty bed. He straightened up stiffly. Took back his hands. Averted his eyes.

"Sorry," he murmured. "Really very sorry."

He got out of there, somehow.

The Dodds were alone in the cuddy finishing the last of their breakfast when Vern entered. Bea glanced at him critically, checking the tousled hair, red-rimmed eyes, the slack lines in his discouraged face, and — remembering what had almost happened last night — she sensed a sudden thrill of satisfaction and power. Then, surprisingly, she suffered a stab of contrition, thinking, I *am* a bitch. A cold predatory bitch. And that's just what he thinks of me.

Vern poured himself a cup of coffee and lit a cigarette. It tasted foul but he knew it would go down easier than food. He sat down at the table with a groan. Harvey grinned at him.

"I understand I missed quite a ball last night."

"Just as well. I don't know yet how many of the members are still living."

"All of them," Bea said. "You were the only one we had any doubt about. The rest have been on their feet for hours."

Was that a slam? He sipped at his coffee and said nothing. After a while he glanced at her, letting his eyes hover on her hair, face and figure. She was beautiful, sleek and smooth, so perfectly put together by God and by her own handiwork. It was interesting just to watch her use her fork. She handled it like a thermometer that had just been removed from the mouth of a typhoid patient.

He looked at Harvey, thinking, I wish you were married to someone else, mama's boy. I wish you were to hell out of this.

Bea was watching both of them, thinking that basically they were a great deal alike. They both fretted about cities and armies and dead history. Somehow they had managed in their thinking to separate the individuals from humanity, and it worried and frightened them because there were so damn many individuals. And yet she knew that they were not alike, because one had a dormant strength where the other had nothing but violent weakness.

"Captain Sim says the weather looks fine. I hope it holds. I'd like to make a quick passage."

Vern worked on his coffee and cigarette. He listened to Harvey with half of his mind on the man's wife.

"Have you talked much with Haki about the wreck? Do you think you'll run into any trouble collecting the gems?"

"Can't say until I get down there."

"I'll be glad to assist you in any way I can. I don't know much about deep-sea work but I'm capable at skindiving. I hope we don't run into anything nasty. I want to get this business over with," he added, almost in undertone.

Vern watched him silently. Harvey Dodd, playboy gone broke, he thought. A little boy who has lost his silver spoon and wants it back desperately. How desperately?

He found Tapley in the fo'c'sle. The seaman's face was a rainbow of colors: pink, red, blue and purple. But he was like a rubber ball and he bounced back easily. He grinned at Vern and raised a hand.

"Hi, sport. Come to see old hamburger face?"

Vern smiled wryly and put his fingertips to his temples. "Can't be much worse than my head. What did I drink last night? Ling-Po's lice juice?"

Tapley shrugged and picked up a small hand mirror and looked appalled when he saw his reflection in it. "Bilge water among other things, I think. Say, that black sonofabitch can sure slug, can't he?"

"That *mate*," he emphasised the noun, "is exactly twice your size. What did you hope to gain besides a broken nose?"

"Dunno. But I always have a try at it when I'm skiffed. Any big man that's handy. Watch me when I'm sober, though. I'm all Yessir and Nosir."

65

Vern didn't exactly believe that but he saw no profit in pursuing it. He sat down next to Tapley.

"You've knocked around a lot in Singapore. What do you know of Dodd?"

Tapley grinned. "Which one? Same one I'm interested in?"

"Come off it. Harvey."

"The Rover boy? He's got him a sort of shady reputation. I don't mean the kind the skipper and the mate got. I mean the kind that a high society gent gets when his morals sink below par."

"Sully?" Vern asked. "What's with his reputation? Is it true he's served time for smuggling?"

"Hell, yes, it's true. The jig got picked up for gun-running. Fact. He was scooting rifles and grenades into the rebels above Penang. He picked up some penal time for that."

So it was possible that Sully was still on the fence and didn't know which side to climb down. The European element in Indonesia looked upon him as a renegade Kanaka and wanted no part of him. But the Reds didn't care about race or color, they wanted any man who could get the job done. And Sully had been the man, a hungry one.

"All right. Come back to Dodd."

"He was a sort of remittance man, see? Only he was a high-class one. But he's a regular heller, gamblin', whorin', you know the bit. Then his dole went sour on him and he started floating a little rubber around the Colony. You know it don't take the Colony long to get down on a guy for that sort of thing. First thing he knew he was ostersized — am I saying it right? So I guess he was goddam glad to listen to Fergus' deal. All he had left in the world was this stinking tub and his hot little mama."

"Yeah." Vern nodded, thinking.

"What are you working on, sport? You want to push that Fergus rumble on little Harvey?"

"Why do you say that?"

"Would get him out of the way, wouldn't it, if you could pin it on him? It would leave Mrs. Dodd wide open . . . you understand I don't mean anything dirty; I just mean it would leave her —"

"All right, cut it out."

"Touchy on that score, ain't you, Rig?"

Vern stared at him blankly. *Was* he trying to push Fergus' murder on Dodd? Was he trying to build up a case against the playboy in order to get him out of the way? He said, "I still haven't forgotten that it was you I found in my room with Fergus that night."

Tapley grinned. "Funny, for a minute I thought you *had* forgotten."

Vern stood up. He'd had enough of Tapley. He felt that if he had to look at that smirking face another moment he'd reach out and push it in. And Tapley's face had had enough done to it for one spell.

"Smart little bastard, aren't you?" he said tonelessly.

"I ain't blind, sport. I know you got the hots for that skirt. Hell, who don't? But also I ain't dumb. She's not going to look at me. I don't have it. But you . . ."

Vern's anger had ebbed, leaving only a backwash of pity for the little man. He was aware of the fury and passion that were in Tapley's soul, and the tragedy lay in the seaman's size.

"Leave it alone," he said.

"Sure. I can, but can you?" Tapley asked, twisting out a different meaning.

Vern said nothing. He turned and went up the ladder.

There was nothing wrong with Tapley (as he often put it himself) that a naughty girl and ten minutes couldn't cure. Well (he always considered extenuating circumstances), say twenty minutes if he'd been drinking, and he usually was. But the problem was where in the hell to find one on this two-by-four tub.

And it was always a problem with him, even in the land of plenty, because of his size. Girls — that kind — liked big manly men, and he was built like a fifteen-year old with an underweight condition. Of course once they got to know him (and here he would nudge you in the ribs and wink) they realized that there was more to him — much more — than met the eye.

Now you take this wop girl — now there was an example of what he meant. Well, this particular girl had happened some time ago back in the States. He was twentyish and she was seventeen or eighteen, somewhere in there and old enough to know what it was for, and built like a brick outhouse. Kay-rice and the gas company, he meant *built!* 37-25-38 . . . oh, let him tell *you!* And sexy-looking? Hey-hey, he should hope to God so! Glossy black hair, all feathered and wild looking, around her face, and long black-mascara lashes over smoky eyes, and

67

soft pouty painted glistening lips, and big hoop earrings, and those damn things sticking out of everything she wore, and . . .

Well, anyhow, he met her in this roadhouse this night, see? And she was with some guys and gals but the guy she was mostly with was already loaded and looking like a pinball machine that had been jarred into *Tilt* and not much good for anything. So he started getting friendly with her in one of the rear booths that hadn't seen an electric light since the black-outs.

He knew the score. She was full of giggles and wiggles and teases, and was just playing him along for the drinks, thinking he wasn't much to worry about. But he kept right after her, making with the drinks and with the hands, and within an hour she was starting to sit up and take notice, and without too much trouble he finally coaxed her out to the parking lot and into his old Ford, and then they became downright friendly.

She punched a hole in the headliner with her highheels, and once there he thought she was going to kick out the windshield, and another time he slipped in his excitement and banged the goddam door handle with his elbow and the door swung open and he almost fell out on the ground, only she had such a grip on him he couldn't fall, and that's how friendly it was.

But the point is — that from that night on she was his. She belonged to him. And he didn't give a damn how big a bastard might come along, or how good looking either; she only had eyes for yours truly.

Well . . . to hell with it. That had been a long time ago, and by now she probably had an old man and ten-twelve little dago brats. And what did he have? All right, he could break the situation down to this: eight men and two females on a schooner for God-only-knew-how-many weeks or even months. And if anyone thought he was going to wait that long for his, they were simple in the head.

The ritzy bitch was out. The fact that she was married didn't cut any ice, because she and her old man had made it plain that they weren't compatible. But there was Rigby. He already had that marked, and Tapley had an idea that she knew she was marked, and you didn't see her kicking about it, did you? Anyway, she was far out of his class.

So that left Lotus Bud.

She wasn't a fool (it was impossible to fool a person of her profession); she knew what he was after when he came up the fo'c'sle companionway and found her standing by the fore-shrouds. Because he came right to her side and stood there — no taller than she — with a crooked smile and with eyes as glassy as a starved tiger's.

It was a limpid black night, moving up, down and away from a single splintery star. They were alone on the deck. Far aft, Ernie was at the wheel. But they couldn't see him, nor could he see them. The lights were on in the galley but Ling-Po was down in the cuddy collecting the dinner leavings.

"Hello, China girl," Tapley said huskily. "You likee one piecee me?"

The girl said nothing. She turned her face back to the night sea.

Tapley grinned and fetched a thick gold-turnip watch from his shirt (Ernie's watch; he had borrowed it from the Dutchman's duffel). He let the slowly-turning orb dangle by its chain, holding it close to her left profile. It said *tic-atic-atic* soothingly. Her obsidian eyes backrolled a little.

"You likee one piecee watch, huh?" he prompted. "All gold. Catchee plenty piecee money, you savvy?"

She savvied. But she wasn't very moved. She looked at the single star.

Tapley allowed himself a quick frown, then hurried his grin back into line. He took her small pale hand — tenderly; no sense in spooking her — and placed the ticking watch in it. Her fingers closed over the gleaming orb. Nothing else about her moved.

All right. Time to bring up the heavy artillery. He reached inside his shirt and drew out a pair of nylon panties. They were black briefs with a little pink bow on starboard and port. They had belonged to Bea Dodd, but she was always careless about leaving her cabin door open, and Tapley (his mind firmly fixed on the course of conquest) had walked off with them that evening.

He hung them shimmeringly in his hand by her face, offering no comment. Visual temptation speaks louder than words.

The girl's eyes slipped around and lingered on the ink-black panties. Slowly she raised her hand and touched them caressingly. Then, just as slowly, she drew them free of his hand, folded them into a spongy square, and looked at the sea again.

69

So it was a game: Him giving, her taking, and the odds in her favor — she thought. He took it easy. There was no sense in acting like he was in a hurry, which he was. He eyed her up and down, resting his perusal on the tight-silk swell of her derriere. She was just the right size (he disliked tall girls); and even if she wasn't very chesty, was he kicking? Hell no. His hands were small. Casually he reached into his shirt again and brought out another bit of filminess that had once clung to Bea Dodd's shapely body. A single nylon stocking.

The girl accepted this little offering with the same stoic calm that she had exhibited during the transfer of ownership on the previous articles. Then she realized that something was missing. There was only one stocking. Involuntarily she looked at Tapley.

The old pro was grinning at her. His hands were empty and he made no movement to reach into his shirt-of-plenty. And of what use was one nylon stocking to a girl?

"You come along with me, Lotus Bud," he said. "You catchee one piecee stocking, you savvy?" He turned and opened the fo'c'sle doors wide.

She savvied.

And in the crowding darkness of the fo'c'sle, with a blending of the lifting and plunging rhythm of the schooner plowing across a chopping sea, matching unconsciously the uniform recurrence of the beat, she forgot about the gold watch and black panties and nylon stockings, and for the first time since he had known her, she spoke.

"Tappy . . . *ohhh* . . . *Tappy!*"

The fight could hardly be called a fight, because Sim happened to be on deck and he wasn't having any of that nonsense aboard his ship.

Once Ling-Po had discovered where the girl had gone, he went down there too, with a butcher knife in his hand and a wild look in his eyes. Nothing was happening right then. Tapley was sitting on a chest rolling cigarettes and the girl was busy remaking the bunk. In a sense it was a very cozy, homey scene. But Ling-Po couldn't see it.

The girl spotted him as he left the steps and she gasped a

sound of warning. Then Tapley looked up and saw him coming with that ten-inch butcher knife and he knew it wasn't going to be a game of tag. He threw the sack of durham at the cook's face as he leaped to his feet.

Inside his shirt he carried a straight-edged razor which hung between his shoulder-blades on a loop of cord, and he snatched it up and over his head, the loop of cord at the same time coming free, and the momentum of his hand flipping the blade open and right on around until its back edge lay between the double knuckles of his fist. And that was the way he struck at Ling-Po's jaw. If he had connected it would have opened the cook's mouth nearly to his left ear.

But Ling-Po skidded, dodged, ducked, and shifted his position fast, leaping back, to the left, and then came in again with the butcher knife aiming from his waist. But the shock of that suddenly swinging razored fist had shot his timing. Tapley was set now and it promised to be an even fight.

Then the whirling belaying pin came banging on the deck between them and leaped away again like a pogo stick and clattered under a port bunk. They jumped away from each other automatically and looked up and around with startled eyes. Sim was standing halfway down the steps, his eyes as cold and hard as two nails left in the snow.

"Now," he said in a voice like a low-strung strand of barbed wire, "I'm going to do one of two things, and it's up to you boys which. I'm either going to go back on deck and enjoy my evening smoke — or I'm coming down there among you." He held them for a moment with his eyes. "And if I do . . . you're going to find out what is meant by a bucko skipper."

"He took my woman!" Ling-Po cried, his voice childish with passion and frustration.

Tapley lowered his razor, looking disgusted. "She's my woman now," he said shortly. "Like it or lump it."

Sim looked at the girl.

"That leaves it up to you, missy. Which piecee fella you catchee?"

There was no doubt or hesitation in her mind. She had discovered Tapley's secret charm. "Tappy," she said, and pointed at him.

Ling-Po started to move toward her but stalled as Sim brought his right foot down on the next step.

"All right, doctor," he said flatly. "You heard the word. She's made the choice and that's how it'll stand. Clear out."

The cook went slowly, backlooking at Tapley and the girl

71

but not looking at Sim at all as he pushed by him on the steps. Sim looked at the girl and a little gleam of sardonic amusement came into his hard eyes. He wasn't so old that he couldn't appreciate the circumstances. She wasn't a bad-looking bit at that. Kind of grubby though. Tapley would have to take a GI brush to her.

"Better have her cook your food after this," he said to Tapley. "The Chink might be tempted to drop a little something in your mush." He turned and went up into the night, carefully and with a smile, closing the doors after him.

They went southeast, and then angled past Billiton and plowed due east with Sumatra on the starboard and Borneo on the port. The Java Sea — that great blue stretch of the Greater Sunda — opened beyond the swollen spread of the flying jibs and the Trades of Karimata Strait hallooed their coming as they drove for the Flores Sea. And on the seventh night Sim made a single entry in the logbook: *Barometer dropping.*

It caught them the following day.

The old schooner ran through a sea of long oily rollers that were visibly increasing in length and steepness. Astern, the western sky was darkening with a sullen copper tint, while forward the early morning sun was already obscured. Sully, watching the barometer, saw it drop to a sickening 29, and when he glanced at the nimbus sky it seemed to him that they were fleeing out of a great tarnished copper bowl.

"For what we are about to receive . . ." he murmured.

Sim was stumping across the deck, watching the sky also. He knew what was coming and in a way he was glad. It had been a long time. It was like seeing a long lost enemy suddenly coming over the horizon. Well, let it come. He enjoyed ferocious environment. It was his nature to pit himself against the vast and mighty titans. It made him feel godlike. Maybe, he thought with grim satisfaction, this will take their minds off that host of spooks they drag around with 'em.

He glanced at the barometer and spun abruptly on his heel, shouting for reduced sail. But it was too late. The soul of the sea turned over with a great sigh and for a moment it was as though the schooner had burst through a giant pane of glass. There was an awesome shimmering between the sky and the sea — a growth of the conflicting pressures; then the foresail was puffed out of existence like a piece of gossamer, and the

72

Sally Lou wallowed aimlessly off course and humped over as if she meant to search out the hidden bottom.

Sully clung tenaciously to the wheel, spinning with it — dark sky and white sails all blurring, balling together in his eyes — until his body slammed into the grating. Through the spokes he saw Sim scoot across the deck with his legs cut from under him as though he'd been raked by machine-gun fire.

Sim fetched up jarringly against the skylight and reached out a hand to hook himself to the scuttle. He looked over his shoulder at the mate. "Bring her head into it, mister! *Her head!*"

For a wild instant, in the midst of great whirls and sucks and eddies, Sully felt like laughing. "Into what part, Skipper?" he shouted. "We got the whole damn world down on us!"

Sim grinned wolfishly and rose to a half-crouched position by the skylight. He didn't have to worry about Sully. He began pounding the deck with his foot, making a hollow, vibrant sound, shouting:

"All hands! All hands on deck goddammit!"

Then he heard Sully shout, and as he turned he saw a huge darksome mass of glassy water hanging over them. But not for long. It toppled with a crash and it felt as though he'd been hit by a house. Airless, blinded, equilibrium shot, he felt the water grabbing, tugging, hurrying him away; then he slammed into the side of the bulwark, his fingers digging for purchase clawlike, saying, You ain't got me yet. Not John Sim. I know you and your bitching ways.

Then it was gone and even before he could get his breath back he could hear water pouring below, surging about in the saloon. The goddam skylight's gone, he thought.

The Dodds and Haki had been sitting in the saloon when the first blow struck the schooner. It slammed their upper bodies violently across the tilted table top, and as they grabbed and clutched at its edges for support, they stared at each other with strained, shocked faces.

"Good God, what was that?" Harvey spoke in a tight whisper.

"It felt like we went through a sound barrier." There was nothing flippant in Bea's voice or eyes.

"Typhoon!"

It was Haki who spoke. And when they looked at him they saw the terror in his face. He was no longer the dapper little diver with a rich secret. He was a frightened Jap fisherman from the remote wastes of the Kuril Islands.

73

Then like a grenade bursting over their heads, the skylight exploded and they were showered with a deluge of glass fragments and water, and from somewhere beyond or above the wet opaque mass that engulfed Harvey, he could hear a sharp scream. That crazy little Jap, he thought angrily. That cowardly little bastard is coming apart. Then, the water clearing from his eyes, he felt hands clutching at his sodden shirt and saw Bea's masklike face in front of him, and her frozen-eyed fear was suddenly very infectious.

"Bea! Get to your cabin. Stay there! I must get on deck."

She left him without an argument — an automaton acting spontaneously through concealed motive power, minus active intelligence. Stumbling and slipping first one way, then the other in the water over the rubbish-covered deck of the saloon, she gained the passageway. The cuddy had disgorged its portable contents the way a drunk will suddenly vomit without a sign of warning. Broken bottles and glasses, newspapers and magazines, biscuits, tea bags and cushions, all rushing aimlessly from side to side.

A paperback novel washed along before her like a child's toy raft, leading the way into the passage. The glossy cover showed a young voluptuous blonde, her size-40 breasts nearly bursting over a tight pink dress, crouching by a prostrate man. She was holding a knife and was laughing with depraved glee. You're all wet, my girl, Bea thought absently. And you're going to get a lot wetter. You'll never be sleek and polished again. You're going to turn into soggy pulp. So laugh that off.

Someone was lurching along the passageway toward her. She stopped, spreading both hands to the bulkheads for support. It was Vern, his morbidly good-looking face tight with urgency. She wondered, femalishly, if he had been worrying about her.

He reached out, catching her shoulders. Then the schooner rolled and they bumped together, and she felt a wild thrill of wantonness as his right arm went around her and slid down to her buttocks. They clung that way for a moment, both knowing that again it was the wrong time.

"Are you all right?" he asked. "What's happened?"

She shook her head, unable to speak at first. "Haki says typhoon. I don't know. End of the world, I think."

"Where are you going?"

"Harv told me to go to our cabin and stay there."

That's right, he thought. He *is* her husband. He gives the orders.

74

"Go on. You'll be safer there." He stood away from her and started aft.

"Vern —"

He looked back, then grabbed for the bulkheads against the crazy tilt of the schooner. "What?"

"Don't leave me down here. If something goes wrong — don't leave me down here."

He nodded, looking at her soberly, thinking, I don't want to leave you now. "I'll be back for you. I promise."

Water was pouring through the broken skylight, making a sharp splashing as it fell into the restless lake below, and as he waded across the saloon a new sound came from a corner beyond the glistening table — a single isolated sound of wailing and terror: the quavering voice of Haki raised in prayer.

A lot of good he'll be to us, Vern thought. A hell of a lot of good.

Almost at once the Jap's voice was drowned by still another sound, faint at first, like the distant hiss of a million snakes, then taking on new force and energy — the unmistakable sound of rushing water. He left Haki to his heathen gods and started up the steps.

The deck was a rubbish heap of spars, canvas and lines. There were no sails but the masts were there, swaying back and forth with a peculiar trembling like giant chalk sticks tracing weird patterns on a vast blackboard. Sim was here, there, everywhere and seemingly all at once, and his roaring voice was equally omnipresent. Now he was at the wheel struggling with Sully, then across the flooded waist chasing after Tapley and Ernie as they stumbled from brace to brace, next on the foredeck clearing out wreckage.

"Dodd! What's the condition below?"

"Flooded!"

"Get on the pump! Vern! Fetch a topsail and stretch it over that goddam skylight! All right, dammit, Tapley —"

The mainsail was down on the deck, bunched and folded like a giant envelope against the port gunwale. It was bloated and blistered, quivering like jelly with the ton of water it contained. Tapley was trying to flatten it out with his body. Sim stumbled toward him cursing, a knife in his hand. He stabbed the swollen sail repeatedly, letting the water out.

75

Vern slid and grabbed his way to the galley and pushed at the door. Jammed. Where was the gook? "Ling-Po!" he shouted. "You in there?" He threw his body against the door and it shuddered open. He tripped and fell, hands and knees, into a foot of flotsam-clotted water.

The galley was in a bad way. Cereal, fruit, canned foods, crockery, hardware, pots and pans, clattered, crashed and clanged over and over in a wild hurly-burly, rushing frantically from port to starboard, forward to aft, gurgling and bobbing in the black backwash. The cook himself was sitting in his own sink, keeping safely clear of the tumbling mess. Something sharp nicked Vern's ankle underwater and he understood the wisdom of the man's elevated position.

He grabbed for a swinging meat hook and heaved himself up on the chopping block just as a stack of dishes contained in a metal cage sprang straight up and shattered, disappearing into the churning wash below.

"Is the storeroom open?" he shouted. "I need a tarp!"

The words didn't completely register in Ling-Po's mind. His almond eyes popped and backrolled and he hunkered his head between his shoulders, as though expecting a blow from the ceiling. Sniping plantation workers, blowing bridges and mining roads he could understand and appreciate, but this war against the elements was beyond his scope. This force, this sea was unsympathetic, monstrous.

"Are we going to sink?" He screamed the question. "Are we going down?"

Vern would have slapped him if he could have reached him. What was it that threw the Orientals into hysterics when they came against the fury of the elements? he wondered, then answered himself: Untold centuries of superstition and awe of the unknown.

"No, you damn fool! Is the storeroom locked?"

The cook nodded finally but his mind wasn't on it. His eyes were still leaping around like swallows trapped in a barn, still looking for the blow he felt certain was going to fall.

The schooner rolled sluggishly to starboard and the galley door sprang suddenly open. Vern waited until the bulk of the dangerous mess had swept over the flange and out onto the deck, and then he leaped across the galley to the storeroom door, Ling-Po shouting frantically after him.

"Aren't there any life jackets on this boat?"

The jib had torn loose from the clew and it was streaming out like a tattered battle flag, flapping itself to shreds. Tapley and the Dutchman clawed at it, fighting it, brought it down, secured it to the sheet and ran it up again. It puffed, billowed, and snapped taut with the sharp crack of a rifle shot. It wouldn't hold for long, but every minute of headway was precious in the turmoil.

Sim loomed behind them, majestic and soaking and swaying with the crazy pitch of the deck, shouting.

"Tapley! Find that playboy! See if the goddam pump is sucking! I can't trust that dizzy bastard! You come with me, Dutchy!"

He handed the seaman a hatchet and told him to start clearing the wreckage. "Overboard! You understand me? Overboard!"

Tapley got the doors open, got himself through them and got them closed again, somehow. He foot-slid down the steps into the fo'c'sle, grabbed the frame of the first berth and looked down at the Chinese girl. She had lashed herself into the berth with one of his belts, and her skirt was way up showing her rolled-stocking thighs and rounded, black-pantied bottom. Her eyes were so wide they were almost Occidental.

He reached her by running with the pitch of the ship.

"It's all right, Lotus baby. We ain't going under. Old Tappy's right here."

And then — through the fear and with the knowledge that the certain degree of gravitation needed for the act was missing — she was after him, her hands on his body like hungry spiders, kissing him wetly, her tongue going like a pneumatic drill.

"Jesus, jesus, baby. Not now. Wait — *wait,* goddammit, Lotus baby. *Not now!* You want the old man to shoot me for dereliction of duty?"

In the whimpering, throbbing darkness of the hold, spear-headed by jerky shafts of weak light from the bull's-eye torch he held clamped between his knees, Harvey knelt before the pulsating, antiquated pump. His boyish face was set in the tight grimace one assumes when undergoing prolonged pain.

He was wondering how much longer the ship could live under this merciless hammering.

The hold was an obscure cavern, dank and foul-smelling, floored with rotten remnants of planking and roofed with black shadows. On either side a narrow shelf ran fore to aft like two continuous bunks, and in some places along the shelves there still remained sets of rusty shackles bolted to a beam. It wasn't the nicest place in the world.

One of the shackles behind him clattered as the schooner rocked into a new angle, and he was aware that he was not alone. No physical presence, but the ghostly entity of the hold and its grim past — the curious air of personality that deserted houses and ships always have. She had her secrets, this old tub. Beneath her aged wood and shadows he sensed something malevolent and threatening: an afterlife of the wicked deeds that had been perpetrated on her decks. I shouldn't have bought her, he thought. She's a trouble ship.

Water was gurgling along the gangway between the two shelves. He raised the torch and shot the beam downward. The black-sparkled water hurried forward with joyous abandon, then retreated, capturing diamonds of light in its backwash. Like an overgrown puppy, he thought, rushing along the hall impetuously, looking for its master and wetting as it goes. Then he thought, That's not bad. Wonder if anyone's ever used it before? If he had a goddam pencil and something to write on he'd make a note of it. Save it for a future story.

"What story?" he asked bitterly. "What future?"

The door to the fo'c'sle jarred open and he started, not knowing what to expect but suspecting the worse. It was Tapley, the man in the boy's body with the big mouth. God, he thought, was a great equalizer.

Tapley came sloshing along the gangway grinning like a satyr. In a sense he was like Sim: he enjoyed the elements, but for a different reason. It was purely an impersonal action when the titans reared to oppose him. To the elements, size had no meaning, everything was tiny and insignificant. Now, cocky with confidence, he hoped to find Harvey frightened. In a way he was disappointed, and in a way he was not.

"Do you know what I thought of when you suddenly yanked that door open?" Harvey asked, smiling.

"No. What?" Tapley was really interested.

"It's absurd, but I saw a mental picture of the *Titanic* standing on its nose just before it made that long dive into the frozen sea. And for a split second I thought that *I* was on her,

78

trapped in one of the compartments, and the opening of the door was the sea sweeping up for me. Auto-suggestion, I suppose."

Tapley didn't quite follow all of that, but he wasn't one to let on. His grin deepened as he squatted on the bench next to Harvey.

"Yammer away, sport. I always talk a lot when I'm scared, too."

Harvey's smile hesitated as he stared at Tapley, then broadened as the enlightenment occurred. It's his pride, he thought. He wants me to be afraid because he isn't.

"You'll have to admit, Mr. Tapley, there's cause for alarm."

Tapley said nothing. He was satisfied. He sang softly: "All, all, all of me. Why not diddle all of me?" Then he looked around at the gurgling darkness and said, "I guess Ernie's sack and gear has all washed away, huh?"

"Pardon me?"

"Ernie. I had him move in here when I set up housekeeping with Lotus Bud."

Harvey had been wondering about that. "I'll bet he loves it in here."

Tapley shrugged. "He's lived in worse. So've I when you come down to it."

Harvey thought about the Chinese girl, realizing that her soiled, sluttish way was not without a sensual quality. His interest stirred.

"Where did she come from?" he wondered. "Ling-Po never did say much about her."

"From a whorehouse." Tapley was indifferent. "Yeah, that's a fact. She was sold to one as a kid. She told me all about it. And, buddy," he tapped Harvey's knee, "these gooks got it all over us when it comes to this whorin' business.

"Why, did you know that they go to school to learn it — the tricks, I mean? Fact. She told me. They got this big old madam, see, and her job is being teacher. And they use some gook stud to practice the lessons on, sort of like we use a blackboard in our Stateside schools. Yeah, and does that gook have a job for himself or don't he? I ask you. I'd swap with him any day.

"Anyhoo, they got to go through their little lessons every damn day, and if one of 'em makes a mistake, then the old madam warms their little bottoms with a switch and makes 'em do the lesson all over . . . which is okay for the gook stud, but kind a tough on the students."

79

My sweet God, Harvey thought, appalled: he's proud of it! This is his girlfriend he's talking about, and he's proud of it. And then his mind — always perverse in matters of this sort — sideslipped and righted itself in front of a mirage. It activated the scenes Tapley had just described.

From far off he heard Tapley ask him something and it was like pulling a tooth to bring his attention back to the question. "What?"

"The old man is worried about the pump. Wants to know if she's sucking — the pump I mean."

Harvey nodded. "Yes. It's holding so far."

"Good. The old man wants you should stick with it. This old tub is taking on water like a Filipino whore takes on sailors on Navy Day."

Harvey, almost fully recovered, smiled genially.

"Mr. Tapley, I wonder if I might borrow some of your descriptive similes? I'm a writer of sorts, you know."

It was okay by Tapley. He didn't know what the hell a simile was, descriptive or any other kind. As long as it wasn't money or Lotus Bud.

The *Sally Lou* shuddered through the living darkness, rolling and plunging with the wind and wave force, the wind sweeping spitefully after her with a following sea, howling and screeching through her skeletal rigging. And across the pseudo-darkness appeared a thick white line of foam as tall as a single-storied house. It seemed to gather a faint gleam of phosphorescent light from the sun that was completely obscured by the driving clouds, and it came at them with a hiss that turned into a roar. A running wall of water.

Vern crawled across the poop toward the shattered skylight dragging his tools and canvas after him, keeping one eye on the charging rampart of water. Sully couldn't outrun it, could he? And what would it do to them if it pooped the *Sally Lou*? And what would happen to Bea down in her tossing cabin?

The skylight was going to need planking, but that was out of the question now. Not only had the glass shattered but the coaming was split as well. It needs a carpenter, he thought wildly. It needs a real carpenter with the right tools and plenty of time on his hands. The wind wouldn't leave the canvas alone. It flapped it brutally, ripping it from his hands. He knelt on it, spreading the canvas along one side of the skylight and began pounding nails into it. The hardwood deck objected to the passage of the small spikes through its skin and it repelled the invasion by bending the nails under the hammer blows. God, he said. Godgodgod.

Sully glanced over his shoulder and saw that it was hopeless. They were going to be had by the screaming wall of water, whether they liked it or not. He turned his streaming face to Vern and shouted.

"Watch out for yourself!"

Vern looked up and saw the monster wave curling high over the fantail, as violent in aspect as a drooling madman running amok with an axe. He didn't hesitate to consider the possibilities. Clutching the hammer in one hand he grabbed the coaming with the other and vaulted over the broken frame, dropping straight into the flooded saloon.

His feet struck the slick table top and whipped out beneath him and he went headfirst into the swirling water, banging the breath from his lungs as he met the submerged deck, rolling, spewing, bringing his head up just as the wave struck the ship, then feeling the reaction under him, the shuddering, flattening force as lumps of cold green water crashed over his head, smashing him back to the deck again and into liquid amber darkness, and his last conscious thought was, It's bad . . . so goddammit to hell bad . . . but it's not painful.

He didn't think he'd been out. Maybe for two-three seconds, but that was all, as if his mind had opened a door, wobbled into limbo, turned around and wobbled out, slamming the door behind. So why not get his face out of the water and see what fresh air was like? He struggled to his feet, using his hands to push himself from the deck. He was holding something in his right hand, something he had blindly caught at during the deluge. He looked at it — a soggy paperback showing a sexy blonde with improbable breasts crouching over a dead man. The title was THE COLD WAKE. It damn near was at that, he thought. He threw it away and looked around for the Jap.

He found him under the table, still alive but as bedraggled and useless as a suit of clothes left out in the rain. If we lose him, he thought with a twinge of fear, we lose everything. He dragged the limp, mumbling man from beneath the table and stretched him out on the port bench. Then he undid the Jap's belt and restrapped it under the bench and about his waist, securing him from toppling back into the water.

He looked up at the open skylight, seeing the attic ceiling of

81

gray sky. A thin cascade of white water jetted down on his upturned face. Have to do something about that. But he hesitated, remembering Bea Dodd, then shook his head and started for the steps. The old schooner was still afloat, still trying. Bea was all right. But if that damn skylight wasn't closed she wouldn't be. None of them would.

The *Sally Lou* bucked her head into a swirling wall of sea, foam and mist, and the bowsprit pierced through the low pressure belt. She scudded into the windless eye of the storm. The waves going on around formed themselves into leaping cones willfully, twenty-thirty feet high; then collapsed abruptly, instantly reforming somewhere else. It was the center of the depression, where the law regulating the strength of the wind proportions the difference of pressure between the place from which it comes and the place toward which it blows. A sort of typhoon clearing house.

Waves like mountains of gleaming black onyx piled up and crashed down on the schooner's deck: thousands of invisible hands reached out and slapped her through the nightmare maze of high water. She shuddered and sprayed like a wet dog coming out of a pool, shaking itself from nose to tip of tail, and went skimming and careening along, as yet undefeated. And Sim, swaying aft on the poop, paused and looked at Vern crouching once again by the shattered skylight, and shouted through the spindrift curtain of spray.

"Don't be afraid! I've been here before!"

At the end of twenty-four hours the worst of it was over. The sea still chopped up lead-colored waves in an aimless fashion, and the wind still blew, but fitfully now, like a continuous sigh of disappointment. It was the time for mopping up, for bringing order out of chaos, and everyone went about his duties silently, weary and thankful. They snatched sleep in shifts, except Sim who seldom left the deck. He had his hand in something he could understand and he milked it to the last drop.

Vern didn't know how the others felt, but he felt like yesterday's cold potatoes. He glanced at the chronometer and put away his tools. It was time for his sack-shift. He welcomed the thought. All he wanted to do was crawl into his damp bunk and sink into deep oblivion. Nothing else mattered. But it did when he reached the doorway of his cabin. Bea was in there.

She was holding a dripping broom in her hands, sweeping water and trash toward him, and when she looked up he noticed that something about her was different: more than the surface observation that she was bare-footed and clad in ill-fitting, rolled-up dungarees and one of Sim's old woolen shirts, and that her hair, once so smooth and glossy, was straggly, damp and dull. The real difference was in her face now that it was shed of its careful coat of makeup. A childlike quality of innocence was evident now, no longer obscured behind a facade of cold disillusionment. Her bone structure, he saw, was delicate: it had the fineness of decadence and over-breeding.

She's tired, he thought empathically, almost tenderly.

She smiled, resting on the broom, looking at him with enormous dark eyes. "Everyone was so busy I felt ashamed of myself sitting in there doing nothing. I wanted to help." Then she lowered her head.

"That isn't quite true, I suppose. I don't have that much nobility of mind. I couldn't stand it in there any longer, alone in that wet cubicle. I felt like a lost soul on a first-class passage to hell."

The schooner rolled easily to port and she caught the rail of the upper berth while he grabbed the door frame for support. The water sloshed musically. Absently he heard the squelch and suck of the pump as its piston hammered mechanically in the hold beyond.

"There's still some bottles left in the cuddy," he said, not because he wanted to hurt her, but because he was suddenly startled by the realization that the moment had come, and having come he found himself afraid to face it.

"Don't, Vern," she whispered.

Then, as the *Sally Lou* slowly righted herself to an even keel, he hated himself for having acted boorishly. He closed the door behind him and reached for her. She stood under the pressure of his hands, childlike, trembling. The deck canted to starboard and, helplessly, they toppled back into the lower berth.

Their worn faces were inches apart. They breathed through open mouths as they studied each other's eyes.

"I didn't mean that," he murmured. "I didn't —"

She touched his hair with her hand, closed her eyes, her pale face suddenly transforming, taking on the gentle aspect of a little girl preparing for sleep. "I know," she whispered. "Don't talk."

83

Then a moment later — "Wait, I'll help you," she said.

"No," he said, his fingers on the clasp. "I want to do it."

Then — minutes later — while the angry sea shook and rattled the old schooner over their heads like a dog worrying a bone, she laughed softly.

"Funny, isn't it?"

"What?" he said, annoyed.

"In a time like this — us."

"Yeah. Funny."

But not funny meaning comical, not funny meaning farcical, or absurd or ridiculous or droll or witty, facetious, humorous, laughable, ludicrous, but that here, now, this place, with eyes closed on the reddish-brown of the inner lids, with breath of her body through her mouth gasping into his body and then back again, with his elbows down on the soft dampness of the mattress and that mattress rising and sinking and yet that rhythm of sea-motion unnoticed, not felt, lost to their own rhythm of needing, searching, finding, having now at last here in this place at this time the nownownow, to him *My God* as the always-to-be startlingly different pain goes highballing, rushing itself down to a narrow explosion-point, while to her the fulfillment of knowing *This is the first time. No other time existed before this.* And then both of them free at last and moving away slowly, softly, and sensing again but not really caring the continuance of reality, the consciousness of the old schooner sailing doggedly on with the fatality of drama, following a destiny to an appointed end, to the finish of her last consignment and the clearing of her account. Funny like that.

Sully came into the cabin just before noon and woke Vern. For a moment, in his drugged condition, seeing the Negro hovering over him, he was frightened. Then, forcing his senses into order, he realized that Bea was gone, that he had been sleeping alone for hours. He focused his eyes on his wrist watch and frowned.

"Why didn't someone wake me before this?"

Sully shook his head and sat down on the edge of the bunk.

"Sim is the only one on this hooker who don't need sleep. The storm has almost petered out. Do you have any dry cigarettes?"

Vern studied the mate's dark face, seeing something in it that went beyond fatigue, a haunting quality. "No, they're up on my bunk drying out." Maybe, after what had happened, he should change bunks with Sully.

"Something bothering you?" he asked half-suspiciously.

Sully shrugged and stood up. "Sim wants you on deck. Wants all of us. The Dutchman is gone. Overboard, I guess."

How many men follow in the wake of a lost ship? How many set out to search for a ship that has passed through the mirror of the sea, with only a rumor, a legend, a twice-told tale behind them and all the vast mystery of the sea before them? Who are these few who find an overwhelming fascination in the mental imagery of a ship sunk in the shallow waters of a hidden lagoon, rife with bright vegetation and inhabited by the colorful creatures of the deep, or a wreck lying somber and forgotten on the shore of a desert island, its secrets and its past lurking unstirred within its decaying shell?

And why? For God's sake why?

Dodd . . .

PART 2

It was a strange tight little group, huddled on the poop next to the shattered and poorly-patched skylight. Tapley was at the wheel with a twisted look of urgency on his narrow face, the Chinese girl standing inscrutably by his side. Ling-Po, sullen and non-communicative, stood as far aside as he could and still remain a part of the group, while Haki, trembling noticeably, leaping his sly, slitted eyes suspiciously from face to face. Bea was leaning against the skylight, hunched and small under the cover of a thick pea jacket. She glanced at Vern, her eyes saying something comforting, and looked away. Sim, Sully, Harvey and Tapley were arguing.

"Overboard," Sim said flatly. "My God, he ain't the first seaman to take the deep six in a typhoon."

"Not Ernie!" Tapley shouted. "He might not have been the cat's prat on brain power but he was a good seaman! He wouldn't go over unless some sonofabitch helped him!"

"Not when he was sober!" Sim shouted back. "But he

wasn't sober this morning. I passed out that bottle to keep you boys on your toes. I didn't know the goddam Dutchman was going to get soused. That's why I ordered him below to relieve Dodd at the pump."

"Well, he did relieve him, didn't he? Ain't no bastard gonna fall overboard when he's down in the hold!"

Sully braced his legs against the movement of the deck and spoke over Dodd's shoulder. "Take it easy, man. Sure he went down into the hold, but the point is he didn't stay there. He was plastered and he must have come back on deck sometime before dawn and caught a wet one. We'd have thought he was still down there if Haki hadn't gone to relieve him."

Harvey nodded four-five short nods. "I think you're right, Mr. Sullivan. But perhaps it wouldn't be prudent to completely ignore Tapley's theory —"

Sim looked disgusted. "Well, what the hell *is* Tapley's theory?" he wanted to know. "What's he getting at? What are *you* getting at? Murder? Is that it? Is that what you damn fools want to make of it?"

He took a step aside, starboard, and turned to face them. His eyes were narrow and hard and as bright as glass, as dangerous as broken glass. The blackbirder, Vern thought again.

"See here," he said to them harshly, "I know you. You're all of the same coin. Oh, you come from different professions, from different backgrounds, different blood, but you all have one thing in common, and my hand is with you. You're blacklisted — for one reason or another — you're blacklisted and you can't escape it. People like us don't get the breaks often, and when chance comes our way we grab her and we hang on like paint. If we don't we'll go under.

"Now chance has given us a crack at a treasure, and we can all come out fat. But start making out that we got a murderer loose on board and we'll all be taking to the boats like scared rabbits. And where will your goddam treasure be then? And where will you be? On the beach again, some of you flirting with suicide, and some of you waiting to be hauled off to some rotten penal colony. Have you ever seen one of those places? I have. Sully can tell you about them, too. I seen 'em in the old days in Caledonia: those white, shaved men in their dust suits and straw hats. They look like preachers, and they look like famine, and they look like the sick. Is that what you're after?"

He checked himself and cleared his throat. The others said nothing. A fine curtain of cold spindrift leaped the rail and peppered them. They mopped at their faces and stared at the deck. But not Tapley.

"All that's so much manure to me," he said. "I want the goddam treasure as bad as the next guy does, but I still say some bastard slipped Ernie over the side."

Harvey bit at his lower lip and looked at him.

"Who do you think would do such a thing?" he asked quietly.

Tapley's eyes flicked around their damp faces. Then he sneered and nodded at Sully. "Ask the mate. He didn't like Ernie," he said suggestively.

Sully started with a jerk and made as if to move toward Tapley, his broad hands open at his sides. Vern caught his arm and held him. The mate stopped and looked at him with an expression of half-surprise. Then he relaxed all at once as though a thread had pulled out a seam in his body. He stared at Tapley.

"What is it you don't like about me, little man? My size, color, or what?"

"Get off it, both of you," Vern said. "Tapley, you know Sully isn't that sort."

"No? What sort is he then? You tell me, sport. He's done time, hasn't he? How do you know what else he's done? How do you know what the hell he's capable of doing?"

"When we come to that," Harvey said, "we don't any of us know what the others are capable of."

"That's right," Sim said easily. "We're all strangers here. We got to take each other at face value. And as far as I'm concerned we're all square Johns trying to turn up a little coin. I'm satisfied that Ernie staggered on deck drunk and went overboard without knowing where he was going. I'm only surprised we lost just one last night after the things I saw. He was careless and he paid for it. We'll go easy on the bottle after this."

He walked to the rail, digging out a cigar from his jacket, and spat over the side.

"You always got to pay the piper," he commented blandly.

Alone in his cabin, Sim made an entry in the logbook after the date.

Ernest Dorp, AB; lost overboard. Drunk on duty.

He hunched back in his seat and lighted a cigar, staring at

the entry with smoke-squinted eyes. He should have guessed that the dumb Dutch bastard didn't have enough sense not to get plastered in the middle of a typhoon. It was hard lines and no mistake; though actually, like Fergus, the Dutchman was no great loss. Fortunately the schooner was easy to handle, and there was always the auxiliary. He and Sully could sail her alone in a pinch. The important people were Haki and Vern. Haki to locate the wreck-site, and Vern to make the dive — if he still had the guts for it.

He frowned and drew deeply at the moist already-tattered end of the cigar, sculpturing the air with thick scrolls of greasy blue smoke. Thinking now of diving and his own lost youth, he leaned forward to remove a thin water-stained vellum-bound book from the small rack he kept above his deal table. He wasn't much on books but he always had a few by his side for off-duty hours: the *Rules of the Road*, Riesenberg's *Men on Deck*, *Merchant Seaman's Manual*, Findlay's *Directory*, Conrad's *Nigger of the Narcissus* (a book he never did quite understand, but liked to study because of the vivid descriptions of men, ships and the sea. He was always a little amazed that the writing was so fantastically accurate), and a slim volume of poetry he had picked up for tup'pence in a wharf-side shop in Sidney.

He had no feeling for poetry, no eye or ear for the rhythm of the words, but two lines from Wordsworth's *Solitary Reaper* never failed to appeal to him. Somehow they touched a streak of melancholy that was buried deep in his savage, battered frame.

The book opened of its own accord to the much-fingered page, and he read the two lines again.

> *For old, unhappy, far-off things,*
> *And battles long ago.*

Battles . . . of one sort or another: with Malays, Kanakas, seamen; with sheath knives, bottles, hand spikes, revolvers, Snider rifles, dynamite sticks; with ships, high seas, burning suns and wild winds; with sharks, squids and morays . . .

He had been a diver once himself in his youth, in his twenties, when the South Pacific was wider, more remote, and laws went by the board or to the man who held the dynamite stick or the Snider; when the square-faced gin bottle and the dog-eared Bible had clashed together in a mighty battle for the mastery of the souls of the unenlightened from the Galapagos to the China Coast, and no man yet could say which had

90

won. He had been a pearl diver in the Tuamotus, for the hell of it, for his own purse, or for the sake of chance which could never be denied but must always be followed.

It had been different in the Tuamotus in those days, the diving. None of your new-fangled lungs, snorkles, peripheral face masks, fins, CO_2 guns, just naked men with homemade bone-rimmed glasses, a knife, a shot line and a pearling basket. It separated the men from the boys, and quick — especially at twelve or thirteen fathoms. But he had had a chest like the bottom of a whale boat, and it had been nothing to him. Child's play, and profitable at that.

He smiled, crinkling his seamed face into a tight grimace, remembering a day and a Kanaka youth called Ofai, who had become careless once while working in the coral beds and had allowed himself to be captured by the wrist by a crevice-dwelling conger.

Like a bullwhip snapping, the conger's head had whipped from its hole and the steel-spring jaws had clamped down and you could damn near hear them clang. Then, the boy snatching for his sheath knife too late, the conger, its starboard eye bright with mad ferocity, withdrew into its black hole dragging Ofai's arm flush against the coral floor. The boy went wild and pressed the panic button and tried to wrench himself loose, only his wrist wouldn't budge because it was chained as surely as if it had been welded to the coral, because a conger eel's jaws are like the jaws of a bull dog and ten strong men cannot drag one from its hole, and the only thing you can do is cut the eel's jaws out of its head and later pry the teeth from your wrist. But there wasn't time for that. The youth's lungs had reached their endurance point and in another minute they would go flat, and Sim, struggling to free him, had seen that the Kanaka didn't have the guts for the job — and it was either that or drown — so he had taken out his knife and done it for him.

Sim took a long reflective drag on his cigar and eased the smoke out between his teeth. He often wondered what had happened to that one-handed Kanaka. He'd been a good diver before the conger incident.

Vern couldn't leave it alone. Sitting in the quietly creaking seclusion of his cabin he made a list of names on a damp notebook he had found in the cuddy.

Fergus
E. Dorp

Sim
Sully
Tapley
Haki
Ling-Po
Harvey Dodd
Bea
China Girl

He stared at the list speculatively, then drew a neat line through the two top names, and to one side of them wrote the word Dead. He moved the pencil to the bottom of the list and put a checkmark after China Girl and one after Bea's name. He was leaving them out of this.

The pencil point hovered over the names for a moment, and then he checked off Tapley. The little seaman wouldn't murder his own friend, would he? He hesitated, looking at the mark. Now wait a minute. Why so cocksure? Ernie followed Tapley about, Tapley didn't follow Ernie. And you discovered Tapley in your room with Fergus, he thought. He frowned and bit at the end of the pencil. Then he erased the check mark. He looked at the list again, moving with deliberation from name to name.

Sim — the hard old man who should have been a pirate. Admittedly down and out on the beach. The treasure his last chance to get fat. A fitting climax to a long violent life.

Sully — also on the beach, blacklisted. A lonely dark man looking for an answer. Gun runner, ex-convict, possible fellow traveler.

Tapley — little man with big mouth and tricky ways. A bad reputation and a burning need for money — to make wealth compensate for size.

Haki — a big secret and a bigger fear. Frightened by intangibles out of his livelihood. Willing to risk almost anything, except go underwater, to gain security.

Ling-Po — the coolie hood-type. Sneering, smirking, sly. In the words of the Peregrine: I'm a good hater, but a bad friend.

And Harvey Dodd — the gentleman from Wits End. Broke, ostracized, perhaps even wanted for passing bad checks. Desperate . . .

He sighed and laid the notebook aside. Any of them, he decided, might adopt murder as a means of expanding his share of the treasure. Once upon a time a quarter of a million dollars (a possible quarter of a million) had been a great deal of money. Today it would be enough for one man, or two or three or four men, but not enough for ten.

He smiled wryly, realizing that already his stock had soared by twenty per cent. Next thing he knew he'd be out on deck pushing his mates overboard. "Jesus," he said disgustedly.

He looked up as Sully entered with his dark face plowing through a burst of cigarette smoke.

"Sully, do you believe that Fergus and Dorp were murdered?"

Sully's cigarette jumped as he said, "Sweet Christ," tonelessly. He dragged on it and slanted his eyes away from the smoke. Then he said, "No, I don't."

"All right," Vern said. "But for the hell of it, let's say you did think they were murdered. Who would you suspect?"

"The gook cook."

Vern stared at him blankly, startled by the abrupt answer. "Why?"

"Dammit, I don't know why. It could be any of us, I suppose. But he's the one I don't trust."

"Yeah, but why don't you trust him? Give me something concrete."

Sully's darkly haunted face twisted around an off-beat smile. "Kind of silly, isn't it? I mean even presuming that there is a murderer, for all you know you might be talking to him right now, and by the same token *I* might be talking to him."

Vern grinned. "Let's forget for the moment that you and I could also be candidates. Let's look at ourselves as outsiders. That's the trouble with all of us: we're so shot in the prat with guilt complexes we can't face anything objectively or constructively. Why the Chinese cook?"

"Because he's bred a little bug inside him called hate. He hates white men and educated men and men with money. He hates anyone that doesn't agree with him. I think he's a Red, or was one."

Vern nodded. "I've thought that for some time, but I don't think it's a valid excuse for murder. I understand that you were affiliated with them for a while."

Sully looked at him sharply, then blinked his eyes away.

"I worked for them, but that's as far as it went. They paid me when no one else would. I didn't like them and I don't think they liked me. But that's not unusual." He took a quick restless turn about the close cabin, throwing a fantastically large shadow among the blue shadows that moved only when the ship rolled and the water reflection stirred them.

"I guess I was looking for something more than just the money," he murmured. "But whatever it was I didn't find it. I never find it."

The Key, Vern thought. The Answer.

Sully drifted toward the berth, not looking at Vern, staring straight out through the open port. "I don't fit in," he said, "anywhere."

Vern shifted uncomfortably, averting his eyes.

"Come off it, Sully."

The mate looked down at him with little sparks of anger. "You're all the goddam time telling me to come off it. Easy words, boy — for a white man."

Vern stared at the shadow-running deck, thinking, There's a truth in that, one I've never stopped to think of before. I can't really know his problem. It's impossible for a Caucasian to have that much empathy. And suddenly he was unreasonably angry at the world that bred men out of the smoke and filth and the damp and blackness and the sanctimonious hypocrisy of civilization. He felt sick and depressed, filled with a sense of numbness and despair, and the feeling, he realized, was the seed of suicide.

He stood up, shrugging. "Have it your own way," he said. "I just think you're hammering nails of self-pity in your own coffin."

Sully let out a long streak of smoke. "You do, huh?" He'd smoked his cigarette down without once touching it with his hands. Now he pulled the butt from his lips and dropped it on the deck, tapped it once with his foot. "Well, it's my coffin, boy." He shoved Vern to one side and crawled into the lower berth.

"Get the hell out of here now, huh?"

Vern went to the door. "Who's at the helm?"

"Sim."

"Where's Tapley?"

"How the hell should I know. Getting some sack-time, I suppose."

Vern went quietly along the passageway, through the morbid hold, and opened the door into the fo'c'sle. The Chinese girl was gone and Tapley was curled tightly in his bunk, face to the wall, asleep.

Vern shook his shoulder. "Hey, Marco Polo, wake up."

Tapley came to life like a stepped-on rattlesnake. He uncoiled, flipped half-around, and flashed a razorblade in Vern's face. Vern recoiled with a start.

"What the hell's wrong with you?" he wanted to know.

Tapley's eyes were bright with the urgency of furious suspicion.

"Don't ever come at me like that again when I'm asleep," he warned in a thin voice. "I don't want to go the Fergus and Ernie bit. No sonofabitch's putting a knife in my back."

Vern relaxed and smiled, and nodded at the weapon in Tapley's hand. "Speaking of knives and sharp things —"

"That's all right," Tapley snapped. "I sleep with it and I carry it all the time. It's my buddy boy."

"All right," Vern said, spreading his hands open at his sides, trying to pass it off. "I don't have a knife or a goddam gun. Can we talk now?"

But Tapley wasn't smiling, and he didn't put the razor away.

"Yeah, we can talk. But as long as it's just you and me down here alone, you keep a few paces to leeward, huh? I don't want to hurt your feelings, sport, but I've decided to call the partnership off."

"Partnership?"

"Yeah, the one we made in your room that night in Singapore over Fergus' stiff. I've decided not to trust anyone anymore except Lotus Bud."

Well, at least he's found someone, Vern thought. "Okay," he said, "we're dissolved. But I still want to ask you a question — about Ernie."

"Back on it again, ain't you?" Tapley sneered. He arranged himself in a better position, throwing back his blanket, sitting up, tucking his legs in, gook-fashion. He placed his hands in his lap and kept the hand with the razor on top of the other hand.

Vern hunkered on the deck, bracing his cocked legs at angles from his body. "Someone's got to do something about it, Tap."

"Yeah, and it might as well be you. You know, you and the Jap are the only ones on this tub that got it made. I figured it out."

"What do you mean?"

"Simple. If one of you is a goddam murderer, you're safe on that score because it's for damn sure you ain't going to knock yourself off. And even if one of you ain't a murderer, you're still safe because nobody's going to knock off the Jap until he shows us where the wreck is, and nobody's going to slip it to you until you bring up the goods."

Vern nodded. "Comforting. But what happens to Haki after he locates the wreck? And what happens to me after I bring up the treasure?"

Tapley grinned with one side of his face. "Better get that gun you was talking about. What did you want to know about Ernie?"

"I want to know about the night, or morning, he disappeared. What was he doing the last time you saw him?"

"Making little ones out of big ones — chopping wreckage. Along about four the old man sprung with a bottle, a little pick-me-up for all hands. Now that I look back on it, I guess Ernie was holding on to that jug more'n anybody else. But I didn't think he was skiffed. Of course he was beat, and he never was the best boozer in the world. Anyhow, he got to stumbling around and the old man tells him to scoot below and relieve Dodd at the pump. That's the last I seen him."

Vern nodded, frowning, rocking with the ship. "Then Dodd was the last person to see Ernie alive," he said.

Tapley grinned. "You always come back to the Rover Boy, don't you, sport? I guess maybe you kind a like it that way, huh?"

"How do you like it, Tapley? Who's your fair-haired bet, aside from me?"

Tapley wagged the razor at him. "Tell you, sport, until I got my share in my pocket and got me off this tub, I'm figuring that you *all* done it. Yeah, that's right. I've made up my mind that me'n Lotus Bud are the only pure lilies on board. And I don't want none of you nasty bastards coming near us. We savvy each other now, huh?"

Vern nodded and stood up. "We savvy one another. Don't cut your throat in your sleep with that Georgia shaver."

"In a pig's ass!" Tapley jeered after him.

It's getting rough, Vern thought as he climbed the steps to the maindeck. As rough as a cob.

All of them had noticed the change that had come over Bea, though none of them, with the possible exception of Vern, divined the secret. She had come to life. Second love had struck her like second childhood. She felt as blindly giddy as a highschool girl. She wanted to be where Vern was, move when he moved, sleep when he slept, eat when he ate; she wanted to smile and think and speak when he smiled or thought or spoke.

Nor did it bother her that there were times when he tried to avoid her, because she knew that he was complex and given to moods of virtue and remorse, and she loved him even more because of it. So she had to keep seeing him again and again, hoping in some way to justify herself in his eyes, if only by being in his presence. And there were moments, rich moments, when from across the cuddy table or across the deck or in the passageway, she would catch him looking at her unconsciously. And in those moments — from the slant of his eyes — she would know that he, too, was hopelessly lost, and her heart would rejoice.

But the justification had to be valid, and that meant that Harvey had to lose his security. So . . .

After the Banda Sea came the Arafura Sea, and then Torres Strait, with Papua — the great darkly smiling land that no white man may ever conquer — on the portside, and the Continent Australia on the starboard. And then the vast blue-color bowl of the Coral Sea.

He came for her in the first night of the last sea. She was in her berth and she was drifting in that half-world which lies between reality and soft images, and heard the door open and knew from the cautious way he closed it and stood there silently for a moment in the swaying dark what he was after.

He's going to want me now, she thought bleakly, because he needs me. And God — I can't help him. I simply can't.

She kept her eyes closed, hearing him step to her side, thinking, Go away, Harv. Please. I don't want to tell you now. I don't want to face it now.

"Bea —"

Even though she had been expecting it and had tightened her flesh and nerves against it, the whisper made her flinch. She opened her eyes and sat up, bringing the single sheet she slept under up to her chin.

"Don't sit down, Harv. Go to bed."

"What?"

"I don't want you to touch me. I'm sorry, Harv. It's over."

He couldn't understand. His voice turned querulous. "Over? For God's sake, Bea. What —"

"We're over. Don't get angry, don't become childish.

97

You're an intelligent man. Accept it and let it end." But he wouldn't. She knew he couldn't. You can't snatch a spoiled child's favorite toy from him and expect him not to bawl and kick and turn blue in the face.

He was silent, building it up, swaying before her in the creaking shadows as the old schooner plodded patiently across the empty sea. His slim hands knotted into tight fists, and when he suddenly spoke, it startled her again.

"Just like that? Sing no sad songs for me and goodby? Why, Bea? *Why?*"

She shook her head, not looking at him now, not really looking at anything in the cabin. "That doesn't matter — can't matter," she whispered. "You know it can't. If it's over, it's over."

His voice went up a step. "But it *does* matter. It matters to me. Goddammit, you *know* how it matters!" Then he sat down on the berth and reached for her knee with his right hand.

"What is it?" he asked. *"Who* is it? That lady-killing diver with the pseudo-tragic Barrymore face and the little sharks running around in his brain?"

"Don't be petty, Harv. That's my line. It doesn't suit you."

"I want an answer."

She shook her head again. "No. It's over — over," she murmured.

A spasm of fury twitched across his little-boy face, snapping it instantly into a mask of insanity. He grabbed for the edge of the sheet at her throat.

Her eyes sparked with the reflected passageway light that angled through the slots of the louvers as her head jerked up. "Don't, Harv. Do it and I'll scream."

He grinned brutally and pushed his face close to hers.

"And who'll come if you do?" he hissed. "Who will kick down the door to get in here? The shark fighter across the hall? Is that who?"

She stared at him icily, thinking, I can't hate him. I've tried but I can't. He should never have left his mother.

They sat that way for a long moment, watching each other, his hand still clutching the edge of the sheet. Then he let go. "Bitch," he murmured. He stood up and left the cabin, closing the door gently behind.

Under the brilliant glow of the midnight moon the old slaver skirted through the Louisiades and approached the hem of the Solomon's sea apron. A day and a night passed and then the long ragged hulk of Guadalcanal appeared against the skyline, and then San Cristobal and Maramasike and Malaita and then the no-man's-land, the nameless sea between Melanesia and Micronesia. And then a day and a night and a day and a night and a new morning, and yet nothing but sea until the late afternoon of that day, when Harvey leaning on the rail by the starboard cathead looked out across the water and saw a low scattered formation jig sawing the horizon. He turned aft and shouted to Sully at the wheel.

"Mr. Sullivan! Look!"

Sully looked and smiled, nodding his head. Sim had made a perfect landfall. The Seven Madonnas were dead ahead.

Sim was in high spirits. He stumped along the deck, his old sea cap pulled smart on his forehead, searching the nearest islands with determined eyes.

"I've passed this way before," he told them, and they were interested, because now that they had finally reached El Dorado they wanted to know all they could about the place, as if every insignificant little bit of information was very relative to their future.

"Back in '23 the first time, then again in '31 or '32, I think. Use to be a Kanaka village down there to the south. On Pauloo, the last island. You can't see her from here."

He dug an old turnip watch from his pocket and glanced at it, darted a professional eye at the sickly green-tinted sky and brought one corner of his mouth down. "All right," he said briskly. "We got to get cracking. Lets have the sails down and we'll run in on the auxiliary."

His eyes rested for a moment on the long white line of foam that marked the reef. He knew there was a channel there somewhere, but as yet he couldn't see it. And the bitch of it was that they had only an hour of daylight left in which to find it.

"It's a frozen fact that there's a pass between Bama and Tapi," he told Sully and Haki. "Don't know why I can't pick her up."

Haki nodded politely, saying, "That is correct. I remember it so well. So sorry for you, Captain, that you cannot see it." He hissed regretfully.

99

Sim shrugged and ordered Tapley up the mast for a look. But minutes later the seaman's voice wailed down on them that he saw nothing.

"Oh, for God's sake!" Sim growled. "All right, Sully. Work her along the reef until we stumble on it. I'll do it by Braille if I can't do it any other goddam way."

The *Sally Lou* skirted within a hundred feet of the churning reef, and she dropped one mile and then two in her whipped-cream wake and Sim knew by then that they had missed, so they went about and worked back again. The long low wall of broken water continued without interruption, and at the end of the second try Sim threw up his hands in disgust. The light was failing. They would have to wait for morning.

"Put her about," he ordered. "We can't anchor here."

Sully ran the schooner out to sea and they let the anchor go.

Sim's spirits couldn't be dampened for long. He put his arms akimbo and beamed benevolently at them. "Well, my sons, lets repair below and hoist one for luck," he suggested.

They crowded about the saloon table and watched Sim unroll a chart which he pinned to the table top with four coffee mugs. He straightened up and pointed a blunt finger into the center of the white spread.

"There's your Seven Madonnas. Fergus dug this old sheet up for us, God rest him. Now see, here we are: Bama, Tapi, Oolam, Norris, Hanara, San Marie and Pauloo." His finger described a circle, tapping each illustrated island in turn. "And there's that damn channel I couldn't find."

Vern hunched forward, his eye wandering away from Sim's finger, going on a tour of inspection of his own. He tilted his head to one side to read the markings. The chart showed the atoll to be in the shape of an oblong frame, ten miles in length by seven in width. San Marie was the largest island, three miles. Oolam the smallest, one-half mile. The others graduated in size between the two. The depth readings for the lagoon were sparse and greatly varied. He suspected they were mostly guess work.

"Well, Haki," Sim said easily. "I reckon the time has come — as the man said. Where is the *Habanera*?"

Vern looked up and found that they were all staring at the little diver from Japan. Staring at him silently with wide unblinking eyes, waiting.

Haki hesitated. His round plate glasses captured the lamplight giving him large dials of white fire for eyes, Cyclopean. He touched his pinched lips with the tip of his tongue and hissed gently when he took breath through his mouth.

This is his moment, Vern thought. Mine is coming later. Now they're asking him to hang himself out on a limb, leaving them with the saw.

"Well?" Sim prompted.

Haki hissed again and pointed a brittle finger at the chart. The finger hovered vaguely over a section midway between Pauloo and Norris at the southern end of the atoll. "There," he breathed.

"Uh-huh," Sim grunted in a businesslike way. He sat down in the captain's chair and hunched himself half over the chart. He tapped at a depth reading, shooting a look at Vern. "Ten fathoms there. Not bad, eh?"

Vern shrugged. "If you can trust it. If that were true we could skindive for the wreck."

Haki hissed again, politely. "So sorry," he said softly. "So sorry that there is a depression in the lagoon floor. It is too bad that the floor slants toward Hanara to the west."

"How deep?" Vern asked.

Haki made a delicate shrug with his shoulders. "Thirty-five, maybe so forty fathoms. The wreck is near the bottom — I think."

Better and better, Vern thought grimly. Two hundred and ten to two hundred and forty feet, maybe more. If there are subterranean holes in the coral reef there will be currents down there, nice swift ones, maybe so. Haki, he knew, was being as vague as possible about exact location and depth. He couldn't blame him; without him they could search the lagoon bottom for months and probably come up with a blank. It was a whole new world down there, a separate universe, a land of crackling silence, painted with vivid splashes of vegetation, marred by endless corrugated hills, ravines, valleys, towering coral fortresses—and all of it vague and obscure under shifting hues, as though the sunlight were being filtered through moving sheets of blue-green glass.

Harvey turned to Vern. "What's our first move, Rigby?"

"To find the wreck." He wasn't trying to be funny.

In the morning, when the sun spread over the subdued hills of Pauloo, the opening in the reef, which had eluded them the evening before, was seen a little to the south of their position.

Sim looked, made a decisive nod with his chin and said, "Let's go."

With Tapley at the masthead to con Sully, the *Sally Lou* swung into the mouth of the wide ring of submerged coral and started down the pass. The slot was deep and navigable but treacherous with sawtooth ledges submerged in depths varying from half a fathom to five. And everywhere lurked coral traps waiting to gut the belly of the old schooner.

Once, during a moment of respite, Sim brushed against Vern and took the time to say, "I guess you don't know much about charts. You didn't notice the big pass they had marked between Pauloo and San Marie. I didn't say nothing about it in front of the others, but later I got Haki alone and asked him how about it. Know what he said? So sorry for you I forgot all about him, please. Hell, we could have drove a battleship through there last night."

Vern smiled wryly. "I have an idea that all of a sudden Haki isn't so hot and bothered about finding that wreck."

Sim snorted. "Wary little bastard, ain't he? Well, if he thinks he's going to shag our ass all over this godforsaken lagoon, then he don't know John Sim. I leave it up to you to either get the exact location from him or to come up with a trick of your own. I want to get this business underway."

Then an underwater canal opened up under the schooner's forefoot and she glided into the lagoon as stately as a child's toy boat on a placid pond. They heard Tapley's call from the masthead:

"All clear! We're in like Flynn!"

A silence disembodied from the rumble of the outer reef greeted them. The nearest island, Bama, lay lapped in bright vegetation with its palm-tufted threads of beach nodding a slow welcome under the sullen hills all aquiver in heat haze. Along the beach, just above the watermark, an industrious animal scurried across the warm sand looking for edible marine minutiae, and from the woods a sudden storm of vivid lorries hit the air and spearheaded the murmuring sky. Out in center lagoon something showed for a moment, breaking the mirror-glazed water cleanly. Then it disappeared. Vern followed it with his eyes.

"Do you think there are sharks out there?"

It was Harvey standing and smiling just behind him. There was nothing friendly about his smile, or about his eyes either.

Vern matched both and said, "Maybe."

Haki and Sim were on the poopdeck, looking at the chart. Haki was pointing across the lagoon to the south, and Sim said something to Sully. Slowly the schooner's head came around on a fresh tack.

The mangrove trees came down to the water edge on tiptoes like a band of shaggy thieves slinking across a headland, and where they stood swamps grew, the water stagnant and sluggish and burnished black and green like the color of a house fly. It was peaceful, somnolent, poisonous.

Bea appeared on deck, looking but not at the shoreline. Her eyes stopped on Vern. He inclined his head slightly, smiling, and went aft. Now it was his turn.

Haki was upset. He had suddenly become very animated and was gesturing from shore to chart. "Closer, please. So sorry that I must say we are not close enough to Pauloo, maybe so."

But Sim was all grins, and he gave the little man a slap on the back that nearly toppled him. "What do we care, son! We'll fish this spot first. Tapley! Stand by!" he shouted forward. And a moment later — "Let go!" With a rush of link-chain the anchor cracked through the lagoon surface like a mallet falling through a pane of glass, and sank in white flames to the bottom.

Sim took Vern aside by the elbow, muttering, "I think Haki is playing coy again. The wreck wouldn't be close to the beach. Not at thirty-five or forty fathoms, it wouldn't. Let's start getting wet now. Or do you want to drag first?"

Vern was in no hurry to get underwater, but he knew that sweeping a coral floor with a grappling iron — hoping to hook a wreck — was a hopeless task. He shook his head. "No, it would be a waste of time. I'll go on downstairs and have a look around."

They laid out the gear under his supervision: life line, air line, lead waist belt, harness, metal-shod boots, suit, and the great gleaming four-port copper helmet. He smoked as he watched them and he didn't have much to say. He felt nervous.

Haki sidled up to him wearing an insecure smile. "Excuse, please," he said hissingly. "If you are so fortunate as to find the wreck you must be very careful, so very careful — the shadow —"

"For crysake, Haki!" Vern snapped. "Do you want me to make this goddam dive or not? Stop trying to spook me. Keep away from me."

Startled, Haki stepped back quickly. "So sorry. So sorry, please, that I was so stupid to upset you. Excuse, please."

"All right. Just leave me alone, huh?"

They dressed him, Sim fussing over him like a proud mother preparing her daughter for her first formal. He was still all grins.

"Don't worry about a thing, boy. Sully will tend the compressor, and I'll be on the telephone. Take your time down there. You can't expect to stumble over it the first crack. Okay, get on the ladder."

The short awkward mechanical-man walk to the rail and the ladder over, they got him turned around and on the steps facing them, and they fitted the helmet to the breastplate, screwing it home on the segmental neck rings, and secured the catch. The front glass port was open. Sim leaned down wearing headphones, and grinned in at him.

"Okay? Let me hear your phone."

The telephone receiver was set in the crown of the helmet, the transmitter between the faceplate and the portside plate. The telephone line itself was inlaid in his life line. Vern depressed the chin push in the helmet for "speak" position, and muttered:

"Onetwothree-doyoureadme?"

Sim's grin deepened and he raised a hand to signify that all was in order. Just before he screwed the glass port in its gunmetal socket, he tipped Vern a wink. "Bring us up the jackpot, son," he said.

Standing on the ladder, Vern looked through the gridiron guard over the faceplate, seeing Haki nervous and tense, Sully by the compressor calm, almost bored, Harvey smiling (over what, for crysake?), watchful, and Bea . . .

She's frightened for me, he realized, understanding the pinched, urgent look in her pale face. Does that make me feel better or worse? He didn't know. Sim slapped the top of the copper helmet with his hand, and Vern let go, stepping backwards.

He had known from the first time he went under in '46 that he had too much imagination to ever be a good diver. Too much imagination to even be a brave man. He had a great respect for the underwater world, and a greater fear. It was like a beautiful prehensile woman folding herself about a man without any conscious idea of what he was and absorbing him, making him a part of herself, willing to destroy him but never willing to say when, never with warning.

And yet, manlike, it was the beauty and mystery that fascinated him, that drew him under time and again, pulling him down and down and deeper. The underwater world was a Mata Hari with a slender sharp knife hidden in her net stocking top, and she made his back prickle as he waited for the blow, but he never refused the summons to her bed.

Always his mind had revolved around water. Even as a boy he had been fascinated by any body of water, even by a rainpool, studying its clear crystal texture, wishing absurdly that he might be microscopic and plunge himself into that cool amber sub-microscopic sea and explore the vast submerged plain of brown and yellow speckled leaves and twisted twigs and lonely pebbles. Or at the beach — not to frolic in the sand and surf, but to stand out on the edge of the rocks and stare down into the swirling, foam-flecked velvety depths, wondering, 'My God, what is down there? What could be seen? How can I get to it?

Psychologists were now saying that skindivers had an unconscious urge to return to the womb. And that was the simple way in which they wrote off the men who explored the bottom of the sea. But psychologists always saw everything — all of man's behavior — in terms of mysterious self-destructive sex drives. It was stupid. Why do men climb mountains? Why do men fire themselves into space? Why did Columbus cross the Atlantic? Womb-bound? He doubted it. To return to the womb was to turn to death. Black zero.

No. Skindivers knew, or at least felt, something which the psychologists did not and could not: that the imaginative aboriginal mysteries of man have mostly grown from the inherent secrets sunken in the dark lonely depths of water, and being men their natural compulsions were directed to solving the riddle. Skindivers were explorers, not escapists.

Now, sinking slowly through the translucent world into the Silent Room, he felt his back prickle and knew he was once again in the sea whore's bedchamber. He glanced out of the starboard and port windows and saw nothing, then tilted the helmet forward and looked down on the subtle shadow rising to meet him. First the Turquoise Room, then the Green Room, and then the Amber Room. That's how it was in the shallows. But in deep diving there was the final room — the Black Room. But perhaps the worst place was the Middle Room, the nowhere place that existed between the surface and the bottom, where his vision was limited by the opaque walls of nothingness, where the unseen things dwelled. He hated it.

Lowering easily through the Middle Room, he was possessed suddenly with the urge to press the chin-push and order Sim to drop him faster, to get him through this zero stage. But he resisted the temptation. He sidetracked his thoughts and listened idly to the hiss of the intake valve. It was his friend, his nostrils, and the compressor on deck was his lung.

His metal-shod feet cracked through the ceiling of the Amber Room and now, looking out at a downward slant, he could see the coral walls materializing around silent chambers, describing fantastic shapes: anything from colorful imitations of soup bowls to shattered cathedrals, and everywhere and everything garnished and decorated by lacy clusters and ragged sawtoothed edges. On the starboard a thick carpet of crimson spread aimlessly over the floor; on the port a staghorn forest, golden, reaching, petrified. Then he tilted the helmet again and looked straight down.

A great round black pit was rising to swallow him.

"Jesus!" he said, and he hit the tele-transmitter button. "Raise me! On deck! Raise me!"

He watched, appalled, as his feet entered the monster's yawning maw. It was like being lowered into a great deep black well. Then he realized it was falling beneath him. They were raising him. He released the panic button and became rational again.

"On deck. That's enough. I've found something."

The black well was the open mouth of a steamer's funnel. From his hanging position he could see all of it stretching beneath him like a huge dead monster out of another age, frozen and preserved in the sea's storeroom. The first crack, Sim had said. It was unbelievable that he should drop blindly right on top of a ship. . . . But it wasn't important. It was too bad it hadn't been the *Habanera*, but that was asking for too much luck.

A sudden current moved in, drifting him over the top of the sunken ship, over the once-white superstructure still gleaming faintly under its thin coat of green growth. The bridge with its wheelhouse and dead-eyed windows passed under his feet, then the dark shadows of the well deck — transfixed by the tilted, reaching foremast with its secured lift boom. Then the current waned and he drifted aft again, recrossing the deck, wheelhouse and funnel.

Now the boat deck with its stubby air ventilators, stiffly

106

vacant davits, and the muted wireless shack. Then the after well deck, main mast, sampson posts, covered hatch; and then the fantail — stark davits port and starboard, ventilators, afterhouse, skylight and emergency wheel. Everything and all blanketed with the mosslike marine animals called bryozoans.

Then he started back again, dragging in the drift.

"On deck. Lower me, slow."

He settled down lightly on the boat deck, aft of the funnel and near the deckhouse companionway. His heavy boots clumped a dull sound on the metal deck — hollow, lonely, vibrant. He adjusted the air within his suit to the right buoyancy by the regulator screw of his exhaust valve. Then he looked around.

Now that he was stationary the amber-blue walls of the room closed in on him again, very softly, very subtly. He looked aft along the boat deck, where it receded into the bleary vistas of changing color and dissolved its form, everything running, dripping, blending together like a water color picture. The railings, fuzzy and alive with wisps of weed, waved at him in the current with little limber skeletal fingers; and the drunken wireless shack leaned at him like a tilted outhouse in an abandoned farmyard.

Haki's steamer. The one he had done the salvage job on. The ship he had been looking for when he stumbled on the *Habanera.*

He looked around at the coral ramparts rising from the gala lagoon floor, chocking the steamer into an almost upright position; at the madrepore, staghorns, sea-fans, whips; at the blares of red pigment dabbing everything like the spatterings from an artist's brush; and he wondered where in this vast riotous fairyland the *Habanera* was hiding.

A four-foot houndfish passed the wireless shack like a silver spear, and, in contrast, a heavy old grouper finned patiently after, as if it had an appointment at the end of the sea. Vern followed them absently with his eyes, then lost them as they vanished under the overhang of the flying bridge. Great sagging pearls had been strung there in the gangway shadows, pressed against the metal walls in foot-long, sticky strings. Squid eggs.

A chill touched him, and the compulsion to look over his shoulder was like a scream behind a closed door. He was suddenly very alone and vulnerable, suddenly conscious of his life depending on a slender thread of air line that reached above his head to the far surface. If something were to happen to that line . . .

It was silly, he knew it but couldn't help it. The monitor of his mind was like a monkey on his back. Out, it said. For Christ sake lets get out of here. This is enough for now.

His chin automatically touched the push button and he spoke into the transmitter, hoping his voice sounded normal, or close to it.

"On deck. Bring me up."

He heard the hum of the control switch depress, and then Sim's voice, cracked and disembodied.

"Anything wrong, Vern?"

"No," he lied. "Take me up. I want a smoke."

On deck they stripped him from his shell and hammered questions at him, all of them except Bea. She offered him an open pack of cigarettes.

Vern took one, smiled at her, then glanced at Harvey Dodd. The ex-playboy was smiling also, watching his wife, watching Vern. But there was a hint of smoldering fury in his dark eyes, like the head of a match burning behind a black silk curtain. Vern looked away from him, turned to Haki.

"I found your old steamer. We're right over her." He looked at Sim and said, "I wasn't more than forty foot deep. We'll have to work out further west, if —" he turned back to Haki again, "if the wreck is west like Haki said last night."

Their heads swiveled to the Jap as if in the control of one master hand. Haki seemed disconcerted under the combined pressure of their perusal. He made a tentative little smile and let his eyes sideslip.

"So sorry," he murmured. "So sorry that I cannot remember the exact location. Excuse, please, but it has been so long, you understand. But I think west, yes . . . maybe so."

"Why don't we have some chow?" Sim said abruptly, giving the suggestion the tone of an order. "You others scatter and leave Rigby alone. He needs rest."

"He's gonna need seven league boots to cover the whole bottom of this fish bowl, the way the gook is leading him by the nose," Tapley muttered. He slipped his arm around the Chinese girl's tiny waist, his hand sliding down to the ample curve of her buttocks as if looking for a place to catch a ride, and took her away with him.

108

When they were alone Sim struck a match for Vern's cigarette and sat himself next to him on the cargo hatch. "What do you think?"

Vern shook his head. "Haki's holding out. I can't say I blame him, after the things that have already happened —"

"Nothing's happened, for crapsake," Sim snapped. "He's just a jerky little bastard, like all them slanteyes. What are we going to do?"

Vern looked at the sky. The air was so brilliant over the atoll it seemed to waver like the halo around a burning match. He didn't want to leave it.

"Well," he said speculatively, "I think we're in the right neighborhood. I think he's at least led us to the right end of the lagoon. But it's still a big chunk to cover. Maybe twenty square miles. And when you're working underwater that twenty might as well be twenty thousand."

"Where does that leave us?"

"Let's go on the assumption that Haki was telling the truth. That there is a depression sloping to the west. That would be west of where we are now, toward Hanara. And let's assume that the wreck is down there. That narrows the search considerably."

"So?"

Vern looked off to the sullen hills of Hanara and at the shimmering stretch of water between them.

"I think I'll ride the anchor," he said.

Sim had the anchor picked up until half its length stood out of the water. Then Vern, naked except for swimming trunks, waist belt, and helmet strapped under his armpits and across his chest, swung down to the hook and stood on the arms. It was an old-fashioned Navy type anchor, giving him a stock to grasp with his hands. He snugged his feet between the flukes and the crown on the throats, and Tapley passed him a line to secure himself to the shank.

He checked his lines: air hose looped under the right arm and life line under the left. The compressor was started and air began to hiss through the inlet valve of the helmet. He tested the telephone again, then ordered Sim to lower away.

At the signal from Sim, Tapley walked back on the windlass and they lowered Vern to six fathoms and started the auxiliary. The *Sally Lou* began cruising northwest at a walking pace.

Riding the anchor was an old pearl-diver method. It saved time and labor, but it was tricky. If a coral pinnacle were to suddenly block the path of the anchor's drag, collision was almost inevitable. An alternate method was to make a bight in the life line, sit on it, and ride the sea bottom; but Vern liked the feel of something solid.

The drag caught him and the anchor lifted into a slanted position, like a giant pendulum frozen in the beginning of its swing.

"On deck. Lower one."

They dropped him another fathom, and he said:

"On deck. Lower two."

After the second drop he could see the floor of the lagoon again. Thick shafts of opaque sunlight pierced down through the water's blue filter and played flickering shadows of light and dark over the coral castles. The bottom looked like a sunken ruined city, like Atlantis. Then he noticed a heavy belt of dark blue shadow beneath him.

"On deck. Sim, stay in the area west of our original position. The salvage people Haki worked for must have had a pretty good idea of where the steamer was, so if they lowered him in its vicinity, and he found the *Habanera* instead, then the two must be close together. The depression is right below me now. Let me have two more."

The shadows were thicker, the sunrays less frequent, and yet there was still coral: the busy polyp was still at its ageless work, building fantastic designs in blues, pinks, whites and crimson. Vern called for more depth.

A long reaching black wall rose hazily out of the gloom before him, like a mired monster shoving up from the depths to dispute his passage. He jabbed at the chin-push.

"On deck! Raise me! Full astern!"

He watched the great coral wall coming at him, wondering if he should slip his secure line and drop off. No. Couldn't. Might snap the couplings out of the helmet. Above, he could hear the distant whirl of the screw reversing direction. The anchor began swinging toward the wall. He sucked in his breath. They were raising him — he could feel the up-drag — but was it going to be in time?

Then, miraculously, the dark ragged battlement passed under his feet, barely scraping the tip of the crown, and he swung clear. He let his breath out.

"On deck. All right now. Resume original course, but reduce speed. I almost had myself mashed like a stepped-on fly."

"Take it easy," the crackling reply came back. Then he

heard some mutter-mutter but no words, and then Tapley came on.

"Hi, sport. Having some fun down there?"

"What are you doing on the phone?"

"Sim had to go youknow. He turned 'em over to me. What did you just say — drop you ten?"

"You goddam fool. Stop clowning around. Who's at the wheel?"

"The chippie's delight, Dodd."

That made him feel better. Somehow he didn't hanker to have Harvey around the compressor.

"Hey, Rig," Tapley called. "You hear the one about the young man from Dundee who diddled an ape in a tree?"

Yeah, he'd heard it: the result was most horrid, all prat and no forehead . . . but he couldn't help grinning. "Look, Tapley," he said. "Get the hell off the phone now, huh? I've got problems of my own."

Tapley chuckled and said, "Okay. Here's the old man. I'm going to go see what Lotus Baby's up to."

At a depth of one hundred and fifty-five feet Vern felt a change in his direction. The schooner was coming about. The anchor swung easily, gliding him through the murky twilight water. It was colder now. He began to shiver sporadically. They were working on a new tack, moving southwest.

One hundred and sixty-six feet.

One hundred and seventy-two.

One hundred and seventy-eight . . .

From the starboard window he saw a shadow passing through lighter shadows; then it was gone, swallowed by darkness. After that he turned from time to time, looking over his shoulder. But he didn't see it again.

One hundred and eighty-four.

One hundred and ninety.

One hundred and . . .

"On deck!" he called. "I think I see something. Hold your position."

It was a blurred lump at first, a battered broken-in block of nothing, a nondescript length of coral . . . only there wasn't much coral at that depth. There was weed and sand and shadow . . .

Then, as the *Sally Lou* ceased her forward progress and the anchor started swinging down, bearing him into closer range, he began to see definite outlines.

She was a ratty, shapeless, caved-in box: mired, weedy,

sand-clogged. Her very aspect was the mute evidence of her long sojourn on the lagoon bottom. Garlands of sea flowers hung down from the shattered rails and spread over the sand floor like a dropped mantle. The high old-fashioned poop had crumbled, giving the suggestion of a rotting shell, and the maindeck had fallen, leaving only a few wreathed cross timbers and oaken knees visible. There were no masts, no spars, no bowsprit or running rigging, and what standing rigging remained was tangled and thickened to the size of a man's arm with sea growth.

The dead ship. The *Habanera*.

She was nearly two hundred feet down, resting on a gradual, weeded slope. Beyond was blackness, indicating greater depth. And there was a current. It prodded him and the anchor swung over the decayed hulk, passed it, hovering over a darkly shimmering weed bed and curved off in a new direction.

"On deck," Vern called. "I've found it."

There was a great spirit of camaraderie in the saloon that night. Harvey even shook Vern's hand to congratulate him, and the pleased look in his little-boy face made Vern think that he was sincere. And that gave him a stab of contrition.

Sim, Tapley and Sully were drinking heavily; Sim and Tapley outshouting each other's plans and proposals. Bea sat quietly in the captain's chair, smiling, smoking, drinking black coffee, watching Vern. Lotus Bud stood waiting in a corner, inscrutable, watching Tapley possessively.

Only Haki seemed to be an outsider (Ling-Po had scorned the celebration, remaining in his galley). The little Japanese diver sat apart from the others, watching them with worried, glancing eyes.

Vern felt sorry for him and approached him to talk about the dive, but Haki seemed to be in no mood for talking. He made a few polite replies, but made no attempt to further the conversation.

Vern gave it up and went back to the table to sit by Bea. She accepted a light for her cigarette and studied him through the pale screen of smoke.

"Was it bad down there, Vern?"

"No," he lied. "It was all right. Bea, I've got to talk to you."

He checked himself and glanced around at the others. Harvey was at the highboy pouring a drink.

"Tonight," Vern said in an undertone. "Meet me in the hold after midnight. Anytime after. I'll be there."

Sim stood up abruptly and raised his voice for attention.

"Well, my sons, I don't like to be the bucko to sprinkle ice water on these festive doings, but here's a matter we got to consider. This here's the Black Belt, or a stepson to it: only it's a little worse than the Belt because it's more remote. This atoll don't see a French gunboat except maybe once a year.

"Now, if there're Kanakas on these islands, we got to consider 'em hostile until we know better. You can't never take a chance with a wooly, specially when the wooly knows he's beyond the realm of the white man's law. What I'm getting at is, I think we'd better have a watch on deck tonight."

He spun on his heel and went to his cabin. A moment later he returned with a 9mm Luger. He plopped it down on the center of the table along with a single clip.

"That's the only firearm we got on board," he commented. "However, that little toy in the hands of the right man can throw the fear of God into two dozen Kanakas. Fact. I've seen it happen. Personal experience."

Haki straightened up, his slitted eyes hard and bright on the gun. He cleared his throat carefully, motioning a finger at Sim. "Please, Captain, excuse. I should be so happy to offer myself as one of the watch. So kind of you."

Sim nodded. "Fair enough. Mr. Dodd, will you take the first trick, eight to midnight? Haki can go second, and I'll do the third."

Harvey nodded, reaching for the gun.

"How do you use one of these things?" he asked.

Vern was pacing the gangway in the hold, weaving a confusion of thoughts through his mind. Some sort of conclusion had to be reached between himself and Bea and Harvey. He was sick of the triangle.

But suppose Harvey decided to be nasty? Suppose the bastard decided to cause trouble. What could he do? What might he try to do? Kill me, he wondered. Kill Bea?

I could kill him.

113

The absurd thought leaped into his mind and he let it stay there for a while, pushed it around.

He said he wanted to help me in the diving, he thought. Yeah. So why not let him? Once I had him down there I could close his air exhaust. He'd never know the difference, and the incoming air would expand his suit, spread eagle him. He'd be helpless and he'd take off like a sky-rocket and explode like a grenade, and I'd be glad because he'd be dead and out of the way and no questions asked, and yet would I be glad if it was my hand that turned the trick? Would it haunt me? Would it come between us every time I looked at Bea, at his wife? His wife.

He didn't know. He wanted him dead and yet knew that if something were to happen to Dodd down there, he'd bust a gut to try to save him because he was made that way.

And Christ, he thought, isn't that a jerky way for a man to be made? I want him dead but I can't do it. But if some outside force takes him I'll do everything in my power to save him and while I'm trying to do it I'll be hoping — half hoping — I fail or that the force is too much for me, and when he's dead I'll be glad and my hands will be clean. Christ that doesn't make sense and yet it has to because that's the way things are. But can you honestly try to save a man whom you are hoping will die? Yes, you can. You can risk your life even. Believe it or not. So we're complicated. Yes, my God, as complicated as you can get. And yet I'm considered normal.

Who said so?

The aft door opened, tentatively at first, then wider as he turned and faced it. Bea looked at him and stepped into the hold, closing the door behind her.

"Dog it," he said.

"Pardon?"

"Lock it."

"Said and done, Mr. Righteous Rigby," she said, turning and showing him an arched smile. She was wearing a negligee so sheer he wondered why she bothered with one at all.

He moved quickly through the pale circle of lantern light into the near shadows, reaching for her, feeling a rip of desire in his body as though he'd swallowed a strand of barbed wire.

"Bea. Bea —"

She held him back a moment, with a provocative look that made him want to tear her apart. At such a moment having her simply wasn't enough. And for the first time he was able to

114

understand a little of Harvey's trouble. The right woman, he reflected, could create satyriasis in any man.

"I thought you wanted to talk," Bea said.

"Yeah —" he breathed. Then he grinned and relaxed somewhat, but it was hard. "Yeah. About you and me and Harvey."

The wanton went out of her face. The little-girl look he remembered from that day in his cabin came back. Then he knew she was frightened.

"I told him it was over between us."

"And?"

She looked away from him, looked at the darkly stained benches that had once bedded cannibals and headhunters — recruits for the Queensland plantations.

"I don't know," she said slowly. "He didn't say much, really. But — he's like a spoiled child. If you hurt him, he'll hurt back. He's guessed about us . . . I suppose they all have. You can't cover a thing like this."

"But what do you think he'll do?"

She shook her head. "I don't know. I don't know if he'll do anything. I only feel a — a shadow of something waiting."

Then I was right, he thought. He's going to be bitchy about it. She knows him better than I do and she can feel it coming. So what'll I do?

"Vern — he mentioned today that he wants to help you with the wreck. Don't take him. If he asks you, promise me you'll say no."

Vern smiled grimly. "I was born down there. He wasn't. I'd have the advantage."

Her hands made two knots in the front of his shirt. "No, you wouldn't. Because you'd be on the defensive."

Maybe, he thought, and maybe it would be the other way around. But he wasn't going to tell her what he'd been thinking. "We'll see," he said.

She tugged at his shirt urgently. "Darling," she said. "I'd rather forget about the treasure completely, than have you go down there with Harv."

"Don't be a fool," he snapped. "You and I have a long life ahead of us. We'll need our share of the treasure."

Looking slightly incredulous she reached up and touched his cheek.

"Do you really mean that, Vern? You want me?"

"Yes. What did you think?"

115

"As your wife?"

"Yes."

"Then everything's all right. Then I don't care about the stupid treasure. We don't need it."

"It's not that easy, Bea. We're caught up in a moment of passion now. Nothing seems to matter to us as long as we have each other. But when we return to civilization our emotions will be replaced by cold reasoning. This is a ship, a little world all of its own —"

She shook her head. "It's the only world I've ever known. It's been a beautiful world, frightening, insecure, but beautiful. It's given me you."

It was a nice thought, but you couldn't live on it. There was a pattern to reality. He'd seen it before, because he'd been married once. Marriage was like a small business with two partners. As long as the company was making money the partners got along fine. Once the company headed for the rocks the partners started falling out.

Enduring love, it would seem, was somehow tied up with money. At first it was the moon and its light on the sea and a boy and a girl walking hand in hand, and their future was like the stars, all icy clean and crystal clear and burning bright. And then he said I Do and she said it too and the kindly-faced man in black said I Pronounce. And a year later the young husband drooped into the small apartment after eight hours of working for someone else for a handful of dollars and started grumbling because his dinner was cold or because it wasn't even ready or because why in hell did they have ground round every goddam night of the week, and didn't she know how to cook anything else, for crysake? And the young wife didn't bother to answer him because she knew if she once started to she would probably end up screaming, and anyhow she was in the diaper-strung bedroom with her hair in paper curlers and no make-up and in a nondescript old dress and was walking up and down carrying a little damp bundle that cried and cried and cried. And then the young husband saw the bills the postman had delivered that day.

But why try to explain all that? The girl in the paper curlers and the squalling baby and the unpaid bills were as foreign to Bea as life on another planet. It was something that happened to other people, little, insignificant people, not to Bea and the men she fell in love with. Well, it had happened to him once, but never again. So he was going to get that treasure if it was there or die trying. So why waste time talking about it?

116

He stepped back a pace and jigsawed his eyes down her body. The negligee she wore was pale blue, except where it clung to the pink of her bare body. And suddenly he was reminded of the mannequin in the shop window in Singapore. Funny, he thought, the way things worked out.

She lowered her eyes from his gaze, as though looking down at herself, seeing what he was seeing. Again she seemed young and immature.

"Don't look at me that way," she whispered. "I was in bed, waiting to come to you. Harv would have wondered if I'd gone to bed in my clothes." She hesitated, not looking at him. "No." Her voice was husky, warm. "That isn't true. I thought that you — we —"

And she was right. Good God, how right.

He reached for her again, drawing her in, and it was like bringing light into darkness or hope into despair or life into the world, and brushed the blue gossamer of the negligee from her shoulders and kissed her shoulder and her neck and then her cheek, working for her mouth as her mouth came seeking his, and knowing all the time that something had to be done about that damned lantern because the stinking old hold would be bad enough in darkness, but not wanting, not able to leave her, her body just yet, not now, and then finally setting her back from him and turning quickly away, his hands and knees both trembling, and taking three-four steps to the lantern and turning it out — blackness exploding like a bomb in a silent film — and then finding her again by braille, by breath.

And in the dark it didn't matter if the benches were hard or if they were stained by the sweat and blood of long-ago savages, because he was thinking: Love doesn't care where. Love is Now. Anytime, any place is always Now. Now that I should become a part of her. Now that she should become a part of me. A oneness through fusion. And it didn't matter to her because she was thinking: It's not Where, but with Whom that counts. Odd I never realized that before. But then life is odd, we're odd, all our behavior is odd, Odd, ODD! Oh God I —

"Oh God, darling —"

And then a sudden high shout, sharply intoned and far out, ripped the fabric of the night, and they heard someone's feet pounding the deck over their heads.

117

Haki had appeared on deck promptly at twelve midnight to relieve Harvey Dodd. Harvey had presented the Luger saying, melodramatically, "God's in his heaven and all is right with the *Sally Lou*." And Haki had smiled nervously, replying, "So nice. Thank you so much." Then Harvey had departed for below, leaving the little man with the big gun alone on the shadowy main deck.

A sense of strength — false courage — had come over Haki once his hand closed around the cold butt of the Luger. A feeling of security (more welcome to him than the sight of a fortune) was now in his grasp. He was a very frightened little man.

He trod the old decks silently, wraithlike, passing through moon pools and shadow belts, his narrow bullet-shaped head turning from side to side in a continuous panning movement. The possible threat of head-hunting savages meant nothing to him. He was scared to death of his own shipmates.

He was not a stupid man, merely a greedy one; and he now discerned just how far into the trap his greed had led him. It had been greed that made him listen to the others and their excuses for Donald Fergus' death. Greed had made him vulnerable. But when the Dutch seaman Dorp had disappeared . . .

It was too much, and yet he had known then that it was also too late. But not being a stupid man, he had been cognizant of the fact that he alone (with the possible exception of Vern Rigby) had been immune to sudden death at the hands of the unknown assailant. Immune until he located the wreck for them. That was when he had begun to balk, to stall for time. That was when his shell of greed had cracked, shattering into nothingness, leaving only the naked, defenseless little bit of vitalized matter that was the man, trembling and frightened inside.

And now that the accursed Rigby had discovered the wreck, he knew only too well what was coming next. Someone was waiting to say *sayonara* to him with a knife blade. Then Captain Sim had brought the Luger from hiding, and in his desperation Haki had rejoiced at the sight of the weapon. He would make it his, would keep it by him, and if any man (or woman: he was in no mood to trust anyone) tried to come against him he would shoot him down cold-bloodedly and without regret.

118

Pacing now, spectrally, he formed a plan in which he might deceive the others and thereby keep the weapon for his own. He must find a momentary hiding place for the Luger. Then when Captain Sim came to relieve him he would say he had lost it, dropped it overboard by accident. He would throw something overboard too, a plate or something from the galley, just in case someone might inadvertently be listening. If they doubted his word he would let them search him (he was above pride now); then, later, he would recover the weapon and hide it under his clothing. Let them beware then!

But where was he to hide the Luger now? He looked around wildly, his eyes darting through the shadows like rapier thrusts. Not the galley, the sullen Chinese cook was forever drifting about in there like a restless spirit haunting a house. No. Nor aft either, too many people about. And by the same token the fo'c'sle was also closed to him. That Tapley and his whore were like watchful hawks, trusting no one, watching every moment, listening to every sound, snooping, prying . . .

The empty hold. Yes! That was the place. Back in a dark nook under one of the benches. Very well, then. If Tapley and the slut were asleep he could slip down there and enter the hold through the fo'c'sle.

He scurried to the scuttle and crouched there for a moment to sound the fo'c'sle darkness for the soft sound of sleepers breathing. But the plummet of his hearing brought nothing but the far-out murmur of the outer reef. Were they asleep down there or were they up to their usual pastime? He must be certain. It wouldn't do to mistake silence for unconsciousness.

So intent was his concentration that for a moment the quiet sound of a gentle footfall behind him meant nothing. It was the shadow spilling over his shoulder and up the face of the open door that caught his attention. He peered at it myopically, thinking at first that it was only a shadow from the rigging above, cast there as the schooner shifted on her cable in the moonlight. But it continued to expand, to take form — like the shadow of a man raising a weapon over his head.

Startled, scared witless, everything in him — heart, lungs, guts — ramming into his throat, Haki spun about swinging the Luger up. And something caught his right wrist, cinched down, and his trigger finger couldn't reflex, and a sharp, bright glint of reflected moonlight winked in the corner of his glasses

119

and in that split second he knew what it was and knew that it was too late and he said "No!"

He felt it coming with a rush and felt it jar in his chest, and it seemed to go right through his chest, burning, ripping, and he saw again the marine he had bayoneted on Guadalcanal so very very long ago, saw him writhing and kicking and sob-cursing on the end of that damned blade as he forced him further and further down into the jungle muck underfoot, and, wonderingly, he thought, It doesn't really hurt so much after all. I had always thought —

"No!" he gasped. And then everything was dropping out, the moon, the deck, the bottom of the sea, and nothing was left — only the dead marine with the bayonet in his chest, waiting for him.

A few minutes prior to four A.M. Sim put a fresh cigar in his mouth and left his cabin. He paused in the darkened, creaking saloon to light the stogy, feeling the *Sally Lou* under his feet working on her mooring, while across the way the mirror above the highboy captured his dim reflection, showing him himself as something unreal. No face, just a pale glimmer of cheek, a bright spark of eye, and the small flare of the cigar end. He whipped the match out and clumped up the stairs to the deck.

On deck he stopped by the patchwork skylight and stood contentedly for a moment with an off-shore breeze fanning his craggy face. He dragged deeply on his cigar, enjoying it, watching the smoke snap into oblivion in the zephyr. Then he stumped down to the break in the poop and looked into the waist for Haki.

The moon bathed the scuffed deck pearl gray, crisscrossing it with thin angular shadows from the taut rigging. The waist was deserted. Sim frowned and called:

"Haki?"

The schooner shifted on her cable, drifting a few leisurely feet, and only the tentative creak of her rigging answered him. He removed the cigar from his mouth, and his eyes, narrowed and hard, searched the quiet deck again. Abruptly he clattered down the steps to the waist and started forward, peering suspiciously into the shadows. He hesitated at the galley door. It was open, showing him the nothingness of a black square.

"Haki?"

He looked toward the fo'c'sle scuttle. Something on the deck gleamed like a blotch of silver. He went to it — a small black pool, as though someone had carelessly spilled oil. The Luger shone dully in the moonlight one yard away.

Sim squared his mouth into a thin strip and pitched his cigar overboard. He stooped and lifted the Luger and stalled for a while as he balanced it in his hand, his eyes speculative and wary. What the hell had happened to the gook? he wondered. Bending, he started down into the fo'c'sle, and stopped halfway on the steps and called again:

"Haki?"

Something stirred, someone mumbled, then a voice, harsh, "Who is it?" sprang through the dark. Tapley.

"Sim."

"Well, excuse the disrespect; but what the hell are you pussyfooting around here for?"

"I'm looking for Haki. Is he down here?"

"How the hell do I know? I ain't no owl. What a you think I'm doing, setting up a peepshow here? He's on watch, ain't he?"

"No, he ain't. I can't find him nowhere. Show a light, will you."

"Sure. But don't get gay, Skipper. I got an open razor in my hand."

Sim grinned in the dark. "Hell," he said, "that's nothing. I got the Luger in mine."

He sensed Tapley's hesitation and his grin ironed out with annoyance.

"Jesus H. Christ. Show a leg, will you. I ain't gonna pot you, you damn fool."

"It wouldn't be wise," Tapley's voice came. "I got me a witness. Cover it up, baby. We got company."

"It's all right," Sim said dryly. "I've seen it before. You see one, you've seen 'em all. Snap it up, can't you?"

There was a rustling of noise in the dark, bare feet scuffing the hardwood deck, then a soundless explosion of bright light, and Sim blinked his eyes against the glare. When he looked again he saw Tapley standing in a pair of dungarees, lifting the lamp to the timber hook. He did it with one hand. The razor was in his right hand.

The Chinese girl was in the first starboard berth (If both of 'em weren't built like toothpicks, Sim thought, they'd never

121

fit), drawn up on the pillow with her back to the bulkhead, her lithe body coiled and tense like a compressed spring under the sheet she held up to her breasts. She had a small dirk in her hand and her almond eyes glittered dangerously as she watched Sim.

He made a wry smile, seeing the humor in the static scene. "Quite the band of thieves we are. If someone was to snap his fingers right now I bet we'd be at each other's throats like wildcats."

"Yeah," Tapley muttered. "I bet we would."

Sim came down the last of the steps, and Tapley moved to the side of the berth to shield the Chinese girl. Sim looked at them with disgust, then shoved the Luger in his belt.

"Relax," he said.

"What's the pitch?" Tapley wanted to know. He gave no indication of relaxing.

"I told you: I can't find the goddam Jap. I came on deck to relieve him, and he's gone."

"So maybe he slipped into the galley for some java, or down to the cuddy for a snort."

"No on both counts, my son. I've been both places."

Tapley smirked nastily. "So maybe he tiptoed into the Dodds' cabin to rape cutie-pants."

Sim sneered. "Very funny — with her husband sleeping there."

"That don't seem to bother Rigby none."

"All right," Sim snapped. "Suppose you worry about your own homework. What I want to know is, where is that Jap? The Luger was on the deck when I came up, and a big spit of blood with it."

The smirk on Tapley's face dissolved. His hand worked around the handle of the razor. "Blood?" he said stupidly.

"You've got my meaning, son. Blood — and no Jap."

Sim turned and went to the door which opened into the hold. He pushed at the handle, then looked back at Tapley and the girl.

"Who dogged the gangway?" he asked suspiciously.

Tapley shook his head. "I don't know. It was clear when I came that way from the cuddy. I sleep like a hungry wolf with one eye and ear cocked, but I didn't hear nobody come down here. Lotus Bud was already in the sack when I came home."

The corner of Sim's mouth tugged down. He didn't look at Tapley or the girl as he started for the companion. "Fetch a light and follow me," he ordered over his shoulder.

122

Tapley closed his razor and looped the cord over his head and tossed the razor over his shoulder to his back, and then took his shirt from the upper berth and put it on. The Chinese girl watched him silently. She lowered the knife in her right hand and then lowered the sheet to her lap. Tapley looked down at her. Her skin was tawny in the lantern light, her stomach flat and firm, her small apple-breasts perky, the nipples reddish-brown and standing up.

He grinned at her wolfishly and cupped one in his left hand.

"Stop looking that way," he said. "Everything's all right. They don't catch old Tappy off base."

Then he let it slide out of his hand and he went over to an old woebegone chest that was secured in the forepeak and he opened it and pawed through the slickers and boots and odds and ends until he found a dented flashlight and he snicked the button to test the batteries and grunted his satisfaction and got up and headed for the steps and shot the beam of light on the girl's bare breasts as he passed her and grinned and said, "Don't catch cold."

On deck he began chopping up the night with the white blade of his light. He hit the pool of blood with it and it glowed like a ruby. Then he shot the beam at Sim.

"Maybe we're knocking ourselves out over nothing," he suggested. "If the Jap got knifed, then I bet he's been slipped over the side."

Sim frowned. "Sounds reasonable. But if that's what happened, must have been someone would hear the splash. You don't dump a hundred and twenty pound man over the side like you do a feather. Now spread out and snoop around. Toss that beam in the galley for the hell of it."

Tapley stepped over to the galley door and shot the white shaft along the deck. The light didn't have far to go. Haki was just inside the door, face down, right arm flung straight before him, left arm bent under his body and out of sight.

Tapley stared and forgot to breathe. Then he sucked air into his lungs and shouted. And then Sim came running.

Ling-Po was the first one there. He ran out of the storeroom in his shorts and right into the blaze of light Tapley threw in his face. Then Tapley cut the light down to the body between them, and Ling-Po made a sharp little sound in his mouth and stepped backwards quickly. He didn't know who the man with

123

the flashlight was and he reached for the knife rack. Then Sim's voice growled through the crystal halo of light.

"Leave them things alone."

The Chinese girl was the first one to reach the deck from below. She went right to Tapley's side and looked at the body and then wrapped her hands around Tapley's pipestem arm. She didn't do anything after that or say anything. She just stood there pressing against his side.

Then Vern and Bea came up through the fo'c'sle and separated among the others. Finally Sully and Harvey came down from the poop. Tapley turned and panned the flashlight across their faces.

"Some sonofabitch . . ." he started to say. But Sim said to stow it, and ordered him and Ling-Po to fetch a tarp from the storeroom to wrap the body in.

Sim went over to the rail and put a cigar in his mouth and struck a match to it. The others watched his gaunt face dip into the cupped ball of flame as he puffed the end of the cigar redhot. The match made a tiny comet's flight as he flicked it over the rail. Then he turned back to them. A lamp was blazing inside the galley and he could see Tapley and Ling-Po rolling the body up in the tarp.

"All right," he said. "Let's go down to the cuddy. I guess we better have a talk."

Sim took the captain's chair at the head of the table and the others spaced themselves on the benches, face to face. Sim nodded his head at the Chinese girl. "Missy, you fetchee one piecee drink all around. I guess we can use it."

The girl went to the highboy and got a bottle of whisky from the fiddle and brought it to the table. Then she went back for the glasses and carried them all in one trip, four to each hand, her fingers inside them. Harvey took his with a frown of disgust and got up and went to the highboy for a fresh one. God alone knew where her hands had been, but Harvey had a good idea.

Tapley got PO'ed about it.

"Are you so damn clean?" he wanted to know.

Sim told him to stow it again. He filled Bea's glass, then his own, and then passed the bottle to Vern on his left. He looked at them.

"I guess it's no secret what Vern and Tapley are thinking," he said finally. "Maybe we're all thinking it. And maybe we're

124

right. I don't know. Haki's dead because someone murdered him. That's all I do know."

"Why not ask the Chink?" Tapley said, turning his eyes on Ling-Po. "He was sleeping right there in the storeroom. Jesus Christ, is he going to sit there and tell us he didn't hear a god-dam thing?"

Ling-Po said nothing at all. He stared fixedly at his untouched drink.

"Well, doctor?" Sim prompted. "You heard the question."

Ling-Po shook his head. "I heard nothing," he said shortly. "I was asleep."

"Oh, Jees-*us*," Tapley complained.

Sully looked at him. "What about you?" he asked. "It must have happened right over your head. How come you didn't hear anything?"

Tapley blinked stupidly. "Well because I — well dammit, I was asleep. What the hell you getting at, anyhow? Listen, buster, don't try to bring that crap around to my door. I got a witness that'll tell you I was in the sack all goddam night. If you're going to start that business, then ask Dodd. He was the last one seen the Jap alive."

Here we go, Vern thought. In a squirrel cage, chasing each other in circles with suspicions and accusations.

Harvey looked at Sim. "What about these savages who are supposed to be on shore? Couldn't they have done this?"

Sim nodded slowly. "Yeah. Sure, they could. But it seems funny they'd go to all the trouble of coming out here, killing our watch, and then not take his head or anything. What do you think, Sully?"

"They're funny people," Sully said. "They've got their own valid reasons for killing — even though it doesn't make sense to us. They don't always do it for heads. And anyhow — for all we know — maybe something scared 'em off right after they hit Haki."

"Jesus," Tapley said with amazement. "You can really stack it around yourself, can't you? Kanakas hell! We all know why the goddam Jap was killed. Rig, you know why, don't you?"

"I think I do," Vern said shortly.

"Bet your butt you do!" Tapley cried. "And Dodd still ain't told us about his last meeting with Haki."

Harvey smiled calmly and reached for a cigarette from a pack that was on the table.

125

"Haki relieved me at midnight," he said simply. "I gave him the gun, said something asinine, and went below. Mr. Sullivan was still in the saloon. I had a cup of coffee with him and turned in. My wife was already asleep. That's all I know. Something woke me at a little after four. I heard the noise on deck. I grabbed my robe and came up. *Finis*."

"What about Mrs. Dodd?" Sim asked. "Didn't she come up with you?"

Harvey looked at his cigarette. "No. She wasn't in the cabin when I awoke."

"But she was there when you turned in. Where'd she gone to?"

Harvey looked annoyed. "Why don't you ask her?"

Vern stared at the table, waiting for Bea to speak, feeling a tight knot in his stomach.

"I sleep like a restless dog," she said quietly, looking at Sim. "Stop and go. Around four I awoke and decided I was thirsty. As soon as I reached the saloon I heard someone shout, so I went on deck. That's all."

That's not so bad, Vern thought. Maybe we won't have to compromise each other after all.

"Wait a minute," Tapley said. "I don't see no alibi there. How do we know Dodd didn't slip it to Haki at midnight when the Jap went on deck to relieve him?"

"We don't," Sim agreed. "But it would take a pretty cool hand to meet a man at midnight, slip a knife in him, drag him into the galley, and then come below a couple of minutes later and have a cup of java with the mate."

"So what?" Tapley demanded. "It don't take any great strain to say 'Howdy do, Jap,' pass him the gun with one hand and ram a shiv into his gut with the other, and then topple him into the galley and get the hell out of there."

"I still say it takes a cool hand," Sim agreed. "Look: he's up there in the dark, knifes a man and then tramps down into the cuddy where another man is sitting. How does he know he don't have blood all over himself until he gets in the light? And then it would be too late."

Harvey leaned back with a wry smile. "Gentlemen, don't you think we could get on someone else's back for a while?"

Sim grunted and said, "Try mine. I went into my cabin after the party in here broke up and did some reading. Little after one Sully came in and we shot the breeze for a couple of hours or so. Shortly after he took off I went up on deck to relieve

126

Haki. That's about right, ain't it, Sully? Must have been after three-thirty when you left."

Sully raised his head and looked at the chronometer across the cabin.

"Yes. That's right."

"Was Rigby in your cabin when you turned in?" Harvey asked.

"No," Vern said. "I was in the hold."

"What's in there, sport?" Tapley asked.

"I couldn't sleep. I was restless. So I went in there where I could pace it off."

"For four hours?" Harvey asked, skeptically.

"Say three. I said I was restless."

"You dogged the forward door?" Sim asked.

"Yes, and the after one. I didn't want to be bothered." He could feel Harvey's eyes on him. He took a drink and reached for a cigarette.

Sim scratched at his jaw and said, "So that's that. Ling-Po says he was sound asleep all night in the storeroom, and Tapley and the China girl say they were asleep in the fo'c'sle. And we still don't know what happened to Haki."

A dull silence pervaded the saloon, intensified by the unflagging tick of the chronometer. No one spoke. They looked at each other blankly, at the table top, their cigarettes, their glasses, and at each other again. The tired old schooner shifted in her mooring, creaking and grumbling in her sleep. Then Sim stood up.

"Well," he said carelessly, "there's only one thing I can say: if the Kanakas didn't get him, then one of us is a goddam liar."

Most of them slept until noon, but Sully came into the cabin at eleven and shook Vern awake.

"Sim says we won't do any diving today, out of respect for the dead. Wants me to take Haki's body ashore and bury him. I was going to have Tapley help me but —" a grin of pure white teeth flashed in his dark face, "he looked all tied up for another half hour. You want to lend a hand?"

Vern focused his sandman eyes on the deckhand. "Yeah," he muttered, not wanting to say it and not able to keep from saying it. "I'll lend a hand."

Sully slapped him on the shoulder. "Good man. Grab

something to eat and meet me on deck. Sim'n I will get a boat over."

They ran ashore in the early afternoon in one of the schooner's small boats, carrying two shovels, the Luger, and the stiff, lumpy parcel of sailcloth. Sully rowed, using a smooth, reaching, perfectly timed stroke, feathering nicely. Vern sat in the sternsheets with the dead man in the tarp at his feet. He watched Pauloo loom closer and closer around and above them, and he thought of Haki.

There was something incongruous in the fact that this frightened little man, the product of countless generations of superstition and evolution, had fought through the most appalling war the world had ever known here in this remote corner of the globe, and had escaped unscathed only to return years later and perish at the hands of a supposed friend.

"Sully, did you fight in the war?"

"Yeah, with the guerrillas in Borneo." Sully didn't lose the rhythm of his stroke. "What were you thinking of, Haki?"

"Yeah."

He had hated them as a kid. Later he had realized they weren't much worse than anyone else. Soldiers, he supposed, were all the same. They lost a basic value — the Golden Rule. After a war they picked it up and attached it to their souls again, seemingly never realizing that they had discarded it for a while.

He remembered a vivid morning on Guadalcanal when a couple of eager-beaver kids from his platoon had fetched six or seven Jap prisoners out of the jungle. Vern had just returned with his squad from a night patrol and all of them were beat and hungry and PO'ed at the war and the world in general and they didn't give a damn about the stupid prisoners. But the eager-beaver kids were all star-eyed and expecting everyone to hang medals all over them and they marched the Japs up to Lt. Daggs and said, "Look what we got, sir. Look what we caught." And there was gaunt old Lt. Daggs with enough satchels under his eyes to take him around the world on a first-class cruise, and all shaky with the dengue fever, and he'd just heard the good news that he was expected to take a hill which would have made Hannibal balk, and when he looked bleakly at those prisoners all he said was, "What the hell you bringing that trash around here for?" And then he pulled his automatic and emptied it into the little pack of tied Japs. "Take the rest of 'em the hell out in the bush and kill 'em," he ordered.

128

No one had said anything, no one had even moved. They just stood there apathetically and watched the Japs go down in clumps and start kicking and twisting and screaming on the ground. Then someone from Vern's squad had said, "Let's go get some chow, for crysake." And Vern had nodded and said Yeah. And his appetite had been fine.

Sully looked at him and brought his stroke to a halt.

"What are you doing?" he asked. "Poking up ghosts?"

"Yeah." Then he told Sully about it.

Sully looked somberly at the water. He made no comment about Vern's story. When he started to speak his voice sounded mechanical.

"One day we caught a Jap sniper near Bengara. There were seven of us—two Aussies and me and four Malays. We'd been in the bush for five months — more animal than human. Those Malays, they strung that gook up and skinned him alive. Skinned him with the Aussies' razors. We just sat there and looked. That's all — just looked."

They beached in the shady shallows of the lagoon on Pauloo, Sully splashing overboard first, then Vern, and pulled the bow up onto the sand, and then they stood for a while ankle-deep in the warm amber water, looking, listening.

There were ghosts there, Vern felt; the omnipresent spirits of a vivid past. Conquistadores, pirates, blackbirders, sandalwooders, pearlers, traders, missionaries, savages . . . they paraded in his mind: brilliant, festive, martial, a gleam of silks and metal, a suggestion of faces, eyes, and far-off voices. . . .

Then a storm of lorries went *bat-a-bat-a-batter* overhead, and Sully said, "Let's go."

The ghosts wavered, shattered.

They raised the body and cleared the gunwale with it and started the struggle up the beach and into the woods. Haki was already rock-hard and because of the humidity there was that wild dead smell that is like nothing else in this world, and again Vern was bothered by an entry out of his life, like a case of delayed bookkeeping.

A platoon of Jap prisoners on Guadalcanal were given the grim job of burying their own dead in a shellhole. The dead men were stiffened on the outside but soggy with maggots inside, like a crust over a spaghetti pie. The goddamned maggots were dripping out of their ears and eyes and mouths and nostrils and from wherever their skins had been ruptured by bullets and shrapnel. The Japs would bring them — good

God how they brought them — up to the edge of the pit and swing them out and in, and then they'd turn away with a greenish tint to their yellow skins and they'd retch and puke and stumble off gasping for air, but there wasn't any air, only that putrifying stench. Some tough-looking Texas boys were MPing the detail, and if those Japs didn't look sharp (if one of the bodies stuck to the slope of the pit instead of rolling down to the bottom, and they tried to push it down with their feet, gingerly, instead of getting in there and doing the job properly with their hands) the MPs would boot them down into that godawful wiggly mess and shout at them, "Come on, for crysake. Get off the goddam dime!"

Vern and Sully labored their silent way into a somber wood and set the body down at the foot of a towering tree in a sort of cleared arena surrounded by trunkless nipa palms. A cockatoo screamed at them once, giving to nature a harsh note of reality, and then there was silence again. They traced a rectangle on the sandy ground and said nothing as they dug a damp hole, not too narrow, not too deep, and nothing as they picked up the dead diver and lowered him into it. Then Sully said:

"You want to say something over him?"

Vern shrugged, feeling inadequate in the face of Shinto. "Rest in peace," he murmured.

They filled the grave.

The first Kanaka stepped from the brush just as they were turning to leave. He was a small ageless man, his knobby, sticklike body dully agleam like mahogany vigorously rubbed with furniture polish. His eyes were wary, lusterless, stupid. He held a kauri club in his right hand, balancing it professionally.

Vern's hand started for the Luger in his belt. Sully stopped him with an abrupt gesture of his hand.

"No. There're others. Keep still."

The Kanaka grinned idiotically. That was all.

Then a stir — a nipa leaf bobbed gently. Then a brightly-feathered headdress loomed slowly above the green foliage. Then another, and another. Black faces with pearl-white eyes stared unblinkingly at the strangers.

The nipa leaves rustled, were shoved aside, and half-a-dozen savages showed themselves. They were all small, their knobby joints suggesting deformity, rickets. They were Negrito, woolen-headed, flat-faced and sullen-eyed. The people of the Black Belt. The inscrutable black islanders. Bred in the bone assassins, Vern thought uneasily. And again his hand edged toward the Luger.

"Whatname?" Sully barked at them suddenly, startling all of them, even Vern.

"Whatname you fella walkabout? You show, you savvy? You no stop to gammon one fella big fella me. You show altogether or I'll knock the whatname from black head belong you!" He took a threatening step toward them.

They stirred, fell back slightly, and raised their crude weapons. A murmur ran through them like a faint breeze stirring black tulips. Sully placed his arms akimbo and grinned at them.

"Whatname?" he demanded again. "Here, don't play the fool with me. I know you. I see that fella bullet in nose belong you. You fella savvy pidgin big bit."

Vern had the feeling that they did understand him, but were not willing to admit it. He too had noticed the earmarks of civilization that they garnished their incredibly dirty bodies with: the bullet cartridges in the soft cartilages of some of their noses, a plastic toothbrush through this one's ear, a cigarette holder through that one's, a ten-penny nail in the ear of the next. And where the white adventurer passed he invariably left that spoken bond between himself and the aborigines — the atrocious *beche de mer* English with its limited vocabulary of fifty words or so.

Suddenly one of them — a younger more healthy looking specimen of savagery — did speak, and Vern thought he detected a hint of intelligence in the man's crafty black-marble eyes.

"Hy, you fella big fella, me fella Tom-Tom, you savvy? Me savvy you big bit. Me *omoo* fella too much long time little bit. Me walkabout no stop. Go along Moresby belong big fella marster white man, me stop altogether. Big fella marster pay me tobacco little bit, cal'co little bit. Me fella Tom-Tom boat boy belong him. That fella big fella marster cross along me too much. Me speak along him, cross, cross, he stop." He grinned slyly and tapped a bone-handled knife in his calico sarong.

"Me like'm too much one fella head belong him. Me tak'm one fella head belong him along boat to Pauloo, stop altogether, you savvy?"

Sully nodded, smiling. But it was a little too rapid for Vern.

131

"What's he saying? He's a headhunter?"

"Yeah. This fella Tom-Tom — that's what the white men call him — is quite a gay little devil. He's been doing some boasting. When he was younger he went to sea and ended up in Port Moresby. Some trader gave him a job as boat boy, but I understand the trader wasn't very nice to Tom-Tom, so Tom-Tom relieved the trader of his head and came home with it. Probably has it on a stake in front of his hut now. Must have made him quite the big boy around these parts."

Sully turned back to the pseudo-civilized Kanaka.

"You fella Tom-Tom no look'm eye belong you along head belong me, you savvy? I bonk'm black face belong you close up. You fella sing out mouth belong you along these fellas belong Pauloo whatname I tell you. You fella sing out gammon, I get cross along you."

The Kanaka Tom-Tom seemed enamored of Sully. He grinned, winked, bobbed his head and went into a sort of shuffling, witless dance.

One of the savages spoke suddenly in Melanesian, and Sully turned to Tom-Tom sharply.

"Whatname that fella sing out?"

Tom-Tom broadened his grin and pointed a finger at Sully. "You fella Kanaka belong Solomons?" he questioned.

Sully shook his head. "I fella Kanaka belong me altogether," he said sternly.

Tom-Tom twisted his monkey face into a comical mask of wonder. Then he turned to his companions and began to speak, pointing at Sully.

"I'm in the cold," Vern murmured.

"He's telling them I don't belong to anyone, that I'm my own man."

"Are they going to be dangerous?"

Sully shrugged. "I don't think so. I've got them going. They can't quite pin me down. They know I'm of their race, but different because I'm twice their size and because I talk to them like a white man. If I don't come from the Black Belt, then they can't understand where I do come from, because to them that's all there is — the Belt and the mystical land beyond the sea where only white men come from. Maybe I'm wrong but I think I've been elected."

"Elected for what?"

"For a god." Sully smiled and looked over his shoulder at Vern.

"What will that make you?" he asked.

Vern matched the smile and motioned toward the lagoon. "Let's get out of here before we get excommunicated on the altar."

Sully looked at the savages again. "You fella Tom-Tom," he called sharply. "You tak'm those fellas along legs belong you, you go to hell along scrub, no stop. I big fella marster too much cross today along all Kanaka." And in an undertone to Vern—"Follow me, but don't show fear."

Sully strode straight for the knot of wary savages. They fell back grudgingly as he came among them. One of them started to raise a kauri club, but Sully's thick arm shot out and his fist went *bok* in the Kanaka's face, and the man went down right now and didn't move. Sully walked on without a change of expression, Vern tight on his heels.

From behind them came Tom-Tom's wail. "Hy! You fella big fella marster! Whatname you no stop? Whatname you fella walkabout? You fella stop along me. I like you too much big bit. You savvy? Hy! You big fella —"

It wasn't until they had reached the beach that Sully turned around and looked back.

"Funny little bastards," he said thoughtfully. "Never did have a show, though I guess they don't miss it much."

Looking at him, Vern suddenly imagined Sully in transition, saw him standing under a sky of polished brass among the hostile green hills of Pauloo, an incredible apparition of power and pride, towering over the stricken ranks of dusky savages, like a black god harassing little black children.

The picture in his mind winked out, as though he had only been allowed a glimpse through the flicker of a shutter, leaving him startled and unsatisfied.

"Do you think they killed Haki?" he asked.

Sully stuck a cigarette in his mouth and cupped a match to it.

"Do you?"

"No."

Sully shrugged and blew smoke. "I don't really give a damn," he said.

Vern stared at him. "You don't care if you're living with a murderer?"

Sully looked across the placid water at the schooner.

"A murderer is a killer," he said flatly. "That means you and
133

me and Haki, because we killed in the war. And I know damn well that Sim has killed in his time. And I imagine Ling-Po has too. And Tapley's done more than shave himself with that straight-edge of his. And the Dodds —" He grunted. "They've been killing each other for years."

He pulled the cigarette from his mouth and looked at the end of it, as if inspecting it for flaws.

"What's the difference if you live on a ship full of civilized killers or if you come to an island full of uncivilized killers?" His mouth jerked into a square, harsh grin.

"What are you looking for, Rigby? A land of brotherly love?"

"Maybe," Vern said. "Maybe you are too."

Between ship and shore a bright dab of orange color was bobbing on the lagoon surface. Vern pointed, asking, "What's that?"

Sully stalled at the oars and looked over his shoulder.

"Marker-buoy. Sim wanted to keep a fixed position on the steamer. Dodd offered to do it for him this afternoon."

He chopped the boat over to the buoy and together they leaned at the gunwale and peered down into the dark crystal depths. A blurred orange-green shape materialized beneath them and Vern saw the tell-tale thread of air bubbles.

"He's still down there. That's him coming up."

But it wasn't. It was Bea.

She spearheaded the surface gracefully, arching her head and neck backwards, letting the rubber mouthpiece slip from her crimson lips, and looked at them through the Cyclopean eye of the face mask and smiled. Then Sully ran the port oar out to her and she clung to it, breathing heavily, working her shoulders against the rub of the lung straps.

"Hello all," she said. "I saw the bottom of your boat from down there, so I came up to give you greeting."

Sully smiled at her. "Like the Sirens of Circe?"

"Why, Mr. Sullivan," she said brightly. "You surprise me. You have a classical background. I'm glad you didn't say like Scylla."

"Uh-huh. She had seven necks and a voice like a young dog."

"Six necks."

134

"Come in here," Vern said sharply. He didn't know what the hell they were talking about; and he was also annoyed with himself because he suddenly realized he was being childishly jealous. Why did she have to go skin diving with Harvey? If something was over, it was all over, wasn't it?

Bea worked her way hand over hand along the oar to the side of the boat, and Vern unstrapped her from the lung.

"Harv's still down there," she told him (as if he gave a god-dam). "He's found a new love. He's crazy about that wreck."

"Get in," Vern said, giving her a hand. He pretended he didn't notice the peculiar look she gave him.

A moment later Harvey split the surface four yards off the starboard bow. "Hi!" he called. "Say, that's something down there! By God, I can't wait to get that wreck with my camera. Give me a hand, will you, before I sink." He held up one hand, showing them a slimy, topless thermos bottle.

"Look what I found in the wheelhouse, Bea. Say, Rigby, I'll bet there's a story behind that steamer. Did you know she's sound? Not a damn hole in her. But her sea-cocks are open. Looks like an open-shut case of barratry to me."

Harvey was like a little boy with a new toy. After they helped him into the boat he insisted that Bea inspect his slimy treasure.

"I'll bet they were drinking coffee from that the very night the steamer went down. Dammit, I wish now I had talked more to Haki. He could give us the story on that steamer. After all, he did the salvage work on her."

Sully winked at Vern. "You could ask Sim about barratry. It used to be in his line."

"Yes sir," Harvey said, studying the water, "that is a fantastic sight."

Vern forced himself out of his wet-blanket mood. "You should see the *Habanera* if you want to see something."

Harvey looked at him, his eyes intent and serious. "I want to. In fact, I want you to take me down there with you."

Vern hesitated, glancing at Bea. She was watching him with a frozen, wet face.

"It isn't for skin divers," he said.

"I know that. I've been down in a suit before."

"How deep?"

"Well, as deep as this steamer."

"There's a difference between sixty feet and two hundred feet," Vern said.

"Maybe, but I want to do it. Will you take me?"

Does he have a trick up his sleeve? Vern wondered. Is he playing a little game of his own? He glanced at Bea again. She was still staring at him. She shook her head slightly.

"We'll talk about it," Vern said noncommittally.

The *Sally Lou* had no diving stage, so they went down on a shot line, Vern leading the way. A second line proceeded them, bearing torches, spades, and a canvas sack.

"Why not take him with you?" Sim had argued earlier in Harvey's behalf. "Jesus Christ, the guy is willing. Besides, you'll need help. We don't want to take all month with this thing. Let's find the goddam swag and haul out of here, I say."

And Vern had shrugged and said, "All right. It's his neck." And he hoped he was right.

Now, sinking into the vast Silent Room, Vern thought about Harvey hanging over his head. The playboy was going to find that the prison of copper and twill at thirty-two fathoms was a more exacting proposition than skin diving through the shallows.

He glanced at his depth indicator and smiled grimly at his own knowledge. At twenty-four fathoms there was a water weight, or pressure, of over four tons on every square foot of the diver's body, and he was carrying a total water weight of about sixty tons. He could do this because he was breathing air at almost five times atmospheric pressure. And it was out of this pressurized air passing into his blood stream to every cell of his body that came the source of divers' diseases and dangers: narks — nitrogen narcosis; bends — caused by nitrogen bubbles lodging in the body tissues; Oxygen Pete — a form of oxygen poisoning. All caused by breathing compressed air.

"On deck. Sim, connect me with Dodd."

He heard the hum of the control switch depress, and said, "Dodd, can you hear me?"

"Yes."

"Don't get rambunctious when we get down there. Follow my lead. Remember, watch your air line. Don't make a move without first checking to see if your hose is clear."

"We've been through all this before. I'm doing all right."

"That's right," Vern snapped, "give me a hard time. That's

what I'm here for. Listen, you silly bastard: you'll do what I tell you. If you lose your air you're dead."

A hollow chuckle sounded in Vern's ears. "I guess it would be rather awkward without air."

Awkward. Vern said, "You wouldn't notice it for long. You'd be punched up into your helmet instantly, all of you."

A pause, then — "Are you kidding? There isn't that much room."

"Water pressure is a law of its own. You, your suit, waist belt and boots would all end up inside the helmet." And that would be a pretty little pulp to bring up to his wife. Here, Bea; here's your husband. We won't need much of a hole to bury him in, and we can use the helmet for a coffin.

He looked down and saw the top of a weed bed rippling under his boots. The line weighted with torches, spades and the sack was waiting for them in a depression of its own making.

"Watch yourself. We're coming down."

Vern peered around at the enigmatic shadows uneasily. There was something intangible about the *Habanera*'s tomb that gave him a strange sinking in his heart, a sensation of moral disturbance that was nearly akin to spiritual dissolution.

He had always felt that there were certain places in the world that were never meant to be, or at least never meant to be seen. Biological mistakes that somehow didn't fit into nature's pattern. He had heard others speak of this curious phenomena before, divers especially, and explorers, and he had always felt certain that the sensation was common among children.

Once or twice in his travels he had come across sections of the world that suffered from this enigma. It was never anything you could put your finger on definitely, but the moment you stepped into one of these earth blights you sensed the utter hopelessness and melancholy that pervaded the air, earth and water, and you wanted to draw back and turn and run.

And the serrated, silt-floored, weed-covered slope at thirty-two fathoms, with its darkly decayed wreck, was like that.

To the left of them the weed bed paused, allowing an inexplicable road to lead mathematically straight to the place where the wreck lay in disintegration. Leaning forward

137

heavily, taking clumsy giant steps, they followed the sandy trace through the slot of undulating weed.

Vern snapped his torch alive and played the feeble light over the stern section of the wreck.

"We'll work aft of the waist. It isn't probable that the chest was stored in the hold with the cargo."

There was a decided pause before Harvey replied, and then his voice seemed strangely awed. "What waist?"

Vern grinned, and turning slowly, peered through his grill into Harvey's shadowy helmet. "Want to call it a day?" he offered.

He saw Harvey's boyish face grimace with annoyance, saw his lips move.

"Stop playing the superior professional, will you? Get on with it."

Vern struck out, wading into the rubble of the waist.

Flowered growth crunched under his heavy boots, rotten timbers and planking coated in a phylum of marine moss crumbled, marl dust swirled up to execute minute dances in the pale circle of orange light. Lifting his feet high, cautiously, he lumbered farther into the ruin, prodding the spade blade before him, shattering deterioration and growth alike, causing a greater havoc with the marl. Now they were blind men, stumbling along without equilibrium.

"I say, Rigby — I can't see."

"You'll get used to it. Three-fourths of this work is done by Braille. I'm leading us toward the quarterdeck — what used to be the quarterdeck."

Then Sim broke their connection and cut in. "How's it look?"

Vern waited before replying. A sagging, flowered shelf stretched vaguely in the marled mist before him. He raised a heavy boot and pressed down on its edge. It crumbled like a chip of frosting on a stale cake, leaving bits of rotten wood drifting in the swirling motes.

The air intake made hearing difficult both for Sim and himself. He pressed a spindle that temporarily closed his exhaust valve. "Not so good," he said finally.

"The maindeck along the waist is completely gone. The upper decks aft are gone. I'm facing a shelf now that I think might be the 'tween-deck forward of the cabin. But it's too shot to hold our weight."

"So what are you going to do?"

"The only thing I can do is to slice through the center, pushing the sides away from us. I don't know. Leave me alone now, huh? I want to fiddle around with it."

He edged toward starboard, following the line of the shelf, stooping once to probe his light under the platform. It was dark and unhealthy-looking and miry with silt and clogged with weed. He wasn't about to crawl into that nightmare. The light picked out the vague form of an oaken knee which looked fairly substantial. He placed a hand on the edge of the shelf and it was like pressing your hand through a layer of garbage.

Closing the exhaust valve he readjusted the buoyancy of his suit and started to rise from the cluttered waist. Then he opened the valve and leaned forward and settled gently down on the sagging shelf. It felt spongy, and he was aware of a slight trembling under his feet. Then the receiver diaphragm in the crown of his helmet hummed and he heard Harvey's voice. It had a sharp little edge of concern.

"Rigby — where are you going? I don't fancy being left alone here."

"Shut up," Vern said. "Stay put till I call for you."

A sudden current buffeted him against the jagged starboard bulwark. He clawed at it for support and it was like being pushed through a panel of balsa wood. It crumpled over his head, raining ragged chunks of wood around him, as he caught at his life line and swung sickeningly into nothingness. Abruptly he regained his equilibrium and settled firmly on the soggy deck.

"Rigby, what in the hell are you doing?" Harvey wanted to know.

"Look," Vern said, "If I want you, I'll pull your goddam chain. Take it easy, will you?"

He inched aft, watching the rubbishy deck beneath him, noting the smooth contours that humped up in strange patterns where long-gone bulkheads must have once met the deck. Pausing, he tried to reconstruct in his mind the original deck plan of the *Habanera*. She had been a collier, not a galleon, so she had had only one raised deck aft. That deck was gone, and that meant that the master's cabin, cuddy, and the mates' cabin had all tumbled down onto the 'tween-deck, and all of their paraphernalia had gone with them. It was probable then that the Manchu chest — which must have been stored aft — was residing somewhere under the clutter of

139

trash which surrounded him, somewhere between his position and the broken stern.

"On deck. Give me Dodd."

They worked diligently in the great dark womb of silence, each absorbed in the center of a separate small ball of pale light, like two fireflies crouching on the limb of a tree, groping, testing, pushing aside, sifting. Sim had lowered two battered grates from the schooner, and the divers had them set up at different angles along the crumbling bulwarks of the wreck. Through them they sifted the silt, weed and rubble.

When they finally called it a day and surfaced, their findings had been of little importance: a brace of encrusted pistols, an almost unrecognizable sextant, a belt buckle, the hull of a ship model made from ivory, and a curious tool which might have been an early version of a doctor's forceps. And Harvey had unearthed three crusty guineas which he showed off with a touch of pride.

"Well, it's not a vast treasure," he admitted. "But it is treasure."

"Yeah," Sim replied dubiously, "of a sort. But you'll have to turn up a lot more than that to suit John Sim, my son. My word, yes. A great deal more."

"Still," Bea said, taking one of the pieces from her husband, "a guinea is a guinea. At least, Captain, the dive was worth something. What was it like, Harv? Were you frightened?"

Harvey grinned all over. "Rapturously so! It was like nothing else I've ever seen. It's a badlands, a dirge in physical form. It's transporting Poe out of *Usher* and putting him at the bottom of the sea. It's the ultimate of all the world's horror and mystery. And, Bea — I can't wait to return to it tomorrow!"

Vern lighted a cigarette and stared at Pauloo. A badlands. He reflected on the term. Yes, it was that, and much more. But how in hell could Harvey find joy in the dreary, clammy vault of the Black Room? Clammy — that was a whacky word to use in relation to anything underwater; and yet the aspect of the wreck, the place in which it lay, was actually that — clammy. So why would anyone in his right mind want to return to it? But he knew, knew it with a sharp pang of jealousy and a dull drag of impotency.

140

The sonofabitch simply isn't afraid, that's all, he thought.

Sully was also staring at Pauloo, but from a different mental angle. He was seeing the island. And he saw something else (in his mind's eye): a race of savage black men with bullets and bones in their noses and anything from dials of alarm clocks to shrunken human heads dangling from their extended earlobes, moving silently across the lush, barbaric paradise. A nation of dark men, divorced from the knowledge and pressure of a civilized world. Needing nothing, asking nothing from the white outside. Taking what they wanted from the land before them when they wanted to take it. Looking for mute gods behind every rock, in every tree, in every wind-trembled leaf.

Looking for a god. . . .

He straightened up, stepped away from the rail and looked at the others. "I'm going to take a turn ashore," he announced quietly. His tone excluded the desire for company.

Sim glanced at the sky and at the swollen orb of sun, where it pinioned itself on the tallest Hanara peak. "Getting kind a late, Sully," he said. "I wouldn't go footing it around the shore now."

"No one asked you to," Sully said quietly. He turned and went over the rail, dropping lithely into the boat secured to the ladder.

All of his life he had wanted to be alone, and in many ways he had succeeded, even in crowded fo'c'sles and bars and the penal colony; but it had been an aloneness of his own making, of his mind, and it had been tragic. There was, he knew, no worse aloneness than being alone in the midst of many people.

What he had wanted was a secure solitude, and yet he had not deceived himself; no man could stand invariably alone. It did not matter how stupid, gross, barbaric or boorish one's companions might be, in the end each man alone must turn back to them — if only to hear their foolish laughter, witless words, to watch their cowlike expressions, to assure himself that he as a man still existed. Because in the aloneness of spaciousness, in total solitude, man was too insignificant; he became a part of the scheme of things and lost his identity in the act of finding his individuality.

What Sully wanted was a solitude that he could turn his back to before the nothingness of being worldly separated

141

could crush him. He was like a man married to a gentle homebody wife, himself forever gadding about seeking the joys of pseudo-bachelorhood, knowing that whenever the ecstasy of freedom palled on him he could return to the loving arms of his understanding wife. He was the complex man that had to eat his cake and have it too. His knowledge that companions were always somewhere in the offering, to take or leave as he wished, was his mainstay in life.

And it was this mood, or want, that brought him at last to the shores of Pauloo, alone and searching.

Walking now through the purity of silence that only a lagoon can hold in such jeweled perfection, leaving behind solitary footprints in the warm sand, crossing the wavering prints of crabs and the four-toed prints of sea-birds, he made his lonely way south, experimenting with solitude.

A pair of graceful ghost terns drifted over his head, banking and turning, gliding with his mood and pace. He lifted his eyes, watching, wanting to touch them in their casual nearness with his hand. Smiling, he spoke to them softly.

"Soar, buckos. Soar like music."

And they answered him, quietly, voicing their soft-wailing *caw-caws* against the brilliant sunset, and their voices were like the wail of a sad little trumpet sounding through a distant echo-chamber.

Suddenly Sully felt drunk.

He was a god floating high and lofty over the far reaches of the Black Belt to the distant tall walls of civilization; free to sneer openly at those white walls and throw mud at them to express his supreme contempt for their proud frailty. He felt sure that he was at that divine state which only drunks and narcotic-takers may reach, where all things — other than self and self's wants — appear to be mundane and childish. The fact that inside he was basically a mass of bruised ideals and damaged illusions no longer seemed to matter.

He tilted his face to the sky and shattered the glassy ball of solitude with laughter, reaching laughter across the illusion of aloneness. Turning abruptly, he viewed his own outgoing track of footprints and found them to be forlorn, lonely, as though they belonged to another, someone going south with no intention of ever returning, with the self-sufficiency to seek out mid-ocean solitude, with the courage to realize that the answer could be found, that the quest was not hopeless, that the key lay over the next outcropping of ancient reef or mound of heaped-up coral.

He looked inland at the mysterious hills of Pauloo and its moist, shadowy growth. *A separate division of the human race.*

Abruptly he stooped and picked up a chunk of purple coral and stuck it upright at the head of his last footprint, as a memorial to the spirit of the man he had been. Then, his look eager, almost ecstatic, he turned inland again and began to run — running faster and faster into his new world, searching.

Two hundred feet above was morning; but to Vern and Harvey in the opaque gloom of the *Habanera* the stages of the day were timeless and meaningless.

Vern did his work — digging, spading, sifting — in a dull web of apathy. The business of finding the supposed Manchu treasure was more and more taking on the complexion of a needle-in-a-haystack joke. He was beginning to suspect that they had gone to a lot of work (not to mention a few deaths) for nothing.

And what about Sully? Why hadn't he returned from his shore party? Had those savage little bush Kanakas brained him?

He tried to picture it in his imagination, but the image wouldn't quite clarify. Sully was too self-assured, too tough and dominant to be suddenly destroyed out of hand. Vern would rather think that Sully had remained on shore because he wanted to. *Maybe he's found a home,* he thought. *Maybe he's going to be luckier than the rest of us.*

He heard the hum of the control switch in his helmet and then Harvey's voice, distorted and a little strained.

"Say, Rigby, I seem to have had an accident. Would you mind telling me where the hell I am?"

Vern peered through his helmet ports. The darkened, disorderly deck appeared deserted. Now what had the dumb bastard done?

"Where are you?" he asked.

"Precisely what I wish to know. I was working aft, near starboard stern, when the deck crumpled under me. Right now I'm in absolute blackness. I'm afraid to move."

"Don't. Wait till I find your lines."

He swept the deck with his torch, but it was like trying to look through yesterday's dishwater. The shaft of light penetrated the marly water for a couple of yards and stopped.

A few hulking shapes vaguely appeared in grotesque attitudes. That was all.

"Do you have your torch?"

"Yes, it's in my hand."

"Do you know which way is up? Shoot the beam upward."

He doused his own light and waited, listening absently to the crackling fire of his exhaust bubbles. A sudden dim glow flickered amidst the blackness aft, and rising through the center of this wan light were Harvey's life line and air hose.

"Hold it," Vern ordered. "I've found you. Now sit tight until I can check your lines. I see your exhaust bubbles; your valve is working all right. Try to protect it with your hand. If it becomes clogged with silt you'll blow up."

Harvey's voice came back with urgent warmth.

"For God's sake, what do you mean *blow up?*"

Vern grinned tightly as he cautiously worked his way aft. Mr. Harvey Dodd, underwater enthusiast, was having a little taste of one of the deep-sea diver's many dilemmas.

"Take it easy. You'll know it if it happens to you."

"Goddammit, I want to know now!"

"Listen, playboy, I don't have time to lead you through the diver's kindergarten now. I'm trying to save your goddam life, remember?"

"Rigby, when I get on deck again, I'm going to punch your lover-boy face in."

Vern grinned again. *"If* you get on deck. Mustn't forget the if, you know."

There was a noticeable pause before Harvey picked it up again.

"That's goddam funny. I'm assuming that you're not quite cowardly enough to leave me in this spot. I have another matter to settle with you—"

"Do you? Why not tell Sim all about it? He's listening in, you know."

That shut Harvey up. But a moment later Sim's voice crackled in Vern's helmet.

"What the hell are you two doing down there? That's no goddam place for a hurrah's nest! If you two think you got something to settle, you can goddam well do it topside. You're down there to find that treasure. What's happening?"

Vern approached a wispy hole that was punched through the garlanded deck. He opened his exhaust valve wide and settled down to his knees, reaching out with his hand for support, and he might as well have tried to do a handstand on the crust of a bowl of cold porridge. His hand sank into the refuse and went right on through the rotten planking underneath and he went sprawling.

All right, he said calmly. We'll have to be careful now or we'll crash down on top of little Harvey.

He began pulling up cautiously, levering his body weight back on his knees, letting his forearm, wrist and hand feel their way clear. His arm came halfway out of the hole and stopped short. He gave a tentative tug. Snagged. He bit at his lip and worked the arm from side to side and then tried to ease it up. It wouldn't come. Then he felt an ice-cold needle pricking down the underside of his wrist. Then it became a trickle, and abruptly after that the sensation flattened out and was solid. It encompassed his entire wrist.

Jesus, he said. Jee-*sus*.

He pressed the chin-push and spoke to Sim.

"We're in a bind, Sim. Dodd has cracked through the deck. He's somewhere beneath me. I'm near the edge of his hole but I've snagged my left arm. I've got a goddam tear in my sleeve and it's filling up. Keep my air coming."

The sudden appalling thought that he might lose his air and drown in his own suit made him repeat himself.

"You hear me, Sim? *Keep my air coming.*"

Sim's reply was caustic. "All right, I hear you. You think I'm going to shut down the compressor and go out for a bite of lunch? Are Dodd's lines clear?"

"I think so," Vern said.

He picked up his torch and traced the beam of light in a line of ascent with Harvey's lines. They rose like two gleaming eels to the pale dome of the torchlight and then dissolved in the nothingness of the void above. He started to speak . . . but stalled.

A giant shadow slipped out of nowhere and coasted to a graceful stop inches from the lines, and Vern's light struck the bright ivory of a long smooth belly.

He stared at the shark blankly, his senses suspended in fascination. Then his hand relaxed on the torch grip, killing the beam of light. Shadows, distorted and undulating, rushed darkness over him.

"On deck. Give me Dodd."

He watched the great blurred shadow hovering over his
145

head, buffing its blunt snout against Harvey's lines. He set the torch aside and reached for his spade.

"Dodd, snap off your light. Quick! There's a shark above me. He's snooping around your lines."

But it wasn't only Harvey's lines now; Vern's set was also there, and the shark was starting to nose them, and each time he did it was as though a current had struck Vern and he wobbled and bounced in a half circle on the weedy deck until he felt like a dribbled basketball, and still his arm wouldn't come free.

"My God, Rigby! He's not going to bite them, is he?"

"Shut up! How do I know? I'm not his brain. Take it easy. I think he's just curious."

Curious. Sharks are always just curious — at first.

You could never tell what a shark was going to do, or what it was thinking, or if it was thinking at all or merely functioning on some atavistic instinct. One knowitall authority would tell you: Now this breed of shark (say a blue or a gray or a white or any damn shark) is absolutely harmless to man; and the next sonofabitchin authority will say: Now this breed of shark (a blue a gray a white, you name it) is without doubt a man-eater. And the trouble was the stupid shark never knew what he was; frightened one moment, ferocious the next; and if he didn't know, then what was the poor slob of a diver supposed to think?

Go away, shark, he said. Go to hell away.

The shark didn't. It fooled around with the lines some more. It dribbled him against the deck.

He closed his eyes despairingly, thinking, It's all up with us. The bastard's going to tear into our lines and our suits are going to deflate through the check valves in our helmets and the goddam water pressure will ram our prats into our stomachs and our stomachs into our heads and . . .

And right then he wanted desperately to speak with Bea, to tell her that he loved her. But he couldn't. He couldn't ask Sim to bring her to the headphone on deck so that he could tell her a thing like that while her husband was listening. Or could he? If this was the end of all three of them, then it didn't matter what was said, did it?

The exhaust bubbles from the two divers wobbled upward, glassy in texture, elongated by pressure. The heavy shadow overhead turned slightly and nosed into them, bursting them into smaller fragments, and then tipped down gradually as

146

though trying to discover the source of the curious objects.

Vern saw the suggestion of a mouth. Was it open — coming for him?

He edged the spade into position between himself and the shark, thinking, A hell of a weapon this is. Why didn't we bring a goddam speargun with us? *Why?*

He could see the faintly luminous starboard eye of the shark now as it dipped its smoothly rounded snout nearer, and the inverted V of the great mouth, open and razor-rimmed.

All of him squeezed into a tight little ball of revulsion. He wanted to rip his arm free, chop at the shark's head with the spade, inflate his suit and skyrocket for the surface . . .

Don't, he said. Don't.

He did nothing. He watched the gape-mouthed shark.

The shark took a dainty nibble at the glassy bubbles and turned a round, expressionless eye on Vern. It hung there effortlessly, staring at him. Suddenly its eye extended as though startled, and it opened its mouth and regurgitated a discharge of bubbles. Its tail whipped the water, twisting the great sleek body into an S shape, and then it was gone like an arrow twanged from a bow.

Vern rolled on his pinned arm and peered through his ports. Then he dropped the spade and picked up the torch and turned it on and pushed the light into the shadows, going on around. Then he started to laugh.

But he had to stop it because it wasn't really laughter. It was a little like the sound of total idiocy.

"Scared," he said. "Scared by its own burp. My God!"

He called for the deck and said, "We're still alive and kicking, Sim. Our fishy friend just took off like a bat out of hell."

Nothing seemed to matter now, nothing at all; not his snagged arm or torn sleeve or Harvey down in the black pit of the wreck. Nothing — now that the shark was gone.

He laid the spade aside and drew his knife and began gouging and scraping at the weed and rotten planking around his arm. He felt good.

But Sim didn't.

He had a sour look as he and Tapley stripped the returned
147

divers. He shot a heavy-browed look at Vern and asked gruffly, "Nothing?"

Vern stepped clear of his soggy suit and went to the cargo hatch for a cigarette.

"Nothing yet. What about Sully?"

"Still gone." Sim glared at Pauloo for a moment, then said, "Think I'll take a turn on shore with the Luger. You boys grab a rest."

Vern lit the cigarette, watching him.

"I don't think he's had any trouble with the Kanakas, Sim," he said. "I think he stayed ashore because he wanted to."

Sim seemed annoyed. "You do, eh? Any special reason why you think so?"

"No, nothing special. Just some things he's said since we left Singapore. I don't know. I think Sully was searching for something . . . but not treasure."

"Oh sweet Christ," Sim grumbled. "Look, Vern: you worry about the diving and stop dragging Sully's soul around by the ear. When it comes to missing mates and Kanakas in the scrub — that's my end."

"Suit yourself. I don't give a damn."

Harvey didn't seem to give one either. He glanced briefly at Vern and said, "I don't feel like going through that again this afternoon. I'll dive with you again in the morning."

Tapley grinned with one side of his face and winked at Vern.

"Kind a going cold on it, ain't he? Maybe you guys got something going. Maybe you're just stringing the rest of us."

Tapley's manner was casual, too casual, Vern thought. He looked at him, wondering what was bugging the little man now.

"How's that?"

Tapley shrugged. "Oh, I don't know. Just a screwy idea that came to me." He was off-hand about it. He was still grinning. "Maybe you guys already found the Manchu ice. Then you could leave it down there and say you didn't find it. Then you could come back some other time and pick it up. Kooky idea, ain't it?"

The four men looked at each other. Then Vern said, "Yeah, kooky is the word for it."

"You have a nice evil little mind," Harvey said to Tapley. He turned and walked away, heading aft for the saloon.

Tapley watched him go, humming, "Your goodby . . . left

148

me with eyes that cry . . ." He looked at Vern and Sim. "Guess I touched a sore spot," he said.

Sim grunted and spun on his heel. "I'll be back before sunset," he said over his shoulder.

The doors to the fo'c'sle opened and the Chinese girl's porcelain-perfect face appeared to be framed in the companionway. She said nothing. She stared at Tapley.

He winked at Vern again, muttering, "Oh-oh, speaking about sore spots . . . guess I better go take care of something, sport."

And suddenly Vern was alone on the sun-yellow deck. It suited him. He stayed there for a while, smoking, thinking of this and that and a few important things, and then threw the cigarette butt overboard and decided he wanted a drink. He stood up and glanced at the fo'c'sle doors. They were closed. He grinned, turning away. Skinny men had an endurance for it that was phenomenal. He'd noticed that before. God gave everyone something it seemed.

There was trouble in the saloon. He could tell as he came down the steps. It was like dropping into a pit of unrest. There was a peculiar aura between Bea and Harvey, in the strained, hesitant silence they emanated as they sat across the table from each other.

"Hi," Vern said to Bea quietly.

She looked at him and smiled but didn't reply.

Harvey turned and said, "Why don't you take a stroll, Rigby." His eyes were about as friendly as two auger holes.

Vern looked at Bea again and said, "Maybe I better stay."

Then Harvey stood up and faced him and Vern saw that he had somehow, somewhere lost his little-boy look, and he was mildly surprised to realize that Harvey had suddenly become a man.

They were standing a little too close for comfort, and Vern thought about taking a step backward. But he didn't because he didn't want to give Harvey the chance to sneer.

"What's going on?" he asked Bea.

She raised her head, her eyes and mouth carefully void of emotion, the same coldly serene look she had worn when he first met her.

"Harv has been making accusations," she said, "concerning the meeting of bodies . . . yours and mine."

Oh, this is nice, Vern thought. A nice sordid little scene.

He looked at Harvey again, thinking it would be a good idea

149

to watch his eyes. "All right," he said. "Let's take it easy and have a drink."

Harvey's hands made fists. He said, "Keep your charm for her. I told you I was going to punch your —"

"Forget it," Vern said. "We were both excited underwater. I don't want to fight you. I want to talk to —"

Harvey got his chance to sneer. "Oh? My apologies, Rigby. I've misunderstood you. I thought you were only afraid of sharks."

The implication was obvious. Vern's eyes went flat with cold warning.

"Take it easy, Dodd. I said I didn't want to fight you. I didn't say I was afraid of you."

"We'll find out about that in a moment," Harvey said. "You've been sleeping with my wife, you sonofabitch. And if you say No, then you're a goddam —"

"Now wait a minute," Vern cut in. "Let's get this straight. Bea doesn't love you, and you don't love her. You've used her, but you can't call it love when you use someone's body like a car to get yourself to the place where you want to —"

Harvey threw a right cross at his chin. But his timing was bad. He telegraphed the blow with his eyes and mouth, and Vern rolled left taking the punch over his right shoulder as he folded the fingers of his right hand at the second knuckles, giving him a striking surface of about two square inches, and jabbed a penetrating blow into Harvey's midriff. Then he stepped clear as Harvey doubled over with a long gasping *Uuuuah!*

"Come off it, Harv. I said I didn't want to fight you, and I mean it. You poor fool, I could break your neck while you're in that position."

Harvey straightened with effort, his face wrinkled and red with pain and fury. "You filthy bastard!" he gasped. "Don't call me Harv."

He lurched toward Vern, cocking his fist again.

Vern stepped aside, keeping his left out, palm flat, to ward off a second blow, and raised his right parallel to his face and showing the straight edge of his hand, swordwise.

"Vern!" Bea said. "Don't."

Vern ignored her. He circled away from Harvey.

"For crysake, Dodd, use your head. What good does it do us to pound each other? It's up to Bea in the end. You can't change anything by fighting me. Call it off now. We'll settle it after we settle the treasure."

Harvey hesitated. His tongue came out and tasted his lips and he blinked two-three times rapidly. Then all at once he relaxed, lowered his fist. But Vern could see that it was common sense and not fear that stopped him.

The bastard has guts, he thought. He knows I can crumple him like a paper napkin, but he's going to try it again anyhow. You can see it in his goddam eyes.

"Keep away from her, Rigby," Harvey whispered. "Keep your hands off her. If you don't — I'll kill you."

Bea's voice startled both of them. It was very quiet.

"Don't say any more now, Harv. Please. Just go. Please."

Harvey looked at her, wet his lips again and looked back at Vern.

Vern said nothing. Harvey, he knew, was going to try to kill him whether he had his wife again or not. He couldn't help himself. He would have to try. And Vern couldn't help himself either. He had to have her and the consequences were immaterial. Funny the way people were made: hell-bent for self-destruction.

He watched Harvey leave the saloon, and then he sat down at the table and leaned his head into his hands. He felt sick, physically and morally sick of himself and everyone around him. Unclean. After a moment he heard a stir, and then he felt Bea's fingers in his hair. He didn't look up.

"What's wrong with all of us, Bea?" he wondered. "Have we changed so much, or were we always like this, only more subtle? What's doing it to us? Fear? The treasure?" He raised his head.

"A little while ago that idiot Tapley suggested that Harvey and I had already found the treasure, but were keeping it a secret from the rest of you. I could see that Sim was wondering about the possibility, and Harvey actually looked at me as if it might be true that *I* had found it and hadn't told him. And you know — for just a moment I was thinking the same thing about him."

"Vern," Bea said softly, "let's call it quits. Let's stop before it's too late. Let the treasure go. If you refuse to dive that will end it. Harvey won't go down without you. I know that. I know him that well."

Vern shook his head. "It isn't that easy, Bea. I can't stop now. We all depend on that treasure. We've gone through too much for it. Three men have died because of it. I can't just turn my back on that and walk off. It couldn't have been all for nothing."

151

She smiled, tenderly, drawing his head toward her, pressing it to her stomach. "It hasn't been — not for nothing."

A knock of wood against wood sounded the hull. Vern looked up.

"Maybe that's Sim returning. He went to look for Sully."

He stood up and took Bea's hands in his.

"One more dive, Bea. I owe this whole affair that much. Then, win or lose, I'm through."

Sim's face was a grim face and his tone was harsh and tinged with anger. He was sitting on the cargo hatch. Harvey and Tapley and the always quiet Chinese girl were with him, the girl holding the long split in her dirty yellow skirt closed with her hand so that the black panties that Tapley had bought her with wouldn't show. Ling-Po was standing silent and sullen and alone by the edge of the cookhouse.

Sim glared at Vern, ignoring Bea.

"I met a wool-head ashore called Tom-Tom. A sly little bugger that savvies plenty pidgin. Little punk told me that Sully came to them yesterday evening. Says Sully beat the goddam hell out of the chief and the devil-devil and took over. Set himself up in state. This Tom-Tom says they made him a god. Fact. I wanted him to take me to Sully but he refused.

"Well, there was only five Kanakas with him, and I thought I'd mess 'em up a bit with the Luger. But then I got to thinking that maybe he was telling the truth. Maybe Sully has thrown in with 'em. That's why I came back — to talk to you. You seemed to know something about it."

Vern nodded, glancing at the ragged outline of silent Pauloo, seeing Sully again in his mind, picturing him standing in savage splendor in a howling wilderness, surrounded by awe-stricken aborigines. Good, he thought. Good for Sully.

"Yes, I thought it was something like that. Like I said — he was searching for something more than treasure. He simply wanted to belong. I think we should leave him alone. He knows what he's doing and what he wants."

Sim chewed it over for a while and, after a moment's reflection, seemed satisfied with the taste. He grunted and nodded shortly.

"Okay, as long as he's alive. That's what counts. We'll let it ride for now."

He fished a cigar from his old sea-stained jacket, snapped one end off sharp with his teeth and jammed the weed into a corner of his mouth. He looked as self-assured, as confident as a victorious gladiator.

"Well," he said smartly, "what about it, diver? Let's get that treasure up. I'll go down with you myself if Dodd won't."

"No," Harvey said, "that won't be necessary." He stood up without looking at any of them. "I'll go with him."

The third dive broke the charm. Harvey found the chest (what was left of it) that afternoon. Vern didn't actually do much searching. He kept his eyes on Harvey, making sure his partner didn't get behind his back or near his lines. But it seemed that Harvey was all business. He ignored Vern and went prowling aft with his spade and torch. And fifty minutes after they had reached the *Habanera* he sent an urgent call to Vern.

"Rigby! Where are you? I've found something, man. I've found a chest!"

Vern killed his own light and peered through his grill until he caught the distant opaque glow of Harvey's torch. Then he started aft at an underwater run — backwards — until he reached a position just forward of the hole Harvey had inadvertently made earlier. Harvey was kneeling there in a little clearing of piled refuse.

The chest itself was nothing. It crumbled into rusty flakes at the slightest hand pressure. And with the shell gone the contents inside seemed to be nothing more than a lump of hardened silt decorated with dull wisps of weed.

"Hell," Harvey said. "I thought I had something."

Vern floundered down next to him and probed his hand into the silt. Feeling small objects in his palm he withdrew his hand and washed it back and forth through the water, freeing it of silt. Then he opened his hand and Harvey aimed a torch at it.

They were lumpy asymmetrical objects, caked with bryozoans and algae. Vern selected one and chipped at it with the edge of his knife. A quick, glassy spark of white fire captured in the torchlight winked at them.

My God, he thought numbly, he did find it.

He looked up peering beyond the crystalline glare of the torch at Harvey, seeing the pale face behind its protection of

153

grid and glass. Harvey was smiling in the shadows of his copper helmet, nodding his head.

"Where's that canvas sack?" Harvey asked. "I'll bet there's hundreds more in the silt here. We'll have to sift."

Vern said nothing. He stared at his hand.

The Manchu treasure, he thought. A handful of stupid, dirty-looking little marbles.

Then he called Sim. "On deck. Sim, we've found the treasure."

The tonelessness of his own voice surprised him. He realized that the discovery had left him void of joy. He felt cold and impersonal toward the fortune he held in his hand. Then he remembered why.

My job's over . . . now I'm just deadwood.

All of them (even Ling-Po) worked at cleaning the Manchu jewels on the saloon table. They rubbed and scrubbed and chipped and polished and reached abstractedly for their drinks, for coffee or whisky or gin or a beer can, and for cigarettes and matches, and no one said a word. They worked in feverish silence, each to his own thoughts.

And when they were through they poured the whole of their labor out on a lumped-up blanket on the table and sat there in the creaking stillness as the old schooner worked on its cable, and their combined senses focused down to the rivulets of glittering wealth spread before them.

In miniature it was a fantastic wonderland of crimson neon lights with pure yellow and white abstractions. The blanket folds were hills strewn with night jewelry, and the canyons between were clustered with snaky sparks and reflections. It took the breath away and sent the mind spinning off into the void of infinite space, trailing a glowing nebulous train behind.

Finally Sim's voice touched them, harassing them back to the reality of the saloon.

"Well, my sons, we've made it. That's short and that's sweet. Now we'll put 'em away before we all go blind from eye-strain or go silly. Tomorrow we'll make up our minds what we want to do about Sully. After that we'll up anchor and haul out a here. Hand me that canvas sack."

Daintily the Chinese girl picked out a sapphire the size of a shelled walnut and, cupping it in her small hand, peered
154

intently into its transparent blue depth as though reading the future. Then, taking it between thumb and forefinger, she held it up to her right ear like an earring and turned to Tapley beside her and almost smiled.

Tapley grinned and slipped an arm around her waist and let it slide down. "I'm going to drape you in them things, Lotus baby," he said, "when we reach the States."

Absently, Vern wondered just what Tapley would do about the Chinese girl when they reached the States. Keeping the girl wasn't consistent with his idea of Tapley's character — not when Tapley would be able to buy himself no end of high-powered peroxided bitches to play with. Perhaps, he thought, this is also the end of the line for Lotus baby.

He looked at Bea. She had a cigarette in her hand but she wasn't smoking it. She was watching Harvey. Vern struck a match and held it over the table to her. "Bea," he said.

She started and looked at him and then leaned her cigarette and face into the light and looked at him again through the smoke.

She's frightened, he thought. Then added, Hell, who isn't?

Sim cinched up the neck of the damp sack and walked it over to the highboy and opened a drawer and casually tossed the Manchu fortune inside. They all watched him and they all said nothing. He slid the drawer closed and turned back to them with a square grin.

"If anybody wants to do sentry-go over this highboy tonight, he's welcome to it. But I don't guess those jewels are going anywhere unless this ship takes 'em. So sleep tight, my sons."

Vern didn't, not at first. It wasn't a black night for him or a white one either, only a mixed-up gray. His mind rambled groggily through that damned somnolent state which insomniacs know and dread, caught between awaking and drifting, seeing vague faceless people whom he knew could only exist in dreams, and yet knowing all the time that he was in his bunk in his cabin on board the schooner.

Then his mind took an erotic turn and he found himself weaving through a maze of dark nylon pictured against the shocking white of bare thighs and on into an endless web of garter straps which were at first black but then became spangled with gleaming jewels and he tried to reach out and grab all of it, wanting to bury his face in it, but it was unobtainable, there but intangible, and then he was out of it

155

and looking up at the dark deckhead above and Sully's face was staring down at him like a black Christ, sad, resigned, apathetic, and he rolled away from it and around to the open porthole by his head and saw a black shape on the water caught in the long blade of moonlight that lay on the lagoon and the shape seemed to be crawling along the path of moon toward the schooner and he thought, maybe Sully's coming back, and then his mind slid over the soft rim of a deep black pit and fell.

Sim shook him awake at dawn. The old man's face was a study in hard horizontal lines, and even in his sleep-stupid state Vern, after one bleary look at him, realized that something was wrong. Very wrong. He shook himself out of the drugged pit he had slid into, shedding sleep like a man getting out of a wet pullover sweater, and sat up.

"What is it?" he wanted to know. "What's wrong now?"

Sim was standing akimbo and his eyes were restless and mean. He snorted and said, "Everything. We're busted. The gook tried to kill Tapley and the whore, and then he jumped ship. He took the goddam swag with him."

And now we are six, Vern thought.

They stood in the saloon, facing each other about the table. Vern, Sim, Bea and Harvey, Tapley and the Chinese girl.

Bea had thrown an unbecoming flannel robe over her body and stood barefoot on the deck, blinking sleep-filmed eyes slowly. Harvey had on his trousers and a pair of worn moccasins. His hair was standing on end and his soft face was puffy and doughlike. The Chinese girl was in her one and only soiled dress and her face showed nothing, not sleep or fear or wonder. She had a good grip on Tapley's arm. Tapley was in his shorts and T shirt, and Vern found himself staring at the ugliness of the man's exposed skinny arms, which were knotted with muscles and pallid in texture, like something dead. Sim, as always, was fully dressed, even to the cap pulled sharp across his forehead.

"The sonofabitch jimmied open the fo'c'sle doors and dumped some burning cotton waste down while me'n Lotus baby was asleep," Tapley said.

"You mean he hoped to burn up the ship?" Harvey asked.

"That's what he thought, I guess," Tapley said. "But you
156

don't burn a ship that easy. But one thing is for goddam certain: if I hadn't smelled it we'd've suffocated."

"Well, there ain't much doubt about what happened," Sim said harshly. "He had it in for Tapley and the girl, and I guess he never did love the rest of us much. So he took the gems and went south. Well —" He shoved his coat aside, showing the butt of the Luger sticking up from his belt.

"I don't know about the rest of you, but I'm going after him."

"Seven islands," Harvey said dubiously. "Seven jungles. He might be anywhere."

"No," Sim said flatly. "He's on Pauloo. I scanned the shore with the binoculars and spotted one of our boats pulled up on the beach. If we look sharp we can get to him before he finds a way to start island-jumping."

"Okay, Skipper," Tapley said. "I'm with you."

"So am I," Harvey said. Then he checked himself and looked sharply at Vern. "What about you, Rigby?" His eyes slid to his wife.

Vern said nothing. He was staring at the table top, bothered by something. A thought, illusive and shadowy, stood half-formed in his mind.

"The women will stay here," Sim said. "There's no sense in dragging them through that damn mangrove swamp."

"Rigby hasn't said that he's going with us," Harvey insisted.

Vern looked up. They were staring at him, waiting.

"No," he said. "I'm not going."

"Why the hell not, buddy boy?" Tapley demanded. "You want the gook to make off with our bundle?"

"I think someone should stay with the women," Vern said.

"So why should it be you?" Harvey's voice matched his eyes and mouth — aggressive.

Vern shrugged and sat down at the table and reached for the coffee pot. It felt lukewarm.

"Because I don't want to go ashore, and you do," he replied.

Sim was annoyed. "What's eating you, boy? You act like you don't care about the gems."

"There's no need for four of us on shore," Vern said evasively. "And I still think one man should remain on board."

Harvey looked at Bea again. "Suppose," he said to Vern, "that I decide that *I'll* stay on board?"

Vern poured himself some coffee that he didn't want.

157

"It's your ship. You can do any damn thing you want to."

But I don't want you here, you sonofabitch, he thought. And not for the reason you're thinking. And I don't want you, Sim or you, Tapley or the gook girl either. Because something is fishy. Something is godawful fishy and it has to do with what I thought was a dream last night but now I don't think so. A black shape in the water in the moonlight. A boat. Must have been a boat. Yeah, but it didn't go away from the *Sally Lou* it came back to the *Sally Lou*. Yeah, and there's other things too, and if you all weren't in such a goddam sweat about those gems you'd realize it.

"Well," Sim said, "I don't know what the hell's going on. But I know we're giving that gook too much of a lead. Are you with us, Dodd, or ain't you?"

Harvey looked at Bea and scowled and looked at Vern and let out his breath. "All right," he snapped. "Let's get going."

But he paused at the companionway before following Sim up to the deck. "Remember what I said yesterday, Rigby."

Tapley grinned and gave the Chinese girl a pat on the bottom.

"That goes for me too, sport. Don't go color blind in a moment of passion."

Bea smiled at him coldly. "I'll see that he doesn't, Mr. Tapley."

Vern and the two women listened to the three men walking over their heads. The muted sound drew out to a vanishing point and then there was nothing but the tic-ticking of the chronometer. Vern looked at the Chinese girl.

"You go along forward, you savvy?"

The girl stared at him, turned the look to Bea, then stood up without a change of expression and went quietly away.

"Isn't all this rather obvious?" Bea asked archly.

"Very," Vern agreed. "If you have a dirty mind. But remember, I'm not called Righteous Rigby for nothing." He grinned at her. "No reflection on your sensual powers, Bea, but I have something else on my mind right now."

She seemed honestly surprised.

"What?"

"Ling-Po. He doesn't add up. Suddenly he's missing and we instantly assume that he's copped the treasure and made off with it. But stop and think: what good would the treasure do any of us if we left the ship? There's no escape from the Seven

Madonnas except by the *Sally Lou*. So where is he going to go with his fortune?"

"Well," Bea offered, "he simply might hide on one of the islands until we tire of searching for him and go away. Then — I would guess — his plan would be to 'go native' until another ship comes along to pick him up. Didn't someone say that French gunboats put in here every so often?"

Vern couldn't see it.

"Sully could do it alone, and probably will. And so could Sim. But not Ling-Po or the rest of us. Look, Bea, do you honestly think Ling-Po had the courage to deliberately divorce himself from this ship to enter a howling wilderness with half-witted headhunters running around loose?"

"But he *is* gone. He isn't on the ship."

Vern nodded. "Yeah, I'm certain he's left the ship . . . but I don't think he left it voluntarily."

"What are you thinking?"

"I think he was murdered."

They sat immobile and unblinking, staring at each other, absently hearing the lap and gurgle of the water under the counter and the creak of the timbers straining against the cable. Then Bea spoke.

"Then where is his body?"

"That's what I'm going to find out," he said.

She helped him arrange his gear on top of the cargo hatch. There was a peripheral vision mask, a two-tank block lung with two-stage constant reserve regulator, a pair of black rubber fins, a watch, a waist belt with five kilos of lead, a knife and a speargun.

He was mighty happy about the duralumin and steel gun. There was a small high-pressure gas tank in the butt, and when the gun was fired the gas blew the spear through the barrel and the spear — which was mostly hollow — gained in speed as it zipped along because of the discharging gas it contained in its hollow interior. The spearhead contained a vial of curare poison which was shattered by the opening of two small wings as soon as the spear pierced its target.

If the Colt tamed the West, he thought, maybe the jet-curare gun will tame the sea.

"Darling," Bea said, "take me with you."

"No," he said, thinking of the shark but not telling her about it, not wanting to worry her with something which might not even exist now. "Not this time." He smiled and touched her cheek. "There'll be other dives for us."

Then — encumbered, grotesque, harnessed and strapped, web-footed and plate-faced — he duck-walked to the rail and looked at the lagoon. Less than midway between the ship and Pauloo was the orange dab of color tugging fitfully at its leash. The marker-buoy.

He went down the ladder to his waist, adjusted his air and mouth-piece and looked up at Bea. She didn't say Be Careful or anything unnecessary like that. She smiled down at him and said:

"What a mixed-up kid you are. The others are searching for a fortune in jewels, and you're looking for a dead man."

Vern grinned around the mouthpiece and let go and stepped clear of the ship.

The wreck of the steamer hulked before him like some long-dead prehistoric monster in a primordial sea — towering, canted, fuzzy, sleeping in silence. He came in obliquely and reached for the truck, the tip of her mainmast, and the instant he looked down through the clear water he went dizzy and had to clutch the mast for fear he would topple and fall forty-some feet down to the deck. The illusion was complete; it was as though the old steamer was still plowing across the familiar blue ocean. He let go and jackknifed.

Every dead ship has a personality of its own. Some are mere mounds of deceiving coral; others are brilliant flower gardens and fish sanctuaries; many are gaping, twisted, dark hulks whose grim aspect warns the diver to be on the alert for something uncanny and unhealthy. This one appeared to be a fish sanctuary.

Droves of green parrot fish sported about the open wheelhouse, and a blue-striped grunt wavered over the bridge seemingly grunting his displeasure at their carefree manner. Four separate shafts of undefined light found their way down to the decks and flickered among the black and amber shadows. And when a squirrel fish wended listlessly through one of the opaque rays it turned a pale pink. It stopped abruptly at Vern's approach, eyes extended, then fled like a snap of fingers, chattering in fright.

Vern hovered over the boat deck, looking, but the shadows told him nothing. The palisade of tall curving ventilators around the stack caught his eye. From the mouth of each vent he saw a black whiplike object undulating gracefully in the current, seven or eight feet long; and as he came closer a squadron of brilliant stingrays rose from the ventilators flapping their winged fins and whipping their seemingly endless tails behind them. They banked and veered and planed around him in agitation. He froze in the water and did nothing. He didn't want any trouble.

After a while the stingrays decided he was harmless and they glided back into their hangers to resume their siesta. Vern gave a push with his fins and skirted the forest of vents.

He curved toward port and corkscrewed down to the deckhouse gangway and finned under the overhang. The saloon door was closed and dogged, but the slime had been scraped away leaving a half-moon of white paint showing where the handle had been forced.

Recent, he realized. Very recent.

He undogged the door, letting it fall inward, and entered.

Darkness encompassed him, but not totally. He could see as well, perhaps, as a myopic man walking in moonlight. A long mirror along the forward bulkhead glowed coldly at him. As he approached it he could see his own black reflection groping toward him.

He reached out with his hand and felt the slimy top of the bar. Then he turned, his legs and fins settling slowly to the carpeted deck, his back to the bar, and peered at the room, waiting for his eyes to grow used to the twilight water.

The carpet was bulged in the center, holding prisoner a giant air bubble. Millions of tiny air bubbles fizzed on its swollen skin, and when he pressed the tips of his fins down thousands of the minute bubbles wobbled crazily upward to give him the sensation that he was drowning in champagne. Many of the bubbles didn't go away, but stuck to the hair on his bare legs.

An overstuffed chair, bloated and obscene-looking, squatted in a far dingy corner like the throne of a night monster. A table was upended, one leg missing. A fifth of Four Roses — half whisky, half air — traced an aimless pattern across the humped carpet, neck down, butt up. It was a screw-cap bottle and unlike the corked jugs that were helpless in water pressure it would stay intact and continue its purposeless meanderings until it fetched up against something solid and shattered.

161

He unhooked his torch and squeezed the beam of light on. Instantly the darkness crowded in leaving only the feeble path of light speared before him. It was worse than not having a light. He switched off and returned the torch to his belt and waited another minute, stirring with the things in the saloon every time a current came.

He was convinced that he was alone in the room. He could make out that much. He leaned into the water and placed his fins against the side of the bar and shoved off.

He hitch-kicked over the huge hump of the pregnant carpet and saw a great black squatty nonidentity grinning at him with a long row of green and black teeth. Piano. Then he approached the swing doors to the cuddy and prodded the right one open with the barrel of the gun and finned into the cuddy and through it, over the pale reddish tiles, leaving the cold gleam of stainless steel counters, refrigerator and dumbwaiter in his bubbled wake, and on into the forward passageway.

He stabbed light into a starboard compartment. Empty. Into one portside. Nothing. Then he hit the first mate's cabin and right now a troop of nail fish — off course for their search of a madrepore meal — broke over him and he rolled in the doorway, ducking, his heart slamming into tilt because he didn't know what they were at first, and then they were gone and he relaxed.

He drifted into a vertical position and looked around. There was a water-stained certificate on the bulkhead and it told him the qualifications of a formless faceless being called William James Lington.

So what?

He got out of there, went down the passageway again, through the cuddy and back into the saloon and headed inboard. Because of the steamer's cant he descended another fathom just in swimming from the cuddy to the head of the staircase leading down to the cabin deck. His depth indicator read forty-six feet.

Then he stalled as he reached the black well of the stairs opening beneath him. He didn't really want to go down there.

But what are you going to do? You've come this far, so why not finish it? Besides, it hasn't been so bad, has it? No, it really hasn't. Not bad at all. *All right then. We've got the gun and we've got the experience. And there isn't a shark in the world over five feet who will put himself in a trap like this, so*

162

we don't have to worry about running into that. No. But how about some nice eels? A conger or a moray? Or how about a fat slimy jolly-eyed old squid? Or a mouth-full-of-teeth barracuda?

How about shutting up?

That was good advice. He jackknifed down the staircase.

The cant of the steamer wasn't really bad (God knows he had worked in worse, including some that were upside down), but any degree that varied from the norm was unnerving. It stole the equilibrium. It was like the feeling a man would have if he were to walk through a house that had been jacked-up on one end. Nothing was out of focus, merely out of balance. It was like looking at yourself in one mirror, catching your reflection in a second mirror, and trying to cut your own hair by using the second image in the first mirror as a guide. It could be done, but there was always that slight hesitation between the hand and the brain. The brain wanted to go in one direction, the hand in the other.

He reached the lower passageway and found himself in a black square containing four gloomy tunnels — two running fore and aft, and two running starboard to port: and he unhooked the torch and played the light along the warped wooden panels and down the four corridors.

He was in the nucleus of the passenger cabins.

A glass-cased notice was set in the wall before him and he hit it with the light and saw that it was a list of lifeboat regulations. Water had worked its way between glass and paper but it was still legible. He got a bang out of the opening:

> *Suitable arrangements shall be made for embarking the passengers in lifeboats, in accord with regulations by the Board of Supervising Inspectors, with the approval of the Secretary of Commerce.*

He grinned around the mouthpiece. That was comforting news — for a man standing inside a sunken ship. He probed the light ahead of him and started along the forward passage.

The corridor was a black sewer pierced with round shafts of wan light from distant portholes and hidden openings. The torch cast a wide circle of red and yellow and black color — sea growth busily planting and spreading, staking a claim on the wreck, patiently building toward that not too far-off day when it would absolve the steamer entirely.

163

He opened a louvered door and cut up the darkness with the torch.

Stateroom. Swollen mattress. Undulating bed clothes. Sink with taps off but bowl perpetually filled. Rug flapping on deck. Porthole gleaming aqua.

Nothing.

He proceeded along the passageway, accompanied with the gasp and gurgle of his exhaust, swimming through an atmosphere of static expectancy, as if the wreck were inwardly watching him, waiting for him to go too far.

A muted slam of sound vibrated toward him, trembling through the plates, and the water stirred gently around him and pressed against his skin. He hesitated and reached for the frizzled wall for support. The wreck was working in the swell. The sound and motion subsided and he moved on.

He finned to an open door with the word MEN set in the panel, and peered inside. The light picked out the greenish-white tub and shower installation and the useless head and sink. An insignificant eel had nestled down in the tub on a matting of marl. Its head snapped up, mouth hinged open, and its eyes had that wild look that homicidal maniacs wear.

Vern pulled back as the eel untwined in fear. It wiggled upward with lightening speed and struck the closed port and turned and leveled itself for the light and shot across the room, whipping itself with frantic motion, and snaked past his face mask and went away all wiggly and horrible.

Vern went in the same direction.

He rounded a corner and turned right, finning up a gradual incline toward the port gangway door. A stateroom on either side. One open, one closed. He poked the light through the open door. Nothing.

Then he tried the handle of the other door. The handle gave but the door wouldn't. Warped in the frame. He shoved and felt a slight give, and so he placed his fins against the opposite wall and shoved again, using the side of his head and shoulder against the thin panel, and this time the door shuddered open and the momentum tumbled him casually to the deck.

He pushed himself up from the porous rug and its welter of tiny champagne-like bubbles, and brought the torch into play. The light struck the figure of a man.

The man was standing up.

Vern snapped back like a rubber band, and for a vivid moment he almost let the damned thing have it with the jet-curare gun. Then he marshalled his wits together and looked again.

The man was floating precariously, toes down and scraping along the deck through the little sparkling dancing bubbles: arms hanging but stirring and lifting lifelike in the current; head down, chin on chest, mouth open, tongue showing . . . Vern centered the grotesque object in the whorling light and stared, sickened.

Ling-Po, ex-sea cook, onetime Communist, the sleek young man with the deep hate, was drifting in his tomb.

The cabin's single porthole was open and that was how the hungry little fish had entered. The Chinese cook's eyes were gone. The fish had blinded the dead man. The slitted eyelids showed black vacant holes that wavered slightly with little thin strands of white recti muscles.

God, Vern said. God. God.

Then a current swept into the cabin and shouldered him aside and gave the body a push, jerking it upright. Head and hands flapped upward. Those empty wiggly good-God eye sockets stared at him. Then the head toppled again as the body swung half around. Then the current receded and the body hulked toward Vern.

He wasn't about to have the filthy thing touch him. He swung his legs up, backfinning frantically, and his lung cylinders went *ka-toooml* against the doorjamb. He aimed the speargun to ward off the body.

The belly-bloated corpse wobbled helplessly as the last of the backwash ebbed out. Abruptly it relaxed into its seemingly dozing, aimlessly tiptoeing state — head down, mouth open, arms hanging, toes dragging.

Vern stared blankly at the deep purple-lipped slit in the dead man's back. He could see it everytime the cook's loose shirt unfurled and fluttered upward.

Now they all know it, he thought. All the little fishes and crawly things of the sea. They know there's a dead man in here because his blood has been in the water. And the shark who burps knows it too. And he'll be hanging around somewhere, wanting in and PO'ed because he can't make it, and ready to eat any damned thing in sight.

He leveled himself, preparing to leave, but looked back at the hanging black silhouette drifting in the liquid silence.

Workers of the world, unite and become fish food, he said. *Sayonara*, tuan Po.

He tried the door that led to the port gangway, but found it jammed. And the same went for the starboard door. The frames and the handles were thick with growth. He didn't feel like struggling with them. He finned back up the stairway into the saloon and left the wreck the way he had entered.

Buster Brown the burping boy was outside, as he had half expected. But it didn't matter because the shark didn't see him. It was nosing low along the portside, trying to find access to the dead man.

Vern finned up to the boat deck, putting the tilted edge of the steamer between himself and the gray marauder. Then he began his ascent, cutting an oblique line to the surface. Oddly enough the near proximity of the shark didn't have much effect on him. He still felt numb because of Ling-Po. Even though he had gone underwater knowing what he would find, it had shocked him.

Death always throws us, he thought. It's like looking in a mirror.

Both small boats were rocking alongside the *Sally Lou*, lashed to the ladder. Vern shoved them aside and hauled himself heavily up the steps to the rail. A tense little group was busy on the deck: the two girls, Sim, Tapley and Harvey. They seemed startled — the three men even angry — by Vern's sudden appearance. They had scuba gear scattered all around them. Harvey was in his trunks and Tapley was still in his shorts and T shirt. Sim was sitting on the cargo hatch with his left shoe and sock off. Bea was doing something with his foot.

"Why did you go down to that steamer, Rigby?" Harvey wanted to know. His eyes were very warm.

"What's going on?" Vern asked. "I thought you people went ashore."

Tapley had one of the lungs standing before him and he was hunkered down fiddling with the regulator. "Sim sprained his ankle in that damn mangrove swamp," he said shortly.

Vern came over the rail and stood dripping on the hot deck as he started stripping himself. "Bad, Sim?" he asked.

Sim was thoroughly annoyed with everything.

"No, it ain't bad. I tried to get those two damn fools to go on without me but they didn't have the guts for it. What's this business Mrs. Dodd's been telling us about you going down to the wreck to find the gook?"

Vern nodded. "That's right. I found him."

They simply stared at him. All except Tapley. His eyes sparked like little flecks of sunstruck glass and he stood up in a hurry.

"You did? You honest to Godly did? Where, for crysake?"

"Down in the steamer. Someone put a knife in his back and hid him down there. Surprised?"

After a blank moment Tapley's face turned crafty.

"Yeah — real surprised. Funny, ain't it? How you knew just where to go to find him."

"I don't think it's so funny," Harvey said.

Vern looked at him, getting the implication.

"Yeah," he said to Tapley. "But I'm a funny guy. I went to all that work last night to drag him down there so I could turn around this morning and go down again to see if I really did it."

"All right," Sim told them, "let's cut it out. We got troubles enough without all that crap. If what Vern says is true, then it's pretty damn plain that no Kanaka did the job this time."

"Yeah," Tapley said, looking first at Vern, then at Harvey. "It was a job for a skindiver."

"You think that, do you?" Harvey snapped. "Well, I noticed that when I started to explain to you just how the lung works, you already seemed to know all about it!"

"Sure I know how it works. I watched you and your old lady messing with 'em the other day. There ain't nothing to 'em. But I've never been underwater with one."

"That's what you say!"

"Harv," Bea said. "That isn't getting us anywhere."

Vern stepped away from his gear and went over to Bea and got a cigarette from her. He glanced at Harvey's trunks. "Why were you showing Tapley how the lung works?" he asked.

"Because we were going to go down there and find out just what you were up to," Harvey said flatly.

"I was looking for the cook. Bea told you that."

"What about the treasure?"

"What do you mean?"

"Oh for God's sake, Rigby! If someone killed the cook and

hid his body, then that same someone also took the jewels and hid them."

Vern nodded. "That follows. But I was taking first things first. I wanted to establish that the cook had been murdered as I'd suspected."

"Fine, wonderful! So now you've established it. But didn't it ever enter your head that if the body was hidden in the steamer, then the jewels might also be hidden there?"

"Yeah — and it also entered my head that they might be hidden aboard this schooner. Perhaps one of us has them in his suitcase or mattress."

"No," Bea said. "I already thought of that. I searched everyone's compartment and baggage while you were all away. Miss O-lan helped me."

"Who?" Tapley said.

Bea smiled and nodded at the Chinese girl.

"No kidding?" Tapley said, looking at his mistress. "O-lan, huh? Kind a pretty, ain't it?"

"Well," Sim said, "I guess it comes to this: someone decides he don't want just a share of the treasure, he wants all of it. So he takes it and he knifes the gook and he sticks the body and maybe the gems too down in the steamer and makes it look like the gook ran off with the swag. That's nice and sweet but I'm damned if I see the ultimate point of it. What good are the gems going to do him if they're down in the wreck?"

They looked at each other, then at this and that and thought about it. Then Vern said:

"Well, if I were doing it I'd hold out a couple of the stones, enough so that when we returned to a commercial port I could cash them in and buy myself another ship, hire a Kanaka crew and return here for the bulk of the treasure."

"Did you think to search Ling-Po while you were down there?" Harvey asked. "His clothes? I assume he's still dressed."

Vern saw the hulking, bloated, eyeless corpse tiptoeing through the bubbles, and shook his head. "No. I didn't think of it at all."

"My God," Harvey murmured. He turned away and started gathering up his scuba gear. "All right," he said, businesslike, without looking at anyone, "let's get ready. I'll go down with you and help."

Bea looked at Vern. "No!" she said sharply.

Harvey straightened up to stare at her.

168

"What's wrong Bea, afraid of something?"

"Look," Vern said, "if the jewels aren't on Ling-Po, you're just wasting your time. You could never search the entire wreck. It would be as hopeless as looking for a lost bag of marbles in a department store."

"But they might be on him," Harvey insisted.

"Well, why the hell we just standing around here gabbing about it?" Tapley said. "Let's get into the goddam swim and go see."

"What about it, Rigby? Are you going to help us or not? You're the professional. We don't even know where the body is."

Vern looked at Bea. She shook her head. He looked at Sim, and Sim nodded. "You better do it, Vern. We might as well get this thing settled. And those boys might get into trouble blundering around down there on their own."

Vern reached for his lung. "All right. Let's get it over with."

Bea started undoing her blouse. "I'm going with you," she said.

"No, Bea."

"Yes. If you go, I go. I'm as good a skindiver as Harv. And compared to Mr. Tapley I'm Cousteau."

"Well," Harvey said nastily, "this is cozy. If he goes, you go. That says a lot, doesn't it?"

Bea didn't look at him. She shed her blouse and then her skirt, stripping down to bra and panties, oblivious to Tapley's warmly illicit gaze.

"Yes, I think it does. I'm sorry, Harv, that it had to be said in front of outsiders. But I mean it, and I'll say more if you force it." She looked up at Vern. "If either of you force it."

Harvey hefted his lung. "I guess we know where we stand then," he said to Vern.

"I guess we do."

Tapley realized that the Chinese girl was giving him a peculiar look and he quickly detoured his eyes to one of the spearguns. It was a stainless steel spring gun, long, brittle and deadly. He picked it up with a grin.

"Hey, are these things dangerous out of water?"

"Only if you shoot it into someone," Vern said.

Harvey duck-footed for the rail. "Let's go."

The shark was gone. But he wasn't really a threat now. Four divers could scare a single shark witless. They could hit him from so many different directions with the spearguns that he would think he was a bull's eye at an archery contest.

They came down over the tuba-like ventilators of the boat deck, Vern leading them single-file like a mother hen — Bea second, Tapley third, Harvey watchdogging the rear. They went over the rearing port rail and peeled off one-two-three-four like a squadron of pursuit planes into the canyon of shadow opening beneath them and slipped under the overhang of the gangway.

The square black doorway of the saloon faced them, and Vern kicked himself for having left the door open when last leaving the steamer. That, my boy, he thought, was not the smartest trick in the world to pull. It was possible that the shark might have entered the saloon, and it was one thing for four divers to catch a shark out in the open—but it was a fish of another color for *him* to catch them in the crowded quarters of a wreck. Then the panic would be on . . . shark smashing around like a two-ton boomerang biting at everything in sight, divers going ankles over appetite through the darkness, through the saloon furniture, shooting harpoons into each other . . .

Oh yes, a merry little ball.

He turned and quickly counted noses and then held up his hand and gave the water three short flat pats. Wait. Then he nosed into the saloon for a look around.

Over the bar a school of small reef fish were disporting themselves before the dull mirror. Instantly they were aware of his presence and they scattered into the interior of the wreck, leaving the illusion of frantic motion behind. That was all. No great dark shadow cruising silently around with hungry banjo eyes. He was satisfied. It was improbable that the shark would have gone any further than the saloon.

He rolled and looked over his shoulder and waved the others on.

Have no fear, group; Rugged Rig is here, he said. He felt pretty good.

The four divers finned into a circle over the stair-well and Vern snapped on his torch and shot the beam downward and then turned it up to his own chest and then to Bea and next to Tapley and finally to Harvey, to show them that he wanted them to keep the same formation. When he flicked the light

170

over Harvey's face-plate he saw the playboy's bright, intense look.

That's right, buster, he thought. You keep your eyes on me. Make sure I don't diddle your wife down here.

He jackknifed down the stairs.

Now they were in the central corridor of the cabin deck, and now it would get sticky. Everything was too cramped, too dark, too tilted and strange for four people. Any untoward happening could cause panic.

Vern brought the light near Bea's face to see if she was all right. Her eyes were enormous and dark and they reminded him of the day in his cabin at the close of the typhoon. The same look was in her eyes again — anticipated excitement.

She nodded at him, and he turned away.

Number 10 portside was the tomb of Ling-Po. The door was still open and Vern came in on the beam of his torch. The corpse was bobbing slowly in the yellow halo of light, seemingly in rhythm with the dancing specks of marl, but his toes were no longer trippling along the deck. He was very bloated and the back of his head was touching the ceiling. He hung there like a lynch victim or a suicide.

Vern glanced at Bea again. She had turned her head aside She wasn't having a second look. Harvey didn't look too chipper either. He had stalled in the doorway. We're like ostriches, Vern thought. We hide our heads. If we won't face it, then it doesn't exist.

But Tapley wasn't bothered with ostrich psychology. He had a single-mindedness of purpose. He gave a push with his fins and went past Bea and then Vern and angled up to the body. He handled himself nicely in the water, as though born to it.

He started going through Ling-Po's pockets.

But it was a waste of time. He shoved the body away disgustedly and jacked down to a closet set in the aft bulkhead and opened the door. The closet contained a coat, two arm-flapping shirts, a pair of shoes and a bulging suitcase. He went through all of them, making a grand mess in the water, and then looked around eagerly for something else to search.

Harvey watched him dispassionately, thinking, Stupid little fool. Running around like a chicken without its head. Without brains, without sight; banging himself against one wall after another, searching for something he was born to go without. But he didn't really give a damn about Tapley.

171

Rigby and Bea, he thought.

The current pushed him. He wobbled slightly, then settled back to an even keel, catching the doorframe for support and letting his body drift level with the canted deck. He watched his wife's silhouette. She was pictured against the bright whorl of Vern's torch.

It was going to happen then, after all; the thing he had always feared. He had seen it in her eyes, heard it in her voice. She was going to leave him, and he would never find another woman like her — not with her qualifications. A stupid woman was enough for lust, but an intelligent woman was necessary for the long drags in between, for the hours of loneliness, despair and self-denunciation. He needed her, had always needed her . . . and now he was being cut out by that goddam frogman.

Tapley darted past him like a hungry barracuda on the make for an elusive bass, a thick foam of bubbles crackling from the exhaust outlet at the back of his neck. He shook Vern's elbow, saying *Uuumm! Uuumm!* in his mouthpiece, and pointed at the swollen bunk.

Vern held the light on it for him.

Tapley leaned his spring gun against the wall and said To Hell with you when it toppled like a falling timber and clunked on the deck. The bed was soft and oozy to the touch and it frizzled bubbles and marl up into his face mask. But he didn't care. He stripped back the blankets and sheets, flapping them out in the water, letting them drift to the deck when he was through with them, and then scanned the bloated mattress with care, looking for rents or tears in its puffy skin. There were none. He shoved it onto the deck beneath him and then tilted himself headfirst to check under the springs.

Jesus, Vern thought, this is stupid. Honest-to-God stupid.

He pulled the light away from Tapley and the torn-up bunk and turned toward the door. Time to gather the clan and get the hell out of there. They were simply wasting time and air.

The doorway was empty. Harvey was gone.

He didn't like that at all. Now what? he wondered. He put the light on Bea. She was looking at the doorway. Then she turned and her oval glass face stared blankly at Vern. Then Tapley nosed into the light and looked at the doorway, then at Bea, and then at Vern. His fins chopped at the water and he scooted out of the room, turned left and was gone.

That's the ticket, Vern said angrily. Go get yourselves lost.

Did the two madmen actually think they could search the steamer compartment by compartment? Then his mind turned a corner and went in a different direction. Or maybe they weren't really searching at all; at least not one of them. Maybe Harvey —

All at once he didn't like the idea that he and Bea had been left alone in the cabin with the dead man. He started toward the door, motioning at her with the light. She finned into his wake.

Out in the corridor he didn't know which way to go or where to start looking first. He doused his light to see if he could catch the glow of Harvey's or Tapley's. Blackness swallowed him, cold and complete, going on around. Bea's hand fumbled on his bare right leg and he started. He switched the light on.

Something's very wrong, he said. We've got to get out of here.

They followed the central corridor to the foot of the staircase and looked up at the telltale-gray square at the head. A shadow, or a suggestion of one, flickered on the ceiling and was gone. Vern cast the beam upward. A pink damselfish glided through the pillar of light, goggle-eyed. That was all. They went up the stairs without touching them.

Right away he was aware of a change in the saloon. Then he realized it was in the lighting. The room was darker than it had been earlier. Someone had closed the door to the gangway.

What is this? he wondered.

From somewhere up forward there came a scrape of sound ... a pause ... another scrape ... then nothing.

What? The hull shifting on the coral? Harvey? Tapley? He didn't know, couldn't guess. He held his hand up before Bea and patted the water and pointed at the deck. Wait here.

She wasn't for it, but he wasn't going to have any nonsense at this stage of the game and he nodded his head vigorously and said *Uum-uum!* in the mouthpiece, sounding like a caveman laying down the law to his woman.

So that was settled and he skimmed across the saloon and through the cuddy, pushing the swing doors open with the barrel of the gun, and came into the forward passage, and way up ahead he saw a light jerking around and wagged his own in the water, and then started toward the light, lowering his own now and wishing that the bastard (Harvey or Tapley — he couldn't tell which) would do the same because the damned torch was

173

like an approaching car traveling on highbeam and he was going blind from it.

Then he heard the releasing *tzzzaaang* in the propulsion unit of a speargun and automatically he barrel-rolled to the right as the headlight up forward blacked out, and he wasn't certain that he actually heard or felt the spear zip past him, but he did hear it go *tooonk!* against something behind him, and then he was bringing his knees up to his chest and trying to get himself rightside up so that he could see and shoot the sonofabitch who had tried to kill him, and he didn't care who — Harvey or Tapley.

But the man didn't give him a chance. He loomed into the light and all over Vern, his left hand grabbing the barrel of the speargun and shoving it off-target, his right over his head and descending with a knife, and just before Vern dropped his torch to grab for the hand with the knife he saw Harvey's wildly glittering eyes behind the face-plate, and he thought, I walked right into it.

He didn't quite catch Harvey's wrist, but he deflected the blow. The knife nicked over his left shoulder and jarred against one of his cylinders, and he wheeled to the right and backlashed, letting the gun go, as Harvey took a swipe at his air hose. Then he kicked forward with everything he had in his legs and piledived into Harvey, his hands clawed and grabbing, trying to keep that damned knife away and trying also to spin Harvey around and get on his back where he could get at his air regulator or get his own knife out and cut up Harvey's hose.

But Harvey was about as easy to manage as a Catherine wheel tearing round and round. Grabbing, warding off, fin-kicking, Vern's shoulder raking fire in the water, he got Harvey bent back over the fuzzy guardrail of a companionway, Harvey's cylinders going *tun-tun-tuunk* against the metal, and then they both went over spinning into a slow somersault, all arms and legs and fins and great thrashings of bubbles, and down down into deeper darkness

. . .

Then the fingers of Vern's left hand fumbled over something he wanted and he ripped it up, over and back, feeling the tough elastic tenacity of the rubber headband, and then feeling it snap loose in his hand. Then he got all of him loose at once and backfinned into the darkness, taking the face mask with him.

Harvey was blinded.

174

Some divers went panicky if they lost their masks underwater; but almost anyone would go wild if he lost his mask inside a submerged wreck. There was simply no way out, nothing to see, just endless crowding blackness. You were an ant at the bottom of an India ink jar. All you could do was bumble around until your air ran out.

He could hear Harvey doing that now, could hear the man's cylinders banging and clunking and blundering along the pitchy corridor. And he knew just how bad it was going to be for Harvey — knew how bad it would be for him if he were in Harvey's fins. And he knew he couldn't let it happen . . . had to do something about it.

He found the companionway and went up to the next deck and retrieved his torch. He didn't take his speargun because he would have to lead Harvey out by the hand.

But he didn't find him. He found Harvey's knife in the lower corridor, but the man himself was gone.

He searched. He honestly tried. He gave it five minutes and that was all he could afford. Time was running out and that business about the saloon door was bugging him and there was Bea to consider. He stalled and looked around at the marl fluttering in the opaque circle of torchlight. It was hopeless. There simply wasn't enough time for it. He finned back to the companionway and started up. But he was sick about it.

I wanted it this way, he thought. And now that I've got it I don't like it.

He rose pikelike into the lighter darkness of the upper deck, leaving Harvey Dodd somewhere below — like a blind man in a dark room, looking for a black hat that wasn't there.

He skimmed back along the passageway, plunged headlong through the dazzling cuddy, into the shadowy saloon, over the hill-like mound of swollen carpet and cut toward the stairwell. One of the shadows took shape, rearing before him, and he swung the gun up instinctively because his nerves had the jump-jumps. Then he saw that it was Bea.

He hooked the torch in his belt and took her hand, wondering how he could tell her what had happened, wondering if he should tell her — and decided to let it ride. It was no place for a woman to learn that her husband — estranged or not — had just been murdered by her lover.

175

Why murdered? he asked. Why start that crap? It was self-defense. But his conscience reserved comment.

He said To Hell with it and tugged at Bea's hand and they started across the saloon. He released her as they approached the door and he nosed down and tried the knob. There wasn't any give. It was dogged.

Tapley.

He said the name and it ran off echoing through his mind. I was right, he thought. I was right the moment I found him in my room that night in Singapore. But I always tried to count him out; tried to pin it on Harvey. Jesus, Harvey . . .

But there was no time for regrets, not for a dead man — and if Harvey wasn't, then he was as good as. And us too, Vern thought, knowing now what the scraping sounds he had heard earlier were. Tapley had been sealing them into the deckhouse.

Bea was watching him. Her eyes were more enormous than ever. He shook his head at her and pointed at the door. She nodded. She knew what the score was, but she didn't know whether it was Harvey's work or Tapley's. Lets keep it that way, Vern thought. They started back across the saloon.

The starboard door had been dogged from the outside also.

Vern removed his hand from the knob, feeling the fuzzy scum it left imprinted in his palm. Fear was crouching on top of his aluminum cylinders with its crooked, spidery little legs hooked over his shoulders. Its heels wore spurs.

There was no sense in trying the forward door because he knew it would be dogged. Was there a way out from the deckhouse to the bridge? He didn't know. Some ships yes, some no. Why the hell worry about it? Tapley would have been there by now anyhow. They would have to try the cabin deck. He gave Bea a sign and they spiraled down the stairs again.

His apprehension was infectious. Bea left him in the central passage to try the port doors while he went starboard. Then they met again and looked at each other and shook their heads. The deckhouse had become a hermetical trap.

Jesus, he said. Jesus.

Of course there had to be a way out of the deckhouse other than the goddam doors. But he couldn't think of it. His brains were leaping about like dice being rattled in a box and all that would come up were snake-eyes. And it would be better, so damn much better if he were alone. If he didn't have Bea to worry about.

He looked at his watch. Bad. It was getting bad. It was later
176

than he thought. At nine or ten fathoms they could stay down about forty-five minutes. Already half an hour had ticked away. If they could get out of the ship they wouldn't have to stage their ascent. That was one thing in their favor. But they would have to ascend at the leisurely speed of their air bubbles.

So all right. But how to get the hell out?

Then he remembered something from his troop ship days and decided it was worth a gamble. Anything was. He had Bea hook her torch to her belt and gave her both guns to hold in her left hand and kept the other torch in his right and took her free hand with his left. Skindiver or not, she was a woman and she would have to be led through this.

He found the door he wanted. It said ENGINE ROOM and he opened it and drew Bea in after him and cleared the rail and hit the void below with the light.

It was a nightmare pit. The steel walls were adorned with bright yellow sponges and hot smears of red pigment and they stood out in crystalline brilliance as the torch brushed them. And below, where the light refused to penetrate, blackness was king. Vern sucked air and jackknifed.

A tall square fuzzy monster reached up for him and he veered sharply to miss the railing and rods. It was a triple expansion Werkspoor-Diesel engine; the stilled heart of the dead ship. He skirted a petrified forest of ladders and pipes and connecting rods, all deceptive under their polychrome skins of alcyonaria, and worked aft.

He breathed with great economy as he descended, hoarding his air supply, hoping that Bea was doing the same, and absently thinking that some places were more attractive to drown in than others. Odd? No — not to a skindiver. If he had it to do and there was no way of getting around it, then he wanted it in clean clear quiet sunlit waters on a soft stretch of blue sand with a tombstone of pink madrepore above him, and he would rest in an endless vault of tranquil color and become a part of the world that had meant more to him than the part he had been born in.

But not in this filthy steel trap of an engine room.

A glittering wall spread before him. He sank to deck level and followed the wall with the torch, stopping when he found what he was looking for. During the war many cargo ships had been equipped with kick-through doors: a thin panel set haphazardly in a staunch bulkhead for use after an explosion if the regulation doors were jammed.

177

Now if the cargo in the hold has tipped against the goddam bulkhead . . .

He kicked the panel with the flat of his foot and fin. It shuddered, giving a little. Jammed with sea growth — he hoped. He kicked again. The panel toppled inward and was swallowed by the black hole beyond. He led Bea into the hold.

They angled up a shaggy canyon between great jumbles of cargo, and then they were in a madhouse of piled cargo and drifting cargo and marled rotten broken nameless cargo, and finning over a sickening heap of wavering refuse and pushing through and around floating things and pausing in consternation and suddenly lost in the swirling water-clouding marl.

Out, he said. Get us out of this.

And then he saw the blind wall of the aft bulkhead. It was piled with decayed cargo. He released Bea's hand and gave her the torch and began digging into the mess, tossing bales, boxes, cordage, clumps of filth aside.

Suddenly he realized that his breathing had become an effort. There was a constriction in his air line.

No. Jee-sus, no!

But there was nothing Jesus could do about it. When pressure within the cylinders falls below an eighth of the original a device in the apparatus causes a constriction, thereby giving warning that the air supply is getting low.

He reached for the control to the emergency tank that would by-pass the constriction, glancing at Bea as he did. She nodded and pointed at her own valve, indicating that she had already switched over.

Ten minutes of air — if they were lucky. And where was the goddam kick-through door?

Then as he cleared a crumpled bale of wire aside he saw it. The panel had already been kicked open. He dragged Bea into the passage and they finned hurriedly for the companionway. There he took one of the guns from her and opened the door and went out first. It was just possible that Tapley was still hanging around the wreck.

But it wasn't Tapley he discovered on the well deck. He saw a heavy shadow working along the hatch cover, saw it pause and edge off. Then he looked up.

The shark twisted casually around with a plate-eyed expression and looked at Vern.

He heard Bea's exclamation of shock behind him, hollow and bell-toned, and a cold little needle went hemstitching up his spine. It wouldn't do any good to retreat. If they chose the sanctuary of the wreck (which he damn well knew they couldn't because their air was petering out) the shark would just hang around outside.

He gripped Bea's hand and they started up slowly.

Maybe the big bastard was just curious. It was nice to think so — but he knew it wasn't going to work out that way. This time he had to face the music. A rhapsody in red and blue.

And there could be no running because the hand he held belonged to the girl he loved, and you can't run out on love. You're through when you do that, he thought. You're truly through.

The shark moved with a sort of dreamy rhythm as though he might suddenly close his great staring eyes and drift to the bottom asleep. He seemed to glide along without motion, propelled by some invisible force. He tilted upward and his underslung mouth swung open.

The magnifying qualities of the water and the face mask were a great help. They exaggerated the shark's size to nearly twenty feet. Vern put him down for fifteen. Pale beige belly, gray-bronze upper shagreen skin, tall slanted dorsal suggestive of a flying jib or a three-cornered sail . . .

Whaler shark. Supposedly aggressive. Carnivorous and predacious.

They rose easily, following their combined foam of bubbles, Bea above Vern, but her right and his left hand still clasped. Her fins flipped against his cylinders. Once a corner of the rubber tip clipped his shoulder. He watched the shark, panning the gun with its ascent.

The gray-bronze whaler edged up to within five yards of Vern's fins. It hung for a moment, its myopic eyes peering suspiciously, reminding Vern of two hungry question marks. Now, he thought. Do it now while he's a sitting duck. But he stalled. He didn't like the range. Then it was too late. The shark spanked the water with its heterocercal tail and executed a smooth beautiful Immelmann turn — half loop, half barrel — going straight up and over and rolling right side up again and cruised off on a starboard tack.

Then it cut back, aimed higher and came on, heading for Bea.

Vern pulled Bea down, forcing her behind him, and turned to place his body between them. The shark slowed to a

179

suspended halt. Its underslung mouth opened and closed as though trying to tell Vern something.

Danger, he realized, had always been an impersonal thing. The time his foot caught in the snag in the swimming hole when he was ten and he nearly drowned, the night he drunkenly put the car over the embankment and himself in the hospital when he was seventeen, that brilliant November morning in '43 when he waded across the Tarawa lagoon through the clumps of dead Marines with the Jap shells and machine-gun bullets whanging the air and spanging the water around him . . . all of these things had been coldly impersonal. Even the near-sighted tigers that took Jimmy Nolan had not been aware of Vern's presence, had left him a bystander floating on the sidelines.

Now all of that had changed and death was suddenly a very personal thing that existed between Vern and the whaler shark. The shark was hungry. The shark had been picking up tantalizing whiffs of blood for hours, but the big steamer on the bottom of the lagoon wouldn't let the shark have what it wanted. No, the big steel fish was keeping the meal in its own greedy gut. And so the shark was ravenous and PO'ed and felt put upon and now here was Vern dangling in the water like a big gleaming hunk of saltwater taffy, vulnerable and . . .

But not defenseless, Vern thought. That's what's got the bronze bastard worried. He doesn't know whether I can hurt him or not. A shark is a wary son of a fish.

He hooted shrilly into the mouthpiece.

The whaler startled. Its pectorals fanned out. The tail undulated. But the shark didn't move.

Great stuff, Vern said. I've really scared the hell out of him. He might break into a yawn any minute now.

Minute — *minutes.* How many left? How long between to have air and *to have not?*

He could feel Bea against his back. Then a long shiny object poked along the left side of his face mask, and he raised his gun-hand hurriedly and brushed her speargun away. The range was too far for a spring gun. Even if she was on target the harpoon wouldn't penetrate old eat-mouth's tough hide. He took a firmer grip on her supple waist.

Poor kid, she was reaching the breaking point. He wanted to talk to her, tell her how much he loved her, tell her that if they had to die he was glad they were going together . . .

Oh yeah, that would be comforting. *Really* comforting.

That was just the thing to tell a girl when she was scared to death. Dumb bastard.

The shark's pectorals flattened.

Vern tensed his hand on the gunbutt, straightening out his arm. Why not get it over? Now, before the goddam air runs out. He began hitch-kicking upward, slowly, panning the gun again on the rising shark. Bea rose above him, still clutching his hand.

The whaler drifted after them, coming like a heavy dark cloud of factory smoke in a clean morning sky. Its blunt snout tilted as though sniffing the aura of their movement and its mouth hung open like a village idiot gawking at a passing parade.

If we strike the surface we're dead, Vern thought bleakly. He'll chop us into mincemeat. Come on, fish! Why diddle around with it? Do it now, you ugly mother!

When he comes for me, he thought, I'll let Bea go. Maybe she can make it to the surface while fish-face and I whoop it up. Sim can get her out of the water. That way it won't matter that I didn't get to tell her how much I love her. She'll know.

The shark did it all at once like the snap of fingers, one instant standing still and the next knifing straight in at Vern's chest, and Vern set and ready and thinking *Here goes everything,* aimed just below the oncoming snout where the wide mouth showed snow-cap dentures all bright and clean and jagged, and the good-God shark coming at him like a wind tunnel, its eyes with that insane look of an eagle swooping on its prey, and then he squeezed off the shot and felt the fast liquid, spastic jolt of the spear in the barrel run up his arm to his shoulder, and then the spear needled the water, going away faster and faster with a trail of gassy little bubbles burping from the circular opening in the rear, and after that nothing made sense.

A welter of turquoise and silver smashed his face mask, ramming the oval plate against his nose and cheekbones, flooding his eyes with glassy bursting bubbles, and then the solid impact of the shark's backwash struck him full-front and he spun off into a great wobbly vacuum-packed ball, seeing far above him the shimmering surface whirling away and he reached out as if to grab it, as if to steady himself.

One thing he was clear on — the only thing that really mattered — he had released Bea's hand.

181

He couldn't seem to shake out of the pressure belt. He felt hammered down to nothing. An elephant was sitting on his chest. And where had the damned thing come from? And why didn't it go the hell away? He rubbed at his body, rolling in the water, then brought his numb hands up to his head and felt the face mask. It was secure but partially flooded. To hell with it. He wouldn't waste air trying to clear it. Then what was wrong? What was missing?

His hands — empty.

Speargun gone, Bea gone.

He spun in the water, looking. Where was Bea? Did she get away? Where was the shark? He didn't know, didn't know anything. He started finning upward, then stopped. Now wait a minute, he said. Which way is up?

He paused, checking the ascent of his exhaust bubbles, and followed them, thinking, I'm in great shape. Someone take my hand and lead me home. A bright darting something fell past his watery vision and he jackknifed and went after it without thinking — reacting.

He caught it and stared at it stupidly. A speargun. A loaded speargun. Then he understood. Bea's gun. Where was she?

A vague form bowled out of the gloom and became the whaler shark. A very activated shark now. Humping, twisting, whipping through long rusty streaks of blood, doing everything that a creature born without hands can do to pull away from the barbed pain that jutted from its snout and not getting anywhere with it at all.

Vern fin-kicked upward. He felt coldly impersonal toward the shark and its death throes.

He found Bea two fathoms below the surface. She was sagging limply in the water, head hanging, rising slowly as the growing buoyancy of her empty cylinders lifted her. Bubbles were crackling from the back of her neck. She was still breathing.

He thought at first she was unconscious. But when he took her arms she rolled sluggishly and fumbled for him with her hands. She must have been slapped by the shark's backwash. Probably in shock. Come on, Bea, he said. We've won.

And then his air conked out.

To hell with it. He was wildly elated. He could go the rest of the road on glory alone.

Sim, his face taut and moist, helped Vern haul Bea over the

182

rail and stretch her out on the deck, and then Vern collapsed next to her with his back to the bulwark, the cylinders propping him up.

Sim stripped the lung, mask, fins and weight belt from Bea and looked at her lying there with her wet panties and bra clinging to her glistening body. She made a noise and opened her eyes and fluttered the long lashes and then closed them again. Her head rolled.

"Her breathing is all right," Sim commented.

Vern nodded. Now that it was over and he was out of the water he felt dizzy and sick, off balance. He couldn't seem to find the norm for everyday reaction and emotion. He felt as apathetic as a fat old cow drowsing over her cud in a sunny meadow. He wanted a cigarette, a drink.

"What happened down there?"

Vern stirred himself back to thought and speech. "Little bit of everything. Tapley locked us in the deckhouse. Dodd —" He checked over an idea, knowing he'd never be certain now. "Maybe Dodd planned on killing me all along . . . or maybe he thought I'd dogged the deckhouse to kill him, and then he decided to get me. One way or another, he didn't make the grade."

"You kill him?" Sim asked. He didn't really seem to care.

"In a way, I guess."

"So how did you and the widow get out?"

"I got rattled," Vern admitted. "I hauled her through the engine room and after hold. There were kick-through doors."

"Uh-huh. That's one way."

Unemotionally, Vern realized that Sim was rather disgusted with him. Sim didn't seem to think too much of his ability. It didn't matter — he'd never thought too much of it himself. He had proved one thing to himself that day and he knew he could never ask for more. Absently, he stared at a dark blotch of water near the cargo hatch and wondered how it had come there. But it didn't matter. Nothing mattered really. The warm sun felt good.

A gurgle and splashing sounded beyond the rail and Vern looked up, startled.

"Tapley," Sim offered.

Tapley? Tapley was just now coming up? That didn't make sense. He should have been on deck long before this — telling Sim lies or planting a knife in the old man's back.

"For — for crysake lend a hand, Skipper!" Tapley's strained voice called. "I weigh like lead."

More splashing. Then — "I almost left *All Of Me* down there. I kid you not, Queeg!"

Vern looked around and saw Tapley sloshing over the rail, the air hose bobbing loose before his neck, face mask pushed up on his plastered hair. He had left his speargun and torch below. He was bleeding.

He spotted Vern and grinned. "Hey, Rig, who locked the goddam jail? Let me christly tell you I had a time getting out-a that rust coffin! Look at me. I feel like I been keel-hauled."

Vern looked at him, wondering. "How did you get out?"

"Went up through the saloon ventilator to the boat deck. No trick a-tall for an un-e-cumbered man. That goddam lung wouldn't fit while it was on my back, though. And I wasn't a-goddam-bout to go off without it! I had to hold my breath and drag it up between my legs. And then I ran into a stupid-looking stingray. Scared us both silly.

"How did you get out?" he asked Vern, finally.

The ventilators, Vern thought bitterly. Why didn't I think of that?

"Through the engine room and hold. You forgot to dog the after companionway."

Tapley stared at him, getting his breath. He smiled crookedly and plumped down on the deck, glancing at Bea. "What happened to her?"

"Shock."

"And her old man?"

Vern didn't say anything, neither did Sim. Tapley looked at Vern, at Sim, back to Vern again. "So it finally worked out for you, huh?" he said. "So he's dead?"

Vern looked at him levelly. "Yeah. Too bad you missed the girl and me."

"What's with you?" Tapley wanted to know. "You sound like you think *I* locked the deckhouse."

"I'm not just thinking it, pal."

Both men were breathing hard. It made talking an effort.

Tapley's narrow face faded to a pasty yellow. Two bright spots of crimson pin-pointed his cheeks.

"What the hell you talking about?" he half shouted. "Some sonofabitch dogged the goddam doors all right, but it was done from the *out*side — and I was *in*side. Don't pull that crap on me, sport. I don't know from nothing. If I was trying to kill you guys down there, why would I try to kill me too? Why did I stay down there looking for those goddam gems till I run out of air? Why did I have to beat my way up that friggin' vent?

"You think it's a joke trying to get the goddam grate off the
184

bottom of a vent with a knife when your christly air is damn near gone? Or to skin yourself alive on barnacles and play Postoffice with a goddam stingray?"

Vern had nothing to say. He was staring at the deck again, at another pool of water. Sim's bare feet were standing in the center of the pool. Sim's bare feet . . .

The pool was draining from the man's soggy pants. Baffled, Vern raised his eyes and realized for the first time that Sim was in his shirtsleeves, and the shirt was wringing wet, and his lank hair was damp, and piled on top of the cargo hatch with his crumpled jacket was a scuba lung and a mask and fins and all the metal and glass were beaded with moisture.

"Sim —" he said slowly, "your ankle doesn't seem to bother you much."

Sim grunted and jerked his thin lips into a one cornered grin.

"It never did," he said flatly.

He turned easily, poked at his jacket, and came back and showed the two men the business end of the Luger. Then he sat down on the edge of the hatch, crossed his legs casually, and looked at Vern with sun-narrowed eyes.

"Finally got around to it, didn't you?" he said.

"Hey!" Tapley cried.

"You —" Sim motioned the gun barrel toward Tapley. "Shut that trap of yours. Unless you want me to put a bigger hole through the back of your head."

His hard face came around to Vern again, reminding him of that first day in Singapore when he had thought he saw youth, like a wisp of sunlight on a far shore, in Sim's eyes. And now he realized he should have seen something else — quiet, uncomplicated madness.

Because Sim was not and never had been a complicated person. There had never been any ratiocination in his motivation. Whatever he had wanted in his life he had transfigured to a goal at the end of a corridor. Some of the corridors had been short and some long, but all of them, for Sim's drive, had been straight — from point of conception to point of accomplishment and attainment. And anything or anyone who had tried to block his path had been treated like a rock and had been kicked aside. There were no tributaries in his purpose.

Now, Sim began to talk, and listening to and watching Sim,

185

Vern realized that madness didn't necessarily mean strait jackets, padded cells, fanaticism, or visitations of the brain; madness could be as purely calm and collected as a nun taking an evening stroll in a cathedral cloister.

Once the thought: *Why give everyone a share?* had entered his mind, Sim had decided to methodically eliminate the deadwood, and he had started his straightaway march down the corridor to the Manchu goal.

Donald Fergus had been first. The opportunity had been there and he had been the least necessary of all. And it was the type of murder which might appear to be the work of Oriental hoods. Simple.

God and the typhoon had taken care of Ernie Dorp — though Sim had planned the deed for himself, but he didn't quibble; and then it was Haki's turn.

Sim broke off suddenly, grinning wryly, his eyes reflective.

"That Jap shook me up some, I'll admit. When I left him on deck at three that morning, I figured he was dead. Never entered my head that he wasn't, that he'd crawl as far as the galley for help before he croaked. When I came back on deck at four — so everything would look normal — and found him gone, well, son, I was blowed!"

Sully, Vern thought wearily. Sully alibied Sim on the night Haki was murdered. Said he was with Sim in his cabin till nearly four. Sully . . .

Sim swung the barrel of the Luger toward Tapley. "It was loudmouth here who gave me the idea of making it look like the gook had gone south with the swag."

He cocked his head, looking at Vern speculatively.

"I made a mistake, though, when I decided to pick the gook. I should have took you. Then you wouldn't have been around to queer my play. Things were looking good until you found Bingo down in the wreck. That was something I couldn't blame on Singapore hoods or Pauloo Kanakas. That meant just what it was — murder."

He shrugged, passing it off.

"Then the whole pack of you swam yourselves into that box, just like you were begging for it. So I went down there and dogged the deckhouse. Simple."

Vern's sense of balance was back. He was looking ahead. He edged his hand up to his waist and rested it on the weight belt. His fingers felt for a pocket flap.

"You must have been out of your mind, Sim," he said. "If you killed us, you'd be alone on this schooner. You couldn't run it by yourself."

Sim's eyes snapped. "Who couldn't?" he roared. "I'm none of your namby-pamby freshwater sailors. I'm John Sim! When I make up my mind to do a thing, *I do it!*"

His hard-rimmed eyes slanted at Pauloo.

"You think I couldn't go ashore and recruit myself a crew of woolheads? Believe me, son, I could get a crew of headhunting halfwits to sail me to Timbuctoo if I wanted 'em to."

Vern believed him. He had always believed in Sim's capabilities. He watched Sim heft the Luger in his square fist, while his own hand lay quietly over the open cartridge pocket of his belt.

It isn't going to work, he thought. It only works in movies. He'll see what I'm up to and he'll blow a hole right through my chest. Or even if I do get the weight out I'll miss the sonofabitch by a mile and he'll still blast me. But, Christ, what else can I do? I've got to try it because there's nothing else.

He glanced at Bea, at her spring gun where he'd set it down beside her. Too far away. Jesus Christ, it's too far away. He eased thumb and forefinger inside the cartridge pocket, felt the lead weight, and waited.

Bea muttered something. Her eyes opened and she put them on Vern and smiled and then moved them to Tapley, then Sim and down to the gun and back to Vern, not smiling now.

"Harv?"

Vern shook his head. "He didn't make it, Bea," he said quietly.

She stared at him and for a long moment her eyes didn't blink. Nothing about her moved except for a slight tremor in her lower lip. Then her eyes shut down.

"I didn't want that," she whispered. "Not that way."

No one spoke. The schooner shifted on the surface, creaking like an old barn door. A ghost tern banked in the sky, turning its wings almost vertical in the breeze, calling its lonesome *caw*. Bea lay quietly on the deck as though taking a sunbath.

"What else?" she asked.

"Sim," Vern said simply. "He's mad. I guess he's going to kill us."

Sim grunted. "Don't seem like there's much else to do, does there?" he said.

Something bright moved in the corner of Vern's eye. Bright and yellow. He glanced quickly at the open door of the galley. Miss O-lan, Tapley's own Lotus baby, was standing there in her soiled yellow sheath. She had Tapley's razor open in her

187

hand and she was staring intently at Sim's back. She started moving on slow, soft catfeet.

That's one thing the old man forgot about, Vern thought with a jolt of hope. That girl would die for Tapley.

"Why me, Sim?" he said quickly. "I thought we were friends."

She isn't going to make it. It's too far. He'll see her or sense her and he'll—

"You?" Sim's look was cold. "What do I owe you? You'd given up like a whipped dog when I found you in Singapore. You're as gutless as the rest of 'em. Sully was the only man who was worth a damn in the bunch. As far as —"

"No, baby!" Tapley suddenly shouted, his bright mercurial face wild with emotion. *"Go back!"*

It was the last thing Vern expected — for Tapley to be more concerned over the girl's welfare than his own; but the wheels were spinning now and the gate of action was swinging inexorably open, and he brought the lead weight out of the pocket as Sim's head jerked toward the girl and the Luger started swinging around, and he whipped his arm back and let it fly and Sim caught the motion in the corner of his eye and reflexed on a snap-shot, the Luger taking a jump in his fist, roared, the slug smashing into the bulwark by Vern's left ear, as the square of lead caught Sim on the point of the chin, snapping his head back and jerking his body halfway about on the cargo hatch, the Luger now spinning into the air and thunking on the hatch and bouncing with a clunk into the scuba lung.

Then Vern lunged forward, hearing Tapley cry something meaningless in his ear, but everything was against him — the fins on his feet, the weight belt around his middle and the goddam cylinders on his back, and he felt himself losing balance and saw Sim, half-sprawling, reach for the Luger, and knew that he couldn't possibly make it in time and that in one split-second Sim was going to blow his stomach through his backbone and said *Jesus Christ!* as —

Something bright, long-drawn and brittle pierced the air and went *thh-wok!* as it skewered into Sim's back. He let out a tight almost inaudible gasp, bowing his spine, swinging half around, reaching both hands crookedly into the sky, the shaft of the harpoon standing straight and firm in the starboard side of his broad back.

"Yah! Sweetheart!" Tapley cried. "How about them apples!" And he waved Bea's spring gun above his head.

Vern snapped the release buckle of the weight belt and lunged upward again, fumbling all thumbs it seemed with the lung-pack harness, as Bea came to her knees and shoved both hands into the back of Sim's legs, sending him lurching and gasping along the deck and past Tapley who was all legs and hands and curses covered with spit, trying to wiggle free of his skindiving gear. Somehow Sim managed to keep himself going.

Bea grabbed for the Luger.

"No!" Vern shouted. "Don't!"

He stepped clear of the lung and shoved the Chinese girl — still going after Sim with that damned razor in her hand — aside and took the Luger away from Bea.

Sim staggered hesitantly into the rail, said something which no one could understand, and rolled over the gunwale. Bea screamed.

Vern rushed after him, tangled with Tapley who was still shouting.

"Did you see me sock it to him? Am I a goddam spear fisherman or ain't I! *By God, I nailed him clean!*"

Vern shoved him away, cursing him savagely, and gained the rail. The two small boats were nestled together in the water. Sim was in one of them. He slipped the painter, ran out the oars, made a loud, drawn sound in his mouth and began pulling away from the schooner.

Vern brought the Luger up and stalled. Then he lowered it. Not in the back. Not Sim. He looked inboard at the others. Tapley had both his skinny arms around the Chinese girl's waist and was leaning back raising her feet from the deck and bouncing her against his chest, and he laughed and laughed and laughed.

Bea stood up slowly as though not quite certain where she was and lurched toward Vern, and caught him and clung to him and began to shiver.

"Vern," she murmured, and then over and over, *vern-vernvern* — and her voice grew louder, became shrill.

Hysteria, he thought numbly. It was bound to come. Little girl, you've had a busy day.

"Tapley," he called harshly. "Stop beating your goddam back with medals and take Bea below."

With Tapley and the Chinese girl helping him, Vern finally got all of himself loose at once and stepped clear of Bea. She looked at him with wide-eyed bewilderment, shaking her head slightly.

189

"You go with 'em, honey," he said softly. "I'll be right here." He slanted a look of warning at Tapley. "You stay with her. Let the other wait until tonight."

Tapley grinned at him. "Hell, it'll keep. Don't worry about me, Rig. We're partners again, for good."

"Wonderful news," Vern said sourly. "Now take her below, will you?"

Alone on the deck, he shoved the Luger into his trunks and went over the side, dropped into the remaining boat. Sim was going to die, but not like a wounded animal crawling off in a hole by himself. All at once, Vern owed him that much, though he wasn't quite certain why he thought he owed him anything. Maybe because Sim was the embodiment of all those now obscured, hard-bitten men who had roved violently and profanely through the Conrad and Stevenson and London books which Vern had read and admired in his youth, and which had endowed the romantic side of his nature with a certain peculiar and wistful regret at having been born too late. Sim was the last of a breed and his death had to be fitting.

He almost caught up with him as they shuttled like two waterbugs across the lagoon, because Sim was in pain and his progress was spasmodic. But when he saw Vern coming he called up hidden energy and shot the bow of his boat into the weak lip of the surf. He piled over the side and ploughed through the wash, his right side hitched high as if trying to draw his body away from that damned thing that jutted from his back. He reminded Vern of the dying shark.

The wall of the distant forest opened like a small green door opening in a vast green room, and Vern paused and leaned on the oars, seeing Sully and five of his Kanakas step through the nipas and onto the beach.

Sim spotted them also. He began lurching toward Sully, signalling with his left hand. Vern couldn't hear anything but the smothering gurgle of the beer-colored water. He rested, staring.

Sully stood statue-still, tall and plateau-shouldered, narrow-waisted and half-naked, watching Sim. The Kanakas spread out along the beach, throwing a semi-circle about the staggering white man. Vern recognized Tom-Tom. The ex-boat boy was holding a war hatchet.

Sully's head jerked.

Tom-Tom went into a poised stance, left arm out for balance, right cocked over his shoulder with the hatchet. He

190

fired the tomahawk, sending it end over end into the back of Sim's neck.

Sim was down and jerking and then not jerking and dead, before the full realization made an impression on Vern.

The Kanakas gathered slowly about the crumpled form. Sully came down to the water's edge and stood with his bare feet in the beery foam and looked out at Vern.

Vern began rowing again, toward Pauloo.

They didn't shake hands or anything like that. They stood in the warm sand and looked at each other blankly. Sully said:

"Do you have any cigarettes?"

Vern spread his hands over his trunks. "Why don't you come out to the ship and get some?" he offered.

Sully nodded, looking over his shoulder at Sim and the Kanakas.

"Yeah, maybe I will later. I'll come out and work you a course to Tulagi. Tapley's good. He can get you there — if he's still alive."

"Very much so. He put that spear in Sim. Dodd's dead, though."

Sully said nothing. He stared at Sim.

"You knew about Sim all along, didn't you?" Vern asked.

Sully looked tired. "No," he said, "not all along. I kind of thought it might be him, but I wasn't certain until the night Haki caught it. Sim told the rest of you I was with him until after three-thirty. That wasn't true. I left him at one-thirty."

"But you backed him up."

Sully looked at him. "What would you have done?" he wondered. "Suppose he had turned to you in front of the others and asked you to help him? I owed him that much." He shrugged and looked away.

"Besides," he added quietly, "I didn't really give a damn. I was already thinking about taking off."

They were silent. Vern scrolled his foot through the sand.

"I didn't think you were going to kill him," he said finally.

Sully nodded as if for his own conviction. "Had to. He'd turned mean. I didn't want him around my island."

"He liked you," Vern said. "He said you were the only one in the bunch worth a damn."

Sully's lips shifted into a wistful smile. He glanced over his

191

shoulder again. "Did he say that? I never knew it — wish I had."

"It's better this way. He'd seen his time. He died like he lived — fighting Kanakas on the beach."

But Sully shook his head.

"No, Sim never had a show today. He died because he trusted me. If he'd looked at me as another woolhead, we'd probably all be dead right now, and Sim would still be on his pins. Tough old bastard."

And that, Vern thought, is that. Tough old bastard. Turned mean. Dead.

For a moment, as Vern climbed back into the boat, he thought about offering his hand to Sully, but decided against it. You don't shake hands with a god.

Sully shoved him off silently. Then he walked back along the beach to his Kanakas. They were stripping the clothes from the body of the white man. Vern pulled his eyes away from the scene and began to row.

He rowed slowly, thoughtfully, feeling and enjoying the warm sun on his bare back. In passing he considered the fact that the Manchu fortune was gone for good. But he was objective about it. It didn't seem to matter, because he was about to start the first voyage in many that was going *toward* instead of going *away*. Escaping from unhappiness, he realized, usually means you have to retrace the route that first brought you to it.

He looked over his shoulder. The chop had gone out of the lagoon, leaving the surface slightly ruffled with long oil-smooth undulations. The old slaver squatted solidly in the water, resting on her cable. Her brittle sticks swayed, nodding at him.